DISCARD

DATE			

7/12
2x
5/12
15
2/14
Some
15

14 DAY LOAN

ADAM AND EVELYN

ADAM
AND
EVELYN

A NOVEL

INGO SCHULZE

TRANSLATED FROM THE GERMAN BY
JOHN E. WOODS

 ALFRED A. KNOPF · NEW YORK · 2011

THIS IS A BORZOI BOOK.
PUBLISHED BY ALFRED A. KNOPF.

Translation copyright © 2011 by Alfred A. Knopf,
a division of Random House

All rights reserved. Published in the United States
by Alfred A. Knopf, a division of Random House, Inc.,
New York, and in Canada by Random House
of Canada Limited, Toronto.
www.aaknopf.com

Originally published in Germany as Adam und
Evelyn by Berlin Verlag GmbH, Berlin, in 2008.
Copyright © 2008 by BV Berlin Verlag GmbH, Berlin.

Knopf, Borzoi Books, and the colophon are registered
trademarks of Random House, Inc.

Library of Congress Cataloging-in-Publication Data.

Schulze, Ingo, [date]
  [Adam und Evelyn. English]
  Adam and Evelyn : a novel / by Ingo Schulze ;
translated from the German by John E. Woods.—
1st American ed.
       p. cm.
"This is a Borzoi book."
ISBN 978-0-307-27281-2
1. Germany—Fiction. I. Woods, John E. (John
Edwin) II. Title.
PT2680.U453A3313 2011
833'.92—dc22 2011009554

Jacket illustration by Emilio Brizzi / Millennium
Images, U.K.
Jacket design by Peter Mendelsund

Manufactured in the United States of America

First American Edition

For
Clara and Franziska

CONTENTS

In our deepest convictions, reaching into the very depths of our being, we deserve to live forever. We experience our transitoriness and mortality as an act of violence perpetrated against us. Only Paradise is authentic; the world is inauthentic, and only temporary. That is why the story of the Fall speaks to us so emotionally, as if summoning an old truth from our slumbering memory.

—CZESLAW MILOSZ, *Milosz's ABCs*

The church fathers, and not only Augustine, condemned as heresy the assertion that Adam, along with Eve, was damned for all eternity. They in fact became saints, their day falling on December 24. They ultimately advanced to patrons—not as might be expected of the planters of orchards, but rather—of the guild of tailors. After all, they were the first human beings to wear clothes. And God the Father had sewn their garments Himself.

—KURT FLASCH, *Eva und Adam*

ADAM AND EVELYN

1

DARKROOM

ALL AT ONCE there they were, the women. They appeared out of the void, attired in his dresses, pants, skirts, blouses, coats. At times it seemed to him as if they were stepping out of the whiteness, or had simply emerged, finally breaking through the surface to reveal themselves. He just had to tip the tray of developer the least bit, that was all it took. First there was nothing—and then suddenly something. But that moment between nothing and something could not be captured—it was as if it didn't exist at all.

The oversize sheet slid into the tray. Adam turned it over with plastic tongs, nudged it deeper, turned it again, stared at the whiteness, and then at the image of a woman in a long dress draped in a spiral around her ample body, but leaving one shoulder bare, found himself gazing at it as devoutly as if a miracle had happened, as if he had compelled a spirit to assume form.

Adam briefly held the photo up with the tongs. The black surface of the background was softer now, but the dress and the armpit held their contour. He picked up his cigar from the rim of the ashtray, took a puff, and blew the smoke across the wet image before dipping it in the stop bath and from there into the tray of fixer.

The squeak of the garden gate unsettled him. He heard the footfall growing louder, taking the three stairs, heard the soft thud of the shopping bag meeting the front door as it opened.

"Adam, are you home?"

"Yes," he called so loudly that she would have to hear him. "Down here!"

The sound of her heels passed overhead as he blew on the negative, wiped it with a chamois cloth, and then slipped it into the enlarger again. He pulled the image into focus and switched off the light. The kitchen tap opened, then closed, the steps returned—suddenly she was hopping on one foot, pulling off her sandals. The empty bottles in the basket behind the cellar door clinked.

"Adam?"

"Hm." He removed one sheet from the package, 18 by 24, and squared it in the enlarger.

Tread by tread Evelyn descended the stairs. Her fingers would be dusty again, from running her hand against the low ceiling to keep from bumping her head.

He picked up his cigar again for a few more quick puffs that left him completely enveloped in smoke.

Setting the timer for fifteen seconds, he pushed the big square button—the light came on, the timer began to buzz.

With a stirring motion Adam waved a flattened aluminum spoon above the woman's head, pulled it away with catlike speed, and as if going for a wade in the water, extended his fingers to shadow the woman's body, but drew them back before the enlarger's light went off again and its buzz fell silent.

"Whoa! Damn, that stinks! Do you have to smoke down here too, Adam?"

Adam picked up the tongs to immerse the paper in the developer. He didn't like to be disturbed when he was working with his photography. He didn't even have a radio down here.

Barefoot, Evelyn was still a good half head taller than Adam. She groped her way over to him now, tapped his shoulder. "I thought you were going to fix us something to eat?"

"In this heat? I spent the whole time mowing the lawn."

"I'm going to have to leave again."

The woman in the long dress appeared on the white paper. It annoyed Adam that she was evidently sucking in her stomach, he thought he could tell from her smile that she was holding her breath. But then maybe he was mistaken. He used tongs to dip the image into the stop bath and from there into the fixer. Now he tugged a new sheet from the package, folded it down the middle, and ripped it in half against the table edge. He stuck one half back in the package.

"What are you eating?" he asked.

"Close your eyes. You're peeking, stop it."

"Have they been washed?"

"Yes, I'm not trying to poison you," Evelyn said as she pushed a grape into his mouth.

"Where'd you get these?"

"Kretschmann's, the old man slipped me an extra sackful. I didn't know what was in it."

The enlarger light went on.

"What do you want me to tell Frau Gabriel?"

"Put her off."

"But I've got to tell her today. If they're going to give me vacation time in August, then I've got to take it."

"She's nuts. We'll take off when we want to take off."

The light went out.

"We wanted to go in August. You said August, and Pepi said August was better for her too. Without kids nobody ever gets vacation time in August. Besides, the visa will expire."

"It's not a visa."

"It doesn't matter what you call it. We applied for August."

"It's good till September tenth."

Adam dragged the paper through the tray, turning it twice.

"Now she's sexy!" Evelyn said, as the woman in a pantsuit emerged, hands braced against her back, breasts thrust forward.

"Any mail?" Adam asked.

"Nope," Evelyn said. "Why don't we take the train?"

"I don't like being stuck in one spot. It's boring without the car. You got any more?"

Evelyn shoved the rest of the grapes into his mouth, then wiped her wet hands on her jeans. "And so what am I going to tell Frau Gabriel?"

"One week at least, she's got to give us a week."

"By then August is as good as over."

"You can turn on the light," he said, once he'd laid the proof in the fixer. He stepped across to the rectangular sink, where several more photos were swimming, fished one out, and hung it on the line with some others.

"Who's that?"

"Lilli."

"And in the real world?"

"Renate Horn from Markkleeberg. Got any more grapes for me?"

"You'll have to go upstairs for them. And this one here?"

"You know her. Desdemona."

"Who?"

"Sure you do. Andrea Albrecht, from the Polyclinic, the gynecologist."

"With the Algerian boyfriend?"

"There's no Algerian boyfriend. You've met, shook hands once. I made this outfit for her"—he pointed at a photo on the line—"back in June."

"Wait a sec—" Evelyn stepped up close to the shot. "Is she wearing my shoes? Those are my shoes!"

"What?"

"Those are mine, there, on the toe, that scratch. Are you crazy?"

"They never know anything about shoes, they show up here wearing clunkers that ruin everything. It's just for thirty seconds—"

"But I don't want your women wearing my shoes. I don't want you taking shots of them out in the garden, and certainly not in the living room either."

"It was hot upstairs."

"I won't have it!" Evelyn was now giving other shots a closer look. "So are we leaving tomorrow?"

"As soon as our new chariot arrives, we're on our way."

"I've been hearing that for three weeks."

"I've called. What am I supposed to do?"

"We're not ever going to go on this trip, I'll bet you."

"You'll lose." Adam pulled photo after photo from the water and hung them up. "I guarantee you'll lose."

"We'll never get another visa. They wouldn't give us one now. They've moved the age limit up to fifty, Frau Gabriel says."

"Frau Gabriel, Frau Gabriel. She's always got lots and lots to say."

"This one's beautiful. Is it red?"

"Blue, silk."

"Why don't you ever do color shots?"

"She had someone bring the silk back with them, and this material here"—Adam held up a photo showing a young woman in a short skirt and loose blouse—"expensive shit, even in the West. You can't feel it against your skin, it's that fine spun."

Adam folded up a wet photo and threw it in the wastebasket.

"Why'd you do that?"

"Wasn't any good."

"Why not?"

"Too dark."

Evelyn reached into the wastebasket.

"The background is all black dots," Adam said.

"Is this Lilli?"

"Sure is."

Evelyn tossed the photo back in the basket and returned to the entryway, where the shelves of preserves were.

"It's like they multiply. You want pears or apples?"

"Is there any stewed quince left? And close the door."

Adam turned off the light and waited till the door clicked shut.

"Some from eighty-five, if this is a five," Evelyn called from the other side of the door.

"Doesn't matter." Adam chose a new negative, focused, pulled the half page from the package, laid it under the enlarger, and pushed the timer button. He hummed along with it.

"You want a bowl now too?"

"Later."

"Are you going to the museum today?"

"Have the tours started up already?"

"Yes, and I'm going to have to miss it again."

"I can't go either, I've got a fitting," Adam called out.

For a moment everything was quiet. He let the page slide into the liquid, pressed it down. There was the snap of the light switch in the entryway.

"Evi?"

He heard the clink of the empty bottles again.

"Evi!" he shouted and was on the verge of following her, but then in the next moment he bent down deeper over the tray, as if trying to make sure that the woman emerging there with her laugh and outspread arms was really looking at him.

LILLI

A FEW HOURS later that same Saturday—August 19, 1989—Adam was kneeling, with a half dozen pins in his mouth and a tape measure around his neck, at the feet of a woman in her midforties. She had taken off her blouse and was fanning herself with an issue of *Magazin*. The heat had nestled into the finished attic, despite open dormers and skylights. The cover had been pulled over the sewing machine, the cutting table tidied up, with shears arranged by size and lined up with spools of thread and ribbons, triangles, rulers, stencils, tailor's chalk, a cigar box full of razor blades, and another small box for buttons, a photo propped against it. Even the tray with two half-full glasses of tea and a sugar bowl had been squared with the tabletop. Rolls of fabric were stacked under the table. From the record player's speakers came music, along with a few scratches.

"Is that Vivaldi?" Lilli asked.

"Haydn," Adam managed to say through tight-pressed lips. "Don't suck your tummy in."

"What?"

"Don't suck your tummy in!" Adam repinned the skirt's waistband.

"I don't understand why you won't take on Daniela as a client. She's beautiful, she's young, and she can pay your prices. She just wants to wear something chic for once. Besides, her father has a repair shop, for

Škodas I admit, but they'd lend a hand when you need one. There's no rush. Daniela will go to the end of the line." She tossed the *Magazin* on the table. "When are you two taking off? Have you got your new Lada yet?"

Adam shook his head. Lilli looked in the mirror, at her left bicep, already half raised, and began to tweak her hairdo. Adam's finger traced along the inside of the waistband.

"You don't have to grumble," she said. "I'm not sucking my tummy in, I'm no beginner."

Their eyes met in the mirror.

"Shorter, I think," Lilli said.

Adam turned up the hem, checked the mirror, and shook his head.

"You don't agree? People won't see any leg at all," Lilli said.

Adam pinned the hem length and smiled, which made him look curiously sad.

"What's with you?" she exclaimed. "What about the belt loops? Those could be bigger."

Adam grabbed Lilli by her hips, turned her around, and removed the pins from his mouth. "There'll be a slit right here—a slit, do you understand? You want them to stare at it, put a crick in their necks. And make sure you find a narrow belt, something elegant. Here are your eight inches, about eight from here down." He fastened another pin and finally got to his feet. "So now the shoes, take a couple of turns."

Lilli slipped into her brown pumps, walked to the window, where she spun once around on her tiptoes, then strode to the dormer opposite, and started back again.

Adam took his cigar from a copper ashtray and puffed away till the tip began to glow.

Lilli stopped in front of him, her hands on her hips. "I can't believe that's me there. Even I look photogenic here with you."

"Keep moving, keep moving," he said.

When Lilli passed him again, she waggled a hand, and in reply Adam took the cigar from his mouth and blew smoke on the back of her neck. "That's enough, come here," he called. "And you did suck your tummy in." Adam tried to tap a finger on the little bulge just above the top of her skirt. Lilli backed away. She pretended not to have heard him, and brushed her hair back. She was sweating, too.

Adam pulled the second mirror over. "Here, I need to take a little out of the box pleat. Otherwise it falls very nicely."

She tensed her butt under Adam's hands. "Actually I'm glad you don't want to take Daniela on. You're liable to take a shine to a spring chicken like her. The lining is marvelous, feels so good to the touch. Where'd you get it? If it weren't so stifling up here I'd purr. Can't you put that smelly stogie out? You'll get lung cancer."

"This flaw here in the fabric, I'll tuck it under, it'll as good as vanish," he said, and inserted a couple of pins beside the box pleat.

"When I get home they can always smell that I've been here with you. Although I always wash my hair."

Adam gave the skirt a gentle tug. "Sits and fits like a glove. Once around." And when she threw him a questioning look, he repeated: "Once around. And take this thing off!"

Lilli undid the clasp of her bra, brushed the straps aside, and let it dangle between her thumb and index finger.

"Satisfied?" she asked as she let the bra fall to the floor. Adam removed the suit jacket from the big tailor's dummy. Lilli stretched her arms behind her, slipped into the jacket, pulled it up over her shoulders, and spun around. She looked straight at him as he pinned the jacket closed. "I found a couple of buttons for it in an antique shop, scarce as hen's teeth, my old man would've said, real mother-of-pearl, prewar stuff." Adam took a step back.

"Well, what do you say? Stretch your arms out in front of you, both of them, and to the sides . . . I fitted the waist. Is it too snug?"

"Not a bit," Lilli said, looking at herself in the second mirror.

"Either find yourself a decent bra or wear nothing under it—nothing would be best. The middle button a tad higher, and a little less here, give some, take some, see, that gives it its shape all by itself." He stepped to one side and watched Lilli turn back and forth between the two mirrors, hands pressed flat at her waist, stroking the fabric.

"Oh, Adam," Lilli said, just as the final duet began. "I ought to bring you a bouquet of roses every time I come."

Adam blew little clouds in the direction of the skylight. For a while music hung in the air, as if they were both listening closely to the voices.

"You deserve a whole rose garden."

Adam laid the cigar on the windowsill, the tip jutting over the edge. "I'll make sure," he said, "that everybody has a great view, from in front and from behind and in profile." He picked up a half-full tea glass, gave it one last stir, licked off the spoon, drank it down, and moved in close behind Lilli. For a moment he eyed the countless copies of her in the mirrors. Then he thrust the spoon handle between her breasts, it stuck there.

"You see, what did I say, you don't need anything else."

The spoon even stayed there once Lilli was lying on her back atop the table and Adam, after carefully working her skirt up, was moving inside her.

"Slow down," Lilli said. "And be careful, you're dripping on my suit!"

Adam wiped his brow with his sleeve and shoved the button box and her photo farther back.

During the final bars of the last chorus Lilli grabbed the tape measure still hanging around Adam's neck and pulled him down to her, until his eyes were looking right into hers. "Adam," she whispered, "Adam, you're not going to cut and run, are you?" She fought for air. "You're coming back, Adam, you're staying here, right?"

"What a lot of baloney!" Adam said. He saw the sweat on Lilli's upper lip, felt her breath against his face, under his right hand her heart was pounding wildly. "Promise me, Adam, promise me!" Lilli suddenly cried so loudly that he covered her mouth out of pure reflex. That's when the spoon slipped from her décolleté. Adam removed it from her shoulder and put it back in his glass, which responded with a low, clear, almost bell-like ring.

3

ADAM, WHERE ARE YOU?

WHEN ADAM HEARD her voice and then her steps on the wooden stairs, it came to pass that he squeezed behind the cupboard to the right of the door. Squatting in the bathtub, frozen with fear, Lilli stared at him. There was a knock, Lilli turned the sprayer off. Evelyn entered.

"I just quit," she announced—and then almost toneless—"my job."

Foam clinging to her arms and shoulders, Lilli got out of the tub.

"I'm sorry," Evelyn said and turned around.

"Adam?" she called as she left. "Adam, where are you?"

She climbed to his workshop. He knew what it looked like up there. Lilli tried to pull up her panties, which had got rolled up and twisted at her knees. Adam looked over her glistening back and out to the garden. Hopping about on the freshly mowed grass were blackbirds, sparrows, and a magpie. Over the last few days he had weeded the bordering flower beds, the fence had been freshly painted in May. The garden hose lay neatly coiled up between the driveway and the spot where he burned trash. The turtle in its little pen had crept out of sight. Evelyn came slowly down the stairs. She stopped at the bathroom door.

"Adam, are you in here?" She opened the door. "Adam?"

"I'm sorry," Lilli whispered. She had yanked her panties up to where they hugged her hips like a cord, and was now clamping a towel under her arms to cover her breasts. "I'm sorry," she said again.

"Have you seen Adam?"

Lilli glanced toward the window as if she might find him there in the garden. Why didn't she say something? I'm far, far away, Adam thought. There was Evelyn standing right in front of him now. He couldn't help smiling—she still had on her white blouse, black skirt, and waitress's apron.

"Who's she?" Evelyn asked, jerking her head back toward Lilli. She picked up a towel draped across the washbasin and threw it at Adam's chest. It fell to the floor.

"Who is this woman?"

He picked up the towel and held it to him like a loincloth.

"I'm sorry," Lilli whispered.

"Is this your fitting?"

Lilli looked up briefly, then back at the floor.

"It was so hot," Adam said.

"Tell her to finish her shower, that won't make any difference now either."

Evelyn hesitated briefly at the door and gazed at Lilli, who with upper arms pressed to her body was standing there bent slightly forward, trying to unroll her white panties and tug them up over her butt.

Adam counted Evelyn's steps. They seemed to linger at the threshold to her room. He was afraid she might turn around and return to the bathroom. Then the door slammed. Her old sofa groaned audibly in the silence of the house.

Adam was sitting at the kitchen table, brushing at breadcrumbs with his fingers. It felt good to prop his head in his hands. In front of him, beside the opened jar of stewed quince, was a paper bag of fruit that looked like little purple onions but felt soft through the paper. He didn't want to risk taking any out. Maybe he had gone too far just carrying the bag up the steps into the kitchen.

Adam, barefoot, a towel around his hips, had gathered up his and

Lilli's things in the workshop, but she had to send him upstairs again because he had returned without her bra, and without the photograph too. He had to pass Evelyn's room again, move up and down the creaking stairs again—but only with the photo. Evelyn had probably stashed her new bra somewhere, Lilli had hissed, and then broken into tears.

She kept saying, "What can I do? What can I do?" to which Adam could only respond with whispers of "It's not so bad" and "It'll be all right."

But what he had really wanted was for Lilli to finally shut up. Every word she spoke only chained him to her all the tighter. And no, he hadn't been in his right mind. Otherwise why hadn't he put clothes on, instead of trailing after Lilli in his bathrobe, and then picking up Evelyn's bike from where it had slid down to the base of the quince tree. So that his bathrobe had spread wide open. He couldn't have made it any clearer to the neighbors what had just happened. Lilli should have done her talking before, not after it was too late: "He's in the garden. I think he's outside in the garden." Just that. He would have slipped upstairs to his workshop—and fine. Nothing would have happened, not one thing.

Back in the house, Adam had for one brief moment actually believed that everything would be all right—just as everything was always all right once he was inside his house. That's why he had hung up Evelyn's keys and carried the bag into the kitchen. She was always leaving stuff lying around. He had found the half-eaten bowl of quince preserves on top of the breadbox and put it in the fridge. Instead of the cutting board, she had sliced bread on a newspaper—she had taken to buying a copy of that fish wrap of late. As usual it had been left to him to shake the newspaper out over the sink, fold it up, and add it to the stack in the cellar. He'd been brought up short by the felt-tip circle around the museum tour: "History of the Laocoön Group," even though Evelyn knew she wouldn't have time for it.

Upstairs Evelyn was moving back and forth. She had slammed

doors and flung them open again, books had fallen to the floor. Hadn't it been his responsibility to go upstairs, to take that first step?

But it was quiet again now, except for the hum of the fridge. Now and then Adam would brush more breadcrumbs away, only to return to the same position. He was thankful for every minute that he could sit at the kitchen table without having to say anything.

Suddenly he felt the pain. A burning under his breastbone, as if a hard lump had got stuck there. Adam could see himself stretched out on the kitchen floor, unconscious, Evelyn at the door.

Suddenly he became frightened that Evelyn might harm herself. But then almost immediately came the sound of the toilet flushing and her footsteps, and that was just as frightening. Adam stood up. Holding the bag in one hand, massaging his chest with the other, he looked up at the ceiling as if he could see Evelyn. All he could think to do was say he was sorry, to apologize. He went to the stairs, sat down on the second step, and placed the bag beside him. Adam was disappointed to notice the pain easing. His elbows on his knees, he propped up his head, which felt unnaturally heavy the longer he held the pose.

4

OUT OF HERE

ADAM GOT to his feet as if about to fight a duel. Evelyn came to a halt a few steps above him and set down her suitcase. The green tent was wedged under one arm. She smiled. "I'm going to Simone's, for now."

"For now?"

"Well yes, and then I'll see. She has a visa too, maybe we'll take the trip together."

Adam wanted to correct her—what was pasted in their papers wasn't a visa. So instead he just asked, "And where to?"

"Why, the Caribbean, where else?"

Adam let go of the newel so it wouldn't appear that he was barring her way. He would have liked to put both hands in his pants pockets, but in getting to his feet he had grabbed the paper bag of fruit, and it was still there in his left hand. "Don't you want to wait?"

"What for?"

"Shouldn't we talk?"

"What about?"

Adam grimaced in agony. "About what happened." He could barely take his eyes off the bright red toenails sparkling at the tips of her sandals.

"If you have something to say to me." She cradled the tent in her arms like a baby and sort of halfway sat down on her suitcase.

"I'm so sorry, I apologize." He looked directly at her, for as long as it took to get a nod. Then his eyes fell to her feet again. While he was dealing with the fear that she might harm herself, she had evidently been painting her toenails.

"I'm so very, very sorry."

"Me too, Adam, very, very sorry." Evelyn said this with exaggerated nods, as if speaking to a child.

"And if I were to tell you that it wasn't anything, nothing at all like what you think it was. Lilli and I have known each other—"

"Are you kidding?"

"What do you mean?"

"You're lying." There was resignation in her voice, as if she had been afraid it would go like this. "I'm leaving, before you can come up with more nonsense."

"What do you want me to say?"

"You're the one who wanted to talk." Evelyn stood up.

"You're going to cut and run, just like that?"

" 'Just like that' is good. I'm trying to get out of here before the other shoe falls."

"What shoe?"

"When it finally hits me what actually happened."

"It meant nothing, not a thing."

"Is that so?"

"That's what I'm telling you."

"To me it means practically everything."

"Go ahead and shine a light in every corner—it means nothing, nothing, do you understand? You can ask me anything you want."

"About what? How long it's been going on? Is Renate Horn from Markkleeberg the only one? Do the plump ones turn you on? Do you need something slutty to get you up to speed? Some things you don't trust me with? Or is it just about variety? Does the designer want proper pay for his work? Is it your services that make them so easy, or do they come to you because they're not getting enough at home anymore?"

Adam sucked in his lips and massaged his chest with his free hand.

"I'd always hoped I'd never be exposed to any of it, that I wouldn't be forced to seriously think about what's going on when silk blouses touch naked skin, about the plunging necklines you create, about those asses that you can tighten better than any plastic surgeon—"

"Evi—" he said, banging his right hand on the knob of the newel post.

"I had hoped that the betrayal only went as far as my shoes, or the garden or the couch, for all I care they could have . . . if that's what you need, fine by me. But I didn't want to know about it, didn't want to see it or feel it, understand? As I was running away from the raths-keller today, suddenly there was this little man in my ear, who said, Watch out, be very careful! But I didn't listen to him. And now I've seen it, and felt it, and that's that. End of story."

Evelyn picked up her suitcase, shoved the tent under her left arm, and descended the last few steps until she was almost touching Adam. Her gaze swept past him. She waited for him to make room for her.

Adam stepped to one side, holding the paper bag against his chest with both hands, like a bouquet.

"And why are you quitting your job?"

"Now's not the time."

"Come on, tell me." Adam leaned against the wall.

"They stole something from me, if you must know, and then they blamed me for getting so upset about it."

"And what was it they stole?"

"Perfume."

"Your perfume?"

"My perfume."

"That I got for you?"

"No. I'd just been given it."

"Aha."

"Simone had stopped by, with her cousin, he brought it along for me, because—"

"The guy from last year? That smug little prick? Put down your suitcase."

"At least he noticed how much I liked the perfume. I put it in my locker, and then it was gone."

"Did these goodies come from him too?" Adam held out the bag to her.

"You don't have to look so disgusted. Those are fresh figs."

"Even after he hit on you like that, you said yourself—"

"Why shouldn't I let someone hit on me?"

"Somebody like him?"

"You mean I should have reported to you about my contact with the West. I really wanted to, but you were busy. Too bad. A real shame!"

"I've told you—"

"And told them I'd be happy to talk about the whole thing, but first I wanted my property back. And that's when Frau Gabriel said that she doesn't allow vague suspicions like that. I asked her if that was her final word, and when she stuck by it, I said that I would take my vacation starting now. She demanded I stay to the end of the shift, and work tomorrow too. And with that I quit. Over and out."

"And the swanky cousin was waiting outside to greet you with a smile."

"Baloney. They'd left long before that."

"I thought you said he was pushy?"

"Should I have said I won't accept it, that I first have to ask my husband and my boss?"

"And now you're moving in with him?"

"Oh, Adam. If that's all you can come up with." Evelyn picked up her keys in the entryway and opened the front door.

"You could at least have dressed right for the occasion," he said.

"I beg your pardon?"

"Well . . . stripes and plaids." Adam followed her out and helped her clamp her suitcase and tent onto the bike's rack.

"Want me to give you a lift?" he asked. "That's not going to stay on."

"Wait a sec," Evelyn said, and now walked back to the garden, where she sat down on the low bench and scratched under the turtle's neck with one finger.

"Be good to Elfriede," she said, giving her right pants leg a couple of rolls. "Fresh water every day. And lay the grating across at night, on account of the marten."

Adam preceded Evelyn, opened the garden gate for her, and handed her the bag of figs.

"Thanks," Evelyn said and rode off. After a few yards the tent slumped to one side. Adam watched Evelyn reach back with the same hand holding the figs. He strode back into the house and closed the door behind him as carefully as if he were afraid to wake someone. "It's not going to stay on," he suddenly said, and repeated the sentence several times while he went back to massaging his chest.

5

WHY DOES ADAM LIE AGAIN?

ADAM WANTED to lie down and close his eyes, at least for a few minutes. But the realization that at some point he would have to get up again kept him on his feet.

He climbed to his workshop. He carefully smoothed out Lilli's skirt and pinned it on the dummy, draping the suit top over it. He slipped the record back in its jacket, turned the record player off, closed the window, left the skylight open just a crack. When he picked up the tray with the empty glasses and sugar bowl and turned to leave, he spotted something dazzlingly white in the space between the wall and the open door—Lilli's bra. On one cup was a dark semicircle, his shoeprint.

Balancing the tray in one hand, Adam picked up the bra between his fingers as if testing the quality of the fabric, but then pressed it to his face like a mask—it had no smell—and hung it back on the door handle.

As he passed Evelyn's room he cast a glance inside. It had been tidied up, the white blouse, the black skirt, the waitress's apron had all been neatly folded and laid on the sofa, beneath them stood her work shoes.

He almost stepped on a fig in the kitchen. It must have fallen out of the bag.

While he washed dishes he was still picturing Evelyn, the way she had stared first at him and then at Lilli. He kept rubbing away at the rim of the glass, although any traces of Lilli's lipstick had long since disappeared. Doesn't matter much now anyway, he thought, and heard himself let out a sound, a groan or a battle cry, and would gladly have repeated it, even more fiercely, with his face to the ceiling. He thrust a fist into the dishwater, Lilli's glass banged against the bottom of the sink.

Adam didn't bother to dry his hands. He slammed the door behind him and walked to the garage. He backed his old Wartburg out.

He used the first rag he found in the garage to wipe dust and cobwebs from the two twenty-liter jerricans and loaded them in the trunk.

Adam drove as far as Puschkin Strasse and turned left to skirt the old city. As he passed the museum he saw a group of people coming out, the tour had evidently just ended. Sometimes even from this point, he could see the last car in the long traffic backup. But Adam was in luck—stinking good luck, Evelyn would have said. There were only seven cars ahead of him. No sooner had he turned off the engine and pulled the brake than traffic was moving again.

Adam's red-and-white Wartburg 311 was one of the favorite cars of the garageman, a short guy with black hair and big glasses. Last fall, without even being asked, he had been able to come up with a replacement for a missing hubcap, and the bill that Adam had folded twice over disappeared into the bib pocket of his blue overalls without so much as a glance.

"Well, things still lookin' up?"

Adam nodded. He was in a hurry to get the cans out of the trunk before the next car pulled in. He opened them and set them down beside the pump.

"Where you headed?"

"The coast. Warnemünde," Adam said. He himself didn't know why he lied.

"Lucky dog. Booked at the Neptun?"

"Private lodgings," Adam replied and walked back to the trunk, where he pretended to search for something. Under the old blanket he found his father's guides to birds and wildflowers. He smiled as he folded the blanket, stood up straight, the books tucked under his arm.

"Anything happening with the castle?" Adam inquired. From here you could see the gap left by the fire more than two years ago.

"They'll have the Junkers' Dormitory restored in forty years or so," the garageman said, never taking his eyes off the cans.

"Along Teich Strasse," Adam said, "there were still twenty pubs after the war. My father kept trying to chug a beer in each one, but never could do it. And now? Now there's one left." Adam suddenly had a hunch that it was the garageman who had told him this story.

"And that one'll be closing soon too," the garageman said, pressing the heel of his hand down on the cap of the second can. He pulled a ballpoint from behind his ear and jotted down the charge. Then he cranked the pump back to zero and started gassing up the car.

"And otherwise?" Adam asked.

The garageman stared straight ahead as if he had to give the question some serious thought. "I was supposed to have taken my vacation by now," he finally said. "But there's my coworker, and if she doesn't show . . ."

Adam gave him a two-mark tip.

"Just a sec," the garageman said. He came back out of the office with a hand on his leg pocket.

"You know this stuff?" He turned around, his back to the Škoda behind them now, pulled out a spray can, shook it, squatted down at the radiator, squirted a blob of foam on the chrome bumper, and rubbed it. "Now ain't that somethin'?" The spot did in fact look shinier. Adam was hoping the garageman would do the rest of the bumper, but he stood up instead.

"You have another can of it?"

"Na-a-a-h!" the garageman bleated. "Got it from some Czechs.

Wanted to ask, just in case you ever head that way, if you might bring me one back."

"We're off to Warnemünde," Adam said.

"Thought you might keep it in mind, if you ever do happen to—"

"Sure," Adam said and nodded. "I'll keep it in mind. Have you got a funnel, by the way?"

"For you I've got it all."

Tucking the spray can back in his leg pocket, the garageman vanished again. Adam was generous in rounding up the price. The money disappeared into the garageman's bib pocket. They shook hands good-bye. Adam could see in the rearview mirror that the garageman was tugging a red-and-white chain across the station entrance, all the while watching him pull away, as if taking note of the license number.

Just after Saint Bartholomew's Adam took a right at Ebert Strasse, crossed Dr. Kulz Strasse, then made a left, bringing him at last to Martin Luther Strasse. Evelyn's bike was beside the front door of number 15, and directly across the street was a red Passat hatchback with West German plates and HH as the first two letters. He couldn't think of any major city that had two Hs in it.

Adam was hungry. Once back home he forced himself to take his time, garnishing his plate of cold cuts with pickles, setting mustard, horseradish, and the bowl of stewed quince on the tray, plus two plates, each with a cloth napkin in its own silver ring.

After he had wiped off the oilcloth on the garden table, he fetched the turtle from its little enclosure and put it on the table, just as Evelyn had always done. The turtle crept closer to his plate. Adam made a point of eating slowly and drinking slowly. There was a pleasant evening breeze, a blackbird was sitting on the ridge of the roof. To finish off his meal he tried peeling the figs, but finally sliced them in half and ate them with a spoon. He laid the leftovers in front of the turtle, which immediately began nibbling away. It felt good having an animal close by, as if he had already been alone too long.

Evening was falling by the time Adam turned the garden hose on the flower beds and shrubs. He always had his best ideas when gardening, which was why he kept a drawing pad in the shed, for a quick design sketch with a carpenter's pencil.

He took time out to set the turtle in the grass, to speak with the neighbors and clean the little pond. Along its rim were four sandstone frogs that spat jets of water. He was as delighted as always with the flat stone he had laid in the middle of the pond last spring—perfect for birds. When he had finished with the garden and the turtle was back to crawling around in its pen, he treated himself to a second beer and a cigar. If Evelyn came by, she would see that not only was she expected, but also he was sticking to his agreement to smoke only in his workshop or outside.

Every thought that entered his head ended up as a kind of self-justification, as if he were being interrogated, as if his mind would allow no uncertainties, no contradictions. It seemed to him as if his just sitting here and smoking had been entered on the police report, with date and time. He still had to take out the garbage, check the windows, including those in the cellar, and make sure that all the doors inside were left open—to unplug everything, wipe up any water in the fridge, pack, and find a box for the turtle. His reward would be a shower and a shave.

Adam was just setting the alarm clock when the doorbell rang. What flashed through his mind was: the garageman. But why him? Evelyn! He turned on the outside light and opened the door.

"Oh, it's you," he said. The telegram delivery boy greeted him and handed him an envelope. Searching for his wallet, Adam frisked his jacket, hung on a clothes hanger dangling from the entryway wardrobe. He pressed a mark into the delivery boy's hand and waited until he had remounted his chug-chugging moped and ridden off.

"Sunday a problem. Monday afternoon? Monika."

Adam grimaced and sat down on the stairs. He had thought of everything, just not of his women.

There was a piece of cardboard tucked between his garden shoes, which he stored in the niche beside the door. He slipped it out and fanned himself. Years ago he had written "In the garden" on it in red pencil, so that if he didn't hear the doorbell his clients wouldn't think he had left them in the lurch. Some came from as far away as Leipzig, Gera, or Karl-Marx-Stadt.

He would have to write about twenty postcards: "Quick vacation till early September. Greetings, Adam." He had time, he was all packed. He had canceled the newspaper clear back at the start of the year. The mailbox was big enough for all the rest. He pushed the sign back into its slot between the heavy shoes.

No lies, no need to hide, he told himself suddenly, stood up, and locked the door from inside. For a moment he thought of leaving the key in the lock—but then pulled it out as always. He was used to Evelyn coming home late. Out of the wardrobe Adam grabbed her straw hat, which he wore sometimes himself for work in the garden, and laid it atop his packed suitcase. He padded the turtle's box with a few fabric remnants and added a water dish.

There were lights in several windows until a little after midnight, Adam included in his imaginary police report while he brushed his teeth. Quickly rinsed and gargled, and went to bed.

6

THE MORNING AFTER

ALTHOUGH ADAM hadn't used an alarm clock for years, he woke up as he always had just before it rang. As on every other morning, he imagined his own death. Today the thought was more unsettling than comforting.

Still in his pajamas, he went down to the living room, opened the old writing desk, took out the jewelry box, and put on his wristwatch, a Glasshütte, Evelyn's present to him on his thirty-second birthday. To make room in the suitcase for the jewelry box he had to remove his extra pair of loafers. He had more stewed quince for breakfast and rinsed out the empty jar. He dried the spoon and laid it back in its slot in the drawer.

When he had finished packing the car, he unscrewed all the fuses for the house.

As he turned into Martin Luther Strasse he spotted the red Passat hatchback from a good distance away. Evelyn's bike was no longer parked at the front of the house.

Adam stopped, rolled down his window, and gazed up at the open windows on the second floor. Compared with those rooms with their high ceilings and fine plasterwork and art nouveau sliding doors, his little house from the thirties looked humdrum, a dump. Adam drove to the end of the street, turned around, and maneuvered his car into the nearest parking space, three down from the house. To keep an eye on the front door over the top of a hedge, he had to sit up straight. The turtle hadn't budged. He got out and lit a cigar. Except for some distant traffic, all he could hear was birds.

Adam inspected the Passat. The backseat was strewn with candy wrappers and crumbs. Adam scowled when he saw that the cover over the driver's seat was made of little wooden balls. The seat was pushed so far back that there was room behind it for a kid at best. From the sidewalk Adam gave the front tire a kick. All he had to do was flip open his pocketknife and do two quick knee bends, and they would be stuck here. He twirled his car keys—one for the door, one for the engine—on his index finger, strolled up the street, tossed the stack of postcards in the mailbox, walked back, and, leaning against his Wartburg, smoked the rest of his cigar. He dropped the butt, it vanished down the storm drain without touching the grate.

Adam pulled the cup from his thermos and filled it halfway. He sipped cautiously, blew on the coffee, took another sip, held the plastic cup to his nose, and smiled. This was what vacation smelled like. Had smelled like for ages now. He couldn't recall the last time he'd drunk coffee from a thermos. Although there was no smell that was more a part of him. It meant fresh air, a girlfriend, freedom.

He felt the pressure ease at his temples, he could breathe again. "It's gonna be a long ride, Elfi," he said, clapped on the straw hat, and then pushed it back with his index finger. Suddenly it all seemed very simple.

7

UNDER WAY

THE KNOCK woke Adam up. "I told you I could smell it." Simone and Evelyn were looking in at him. Although he was sitting up straight by now, Simone kept on rapping at the window. He had no idea how long he'd slept.

Adam took off the hat and opened the door. "Good morning," he said.

"What do you think you're doing?" Evelyn asked. "Are you a spy now, too?"

"I knew it!" Simone gave the car roof a slap. "That's Adam standing down there puffing on a stogie."

"Since when is smoking on the sidewalk forbidden?"

"What do you think you're doing, Adam?"

"I didn't want to wake you up, had no way of knowing when you'd be getting up. But here's your straw hat, you should take it with you."

"Thanks," Evelyn said. "Anything else?"

"It's nice to see you."

"That's not the impression I had yesterday."

"Yesterday was a horrible day."

"You're right for once."

They eyed each other.

"Is there anything else?"

"Yes, in fact there is." Adam looked from her to Simone and then back at her.

"I'll be right there," Evelyn said.

Simone rolled her eyes. "Don't let him sweet-talk you," she said and walked across to the red Passat. The hatch was open.

"I'm on pins and needles, Adam. So what is it?"

"I wanted to ask you if you'd like—or better, ask you if you won't please come along with me to Hungary."

Evelyn burst into laughter. "You can't be serious."

"Sure I am. Everything's all set to go. And Elfi's in the car too."

"You're crazy!"

"Our Heinrich here," Adam said patting the roof of the Wartburg, "is going to make it all the way, really, he promised me."

"No, it's too iffy, in all sorts of ways. See you."

"Then we'll take the train, like you wanted, Evi, please."

"You're one day too late with that, Adam. Bye. We're on our way." Evelyn turned around and walked off.

"Evi!" Adam called. "Evi!" He wanted to ask her why she was wearing one of Simone's skirts. Evelyn tossed the hat in the back, someone was pushing down on the hatch door—and now he saw the cousin, and it came to him. His name was Michael. Michael was tall, midforties maybe. He was wearing jeans and a loose white shirt that made his face look even redder. It took several tries to close the hatch. A flame shot up from Michael's lighter. He fiddled with it until the flame was almost invisible, lit a cigarette, and stuffed the pack back in his shirt pocket. Spreading his arms wide, he opened both car doors at once. Simone beat Evelyn to the punch and squeezed into the back. Evelyn protested, they argued and laughed. Michael just stood there, like a silent chauffeur.

Adam flung himself behind the wheel. Although he was looking straight ahead, as the Passat drove by he could see that they were staring at him. Michael even gave him a nod.

Adam wanted to make a slick U-turn at the next intersection, but was forced to back up to complete it. But as he started down Martin Luther Strasse again, the Passat was just pulling away, and Adam sped up close behind them—closer than the traffic law allows.

He followed them down to the Polyclinic, they turned right at the gas station, drove along below the castle and past the theater, then took a left into the Street of Worker Unity, which would lead them to the Large Pond. The light turned yellow, the Passat came to an abrupt stop, and Adam could already hear the crunch—but nothing happened. He got out, walked up to them, and rapped at the window behind the driver's seat. The music was so loud they didn't hear him. Even Evelyn was smoking. Simone let out a quick shriek when she saw him.

"The hat, you're squashing your straw hat!" Adam shouted. He was amazed she hadn't noticed, Michael at any rate ought to have spotted it in the side mirror. Adam walked back to his car, shifted into first gear, and waited.

When the Passat pulled away and picked up speed as it climbed the hill leading out of town, Adam fell back. But he knew the way. They were taking the road through Gössnitz, at Meerane they would cross the autobahn and then keep going in the direction of Zwickau. He guessed Bad Brambach would be their border crossing, on the Czechoslovakian side that would take them through Cheb. Or they might try the eastern route via Oberwiesenthal and Karlovy Vary/ Karlsbad, the first foreign city he had visited with his parents. Or were there other crossings? What Michael gained by driving like a maniac, Adam planned to make up for with slow but steady.

At the light in Gössnitz the Passat was stuck behind a truck. The straw hat was still squashed against the back windshield. Once they were moving again, Adam fell back to avoid the truck's dense exhaust fumes.

No sooner were they through town than the Passat came to a stop on the shoulder without signaling. Adam pulled off to the right as well. Evelyn jumped out and walked toward him. Those sandals with low heels were new, too.

"You're making an ass of yourself, Adam. What do you think you're doing?"

Adam tried to get out, but Evelyn was standing too close to the car—he would have had to shove her out of the way with the door.

"You trying to trail us? You can't be serious."

A car raced past, honking its horn. Evelyn pressed up against the Wartburg.

"Let me out!" Adam cried. Evelyn tried to say something more, but several strands of hair got blown across her mouth.

"Adam," she said, now that they were standing face-to-face, "what you're up to is not funny."

"And what am I supposed to be up to?"

"Nothing. Zilch. Hasn't it got through that thick skull of yours, what happened yesterday, what you did?"

"I love you."

"You've thought of that too late."

"I want us to be together."

"And I don't!" Evelyn let Adam maneuver her to the front of the car, so that she wasn't standing in the road.

"And you're going to leave me alone now, got it? Besides which it's cruelty to animals. Drafts can be fatal for her."

Evelyn looped her hair into a knot as she tried to talk above the noise of passing traffic. It was all Adam could do not to reach out an arm and pull her to him.

"We can vacation together, the four of us, those two and—"

"Leave me alone! That's all I want from you."

"Are the sandals another one of his presents?"

Evelyn let out a screech. "That's none of your damn business!"

"Have you taken up smoking again?"

"None of your business!" She snapped her fingers. "Not this much."
She bungled the second snap.

She ran ahead to the Passat.

"You're crushing the hat!"

Evelyn waved him off without even turning around. The knot in
her hair came undone.

"It's pointless, pointless!" he heard her say as she got into the car.

She slammed the door, the Passat sped away. The distance between
the two cars grew rapidly. But, much to his satisfaction, he still managed to catch sight of the straw hat vanishing from the back window.

8

DETOURS

ADAM SMILED—Michael was obeying the speed limit. They drove through Meerane, where one row of buildings always reminded him of his toy train set. Adam was startled when the Passat signaled a turn. They were turning onto the autobahn in the direction of Karl-Marx-Stadt. The autobahn was the riverbed where he was supposed to lose the trail. But what difference did it make if they shook him off here or in Czechoslovakia. Even if they spent the cousin's Westmarks to stay somewhere else on Lake Balaton, rather than with Pepi's family, he would find them. And that was what it was all about. And at some point Evelyn would realize just how serious he was.

He almost lost control on the curve of the on ramp. Then he had to yield to a long caravan of cars. But just a few kilometers beyond Glauchau he again caught sight of the red Passat up ahead, doing barely a hundred. Adam even passed it. At first he thought he would pretend not to notice, but then turned his head and waved. Michael smiled, the women were back to talking—and smoking.

He floored it as they started uphill. Once they had the long grade behind them and were on the other side of Karl-Marx-Stadt, Adam picked up speed. The red Passat did the same. Adam suddenly let up on the throttle and looked in the rearview mirror, ready to take the exit at the last moment along with the Passat.

Approaching Dresden, Michael signaled well before the Wilsdruff gas station. Adam threaded into the lane on the right, the Passat took the one to the left, so that Evelyn got out right beside him. She disappeared together with Simone.

Adam turned off his engine and opened the door. It was hardly worth it for him to get gas, but who knew if these couple of extra liters might not come in handy.

"We've met before," Michael called. He had leaned across the passenger seat and thrust a hand toward the open window. "Michael, Mona's cousin."

"I know," Adam said and took two steps in his direction. "Hello." Talking with men from the West, even if they were older than he was, always made Adam feel uncomfortable.

"We've got quite some drive ahead of us!" Michael shouted.

"You can say that again." Adam looked at Michael's hand, the fingertips resting on the rolled-down window. The brown splotches on the index and middle fingers formed an oval. A man with nicotine stains like that was out of the question for Evelyn.

"See you later," Michael said.

"Where you headed?"

"Dresden, main station, Mona knows the way. I can't very well chauffeur two women over the border in my Passat."

"Well then," Adam said and, making sure it was in neutral, pushed his Wartburg ahead. When the women returned he noticed goose bumps on Evelyn's forearms.

Adam stayed calm and cool when the Passat pulled out first.

He let the car coast down into the Elbe Valley. He gazed across to Dresden's steeples, the Rathaus tower, as well as the television tower on the ridge of hills farther up the river, where it turned so hazy you could only surmise the rocky plateaus to the right and left that marked the river's entrance into the Elbe Sandstone Mountains.

Adam decided to take the first exit, followed the direction signs, and got lost. Not until the minaret of the old tobacco factory rose up before him did he know where he was again.

He found a parking space on the square in front of the station. He left a window cracked and slipped his camera into his shoulder bag. He couldn't spot a red Passat anywhere.

The Pannonia, leaving for Sofia via Budapest, was scheduled for a little past three, in about half an hour. The Metropol, ending in Budapest, didn't depart until seven thirty in the evening. He traced his finger down the columns of the schedule—he hadn't missed any.

Adam lined up at the wurst stand. The three of them would probably make an afternoon of it in Dresden and not leave till evening, since if they took the Pannonia they would arrive in the middle of the night. It annoyed him that they had got such a late start. You could drive to Lake Balaton in one day. He decided to drive on alone and wait for Evelyn at Pepi's—who wasn't just her friend after all.

Adam asked for two bockwursts, collected his change from the saucer, hung his pack around his neck, and was just about to pick up his wurst and buns from the counter, and there were the three of them hurrying past—Evelyn with the hat, the green tent-bag under her arm, her heels click-clacking. Michael was carrying her suitcase on his shoulder, something Adam had seen only in old movies. Simone slid across the tiles in her sandals. They made for the upper-level platform at the south end of the station and started straight up the first set of stairs. Prague, departure 14:39. Why hadn't he thought of Prague?

He passed an elderly man panting up the stairs, who suddenly stopped, bent over, his two suitcases set at an angle to the steps. For a moment it looked as if he would lose his balance. With one bun crammed in his mouth, the other pressed to the cardboard tray of wursts, Adam picked up one of the suitcases and carried it to the top. The man dragged the other one up with both hands. No sooner were they at the top than Adam heard the departure whistle. He threw open a door of the nearest car, heaved one suitcase in, then the other, helped the man in the gray suit up, and slammed the door behind him. Adam extracted the bun from his mouth, the train pulled out, the man's hands were moving behind the window.

Michael was coming toward him. He was twirling Evelyn's straw hat on his raised index finger. Adam waited for Michael to recognize him.

"Want one?" Michael shook his head, but then reached out his hand at last. He took the second bun too.

They sat down on a bench. Adam held the cardboard rectangle in his hand like an ashtray, although Michael didn't dip his wurst in the mustard unless Adam gestured for him to do so.

"Where you headed now?"

"We're going to meet in Prague."

"By way of Zinnwald?"

"Mona thinks Bad Schandau is better."

"Everybody goes the Elbe route."

"I don't know the roads," Michael said.

"Didn't she want her hat?"

"Oh sure."

"Probably afraid she'd lose it, was that it?"

"Hm. You think Zinnwald is better?"

Adam nodded, dragged the tip of his wurst through the last of the mustard, and stuffed the tray into the overflowing litter basket.

In the main concourse Adam stopped in front of a schedule.

"At the base of the statue of Wenceslas on his horse, every hour on the hour," Michael said.

They left Dresden heading south. As they waited at one of the last stoplights, Adam hastily filled the white thermos cup with coffee and drank it down. As if on order, the taste of vacation returned, and Adam could in fact think of nothing he would rather be doing than sitting behind the wheel of his car, on his way to Lake Balaton. His only worry was Elfi.

9

THE FIRST BORDER

BETWEEN ALTENBERG and Zinnwald, where serpentine curves wound toward the ridge of the eastern Ore Mountains, Adam drove off at a rest stop. Two men were hunkered down at a table, one of whom Adam first took to be his garageman, because he was staring directly at him as if he recognized him.

Michael followed Adam into the woods. They stood side by side as they peed down the slope. From down below came a foul odor.

"I've still got one of Evelyn's bags with me," Michael said, not turning his head.

"That's not a good idea."

"You think?"

"Yep."

"So what should I do?"

"It may be too late to do anything."

"You think they may be taking pictures?"

"Those two guys are on discipline detail, they have to picnic here day after day."

"Merde," Michael said.

Returning from his car, Adam set the thermos and his bag of provisions on the wooden table. It was sticky, with a layer of dust and insects. The two men had retreated to their white Lada.

"It'd be better if you'd join the picnic," Adam whispered as he unscrewed the thermos.

Michael laid a bag on the bench and put Evelyn's straw hat over it. "She had it in her suitcase."

A gust of wind rustled through the pines and firs, the tips of the needles were brown and bare.

"Damn, it stinks," Adam said.

Michael pulled an unfiltered cigarette from the pack with his lips and flipped open a silver lighter. The flame was way too high again.

"Is that coffee?" Michael blew his smoke above Adam's head.

"Want some?"

"Real coffee?" Michael sniffed at the thermos bottle.

"It's good," Adam said. Michael cautiously took the cup and sipped.

"That was a stupid move on Evi's part. They're sure to search it."

"Mona said they wouldn't be interested in me because they're more concerned about you folks. I have no idea what to expect."

"I spotted those two guys too late, I shouldn't have stopped here."

"And what do I say if they find the bag?"

"A hitchhiker's. She forgot it."

"I don't know if we're allowed to do that."

"What?"

"Pick up hitchhikers."

"So what. Did you look inside?"

Michael shook his head and passed the cup back.

"It's the genuine article."

Adam poured another cup.

"Thanks, that'll hold me till tomorrow."

"There's plenty."

With the cigarette still between his lips, Michael set his hands to his hips and moved his upper body in circles. Then he laid his hands on his shoulders and rotated his arms. The Lada with the two men drove past them, heading toward the border. Finally Michael stretched his arms straight ahead as if for swimming practice. His fingers trembled.

"Surely you don't think you're the trafficker type, do you?"

"I smoke too much."

"Whatever you do it's the wrong thing," Adam said, putting on Evelyn's hat. He picked up Evelyn's gym bag—it was light as a feather—and stuffed it behind the driver's seat.

"Don't you want to look inside?"

"Evi wouldn't like that."

"Got it."

"Did she say anything? About me, I mean?"

"Just to Mona."

"And?"

"That there was some other woman, you and—"

"I'd designed a suit for her. And it was so damn hot—Evi went off the deep end."

Michael nodded. "But what if they do a search?"

Adam shrugged. "Don't think about it. They're like animals. They can smell your fear, they've got great noses for fear."

"Killer instinct, huh?" Michael asked.

"Where are you three headed?"

"For the Plattensee—wait—Lake Balaton, that's what you guys call it. I promised Mona."

"Let's meet at the first rest stop across the border," Adam said.

"And if you don't get through?"

"Then I'll take off for Warnemünde."

"And Evi's bag?"

"You'll be able to see what happens. And remember, you are a free man and visiting the homelands of the proletariat, your natural allies. And don't drive over sixty in towns or ninety on the highway."

Adam took out the box with the turtle, opened the trunk, and put it back there. "Sorry, Elfi." He closed the lid. "We need to move out!" he shouted, and pointed back down the road.

A container truck was creeping around the curve, a long line of cars behind it.

At the border station he pulled up behind the white Lada with the two men and Dresden plates. He turned off his engine, got out, and lit a cigar. With his back to the driver's door, he closed his eyes. It was definitely cooler up here.

Whenever the line moved, Adam just released the hand brake and pushed his car in the direction of the border, the red Passat behind him. He noticed too late that it was two women who were checking his lane.

10

ONE GETS THROUGH

HER BLOND CURLS springing out from under her cap, she leafed through his papers. Despite the short olive-green skirt of her uniform, which showed off her beautiful legs, she seemed stiff and unsure of herself.

"Are you traveling to the Hungarian People's Republic?"

"I originally intended to, but it turns out my vacation time is too short. The car's been having serious problems. I didn't want to risk going too far with it anymore. So now I'm on my way to Czech paradise, to hike and so on."

The brunette with permed hair circled the car, her polished fingernails gave the hood a quick drum. "Customs control," she said, and accepted his opened papers from the blonde.

"You've exchanged koruny for forints."

"Did that a while ago in June. I'll exchange the forints back."

"What are you taking out?"

"Nothing, all the clothes are mine, some food, and eleven cigars. Personal use."

"No presents?"

"No."

After they had exchanged glances, the blonde stamped his papers, handed them back, and gave a perfunctory salute.

"Thanks," Adam said and tucked his papers away in his shirt pocket. In the side mirror he watched the two curly-locked women in short skirts stalk toward the red Passat. Michael's face looked as if it were pasted to the windshield. Adam started his engine and drove on to the Czech crossing.

"Dobrý den," Adam replied and handed over his papers. He adjusted the rearview mirror.

Adam repeated the border guard's "Na shledanou." The barrier ahead rose. As he looked back the red Passat was being waved out of the line. Michael got out. A cluster of uniforms surrounded him.

After the first curve Adam fetched the box from the trunk, placed it on the passenger seat, and opened it. The turtle didn't budge. While still an apprentice he had sped on his bicycle down this same splendid asphalt highway with its serpentine curves. At the bottom he found a parking lot and a little grocery that was closed.

Adam spread the road map out on the hood, setting the thermos at the top. From Teplice he had to drive to Lovosice, then straight ahead on the E15, which was also Highway 8, all the way to Prague. Even in the city, it was the No. 8 that he needed to stay on. He would cross the Moldau twice. If he found the right exit he would end up at Wenceslas Square. He folded the map so that he could hold it in one hand, and slipped it halfway under the box.

Adam poured the last of the coffee into the cup. If they had agreed on a meeting place, then it certainly wouldn't have been Prague, but somewhere in the area, at the train station in Ústí nad Lebem, that way they would have been reunited quickly. But since it might be hours before Michael arrived, he decided to drive on. On the other side of Terezin he picked up two women who weren't much older than he, but had gold teeth that made them look like grandmas. Each held on her lap a huge tin can filled to the brim with dark cherries.

The women were crazy about the turtle. Adam gestured for them to stay nice and calm and leave the animal in its box. The word *ticho* occurred to him. "Ticho." Which sent the women into gales of laughter, and they cried, "Ticho, ticho!" themselves. The woman in the backseat pressed the turtle to her breast. Then they sang a duet for him, occasionally rubbed a cherry on their sleeves, and stuck it in his mouth. The turtle began to move its legs and stuck out its head. In Doksany they got out. The woman who had sat up front with him waved an open palm at the road ahead and cried, "Praha, Praha," which set them laughing again, for no reason Adam could fathom. He spat a whole battery of cherry pits through the window onto the road, which inspired still more golden-toothed laughter before they finally walked away with their tin cans, but not a word of good-bye. He was about to follow them—the turtle was missing—but when he lifted the box he saw it. "Elfi," he said as it drew its head into its shell, "there's no reason to be afraid."

He hoped to arrive in Prague not much later than Evelyn and Simone, but ended up in a detour at the edge of the city. He tried in vain to orient himself by the position of the Moldau and Hradčany Castle, but drifted through the city like a ghost, and noticed too late that he had passed Wenceslas Square. When he finally found a parking space it was already growing dark.

Adam scratched the turtle behind its head in an effort to calm it, put it back in its box, and tried to open Evelyn's bag. After just an inch or two the zipper got caught, and he was afraid of ruining it, he advised all his clients against zippers—and was happy to be able to close it again without damage.

His shoulder bag with the camera under one arm, her gym bag over his shoulder, her hat on his head—he locked the car and set out.

It was a warm evening. He considered getting some ice cream, but wasn't in the mood to stand in line.

Evelyn and Simone were sitting on the top steps of the monument's pedestal—the horse's head above them; suitcases, tent, and backpack in front—and gazing out over the square.

Evelyn looked at Adam as if she were trying to remember who he was. Simone had leaped to her feet. "How did you get here?"

"By way of the German Democratic Republic. They netted Michael."

"Bastards, bastards, bastards!" Simone shouted.

"Where'd you get my bag?" Evelyn asked.

"Just sort of happened. I found—"

"What happened?"

"He was a little edgy about it, so I took it. They've got a nose for fear."

"You've lost me," Evelyn said.

"Before the border, a quick pit stop, and I took over the bag. What a couple of cuties, the women who did the once-over. Plus those pouty faces, as if it was our fault they have to run around in those getups."

"Will you just tell it like it happened."

"I waited, but thought it'd be better if I got here sooner, so that you'd know what's up."

"Did they arrest him?" Simone asked.

"Don't think so, they'll just frisk him."

Evelyn took the bag. Adam tried to set the hat on her head. She dodged it. "I'm not going to hurt you," he said, and hung the hat on her knee.

"Did they send you on ahead to track us down, Adam?" Simone stepped between him and Evelyn. "Is that your assignment?"

Adam hoped Evelyn would say something. She held her bag and hat on her lap and didn't respond.

" 'Course I've been assigned to you two. But especially you!"

"This is no time for jokes, so don't make them."

"Be glad I'm joking, because otherwise I'd slap your face."

"You have no right to follow us, Adam. Isn't that so, Evi? He has no right. Besides, you're just making it all that much worse."

Evelyn stared straight ahead.

"You can talk to me at least," Simone said, crouching down beside her.

Pigeons landed on the hand of a man feeding them breadcrumbs. Simone made a disgusted face.

"How long does it take to drive from Bad Schandau to here?"

"We crossed at Zinnwald."

"Why Zinnwald? Was that your idea?"

"What do you mean, my idea? I said I was going to cross at Zinnwald. He was happy that all he had to do was follow me."

Simone shook her head. Adam sat down below Evelyn, but a little to one side. After a while he got to his feet and walked back to the ice-cream shop. He returned with three bottles of Pepsi and three vanilla-and-chocolate cones.

"Just leave me alone," Evelyn said without even getting up. Simone took one of the cones. When Adam had polished off the other two, he opened the Pepsis with his pocketknife.

"Don't make such a face," he said, after toasting them both. "Nothing awful has happened. If you like, you can spend the night in Heinrich, Elfi would like that."

"Elfriede," Evelyn said.

"Elfi suits her better, comes from 'elf.' There's nothing to worry about. What have they got to hold him on? Nothing! They'll harass him a little, that's all."

Adam stepped out in front of the monument and opened the leather case of his camera. But before he could even choose a stop, the two women had sprung to their feet.

"Don't you dare!"

"Are you nuts, Adam?"

"You can't just take our pictures!"

Adam lowered the camera. "Why not?"

"Because I don't want you to. We don't want you to," Evelyn said.

"Put that thing away!"

Adam snapped the leather case shut and returned to his spot.

He was suddenly reminded of those two women with gold teeth and how they had brushed his lips with cherries. Behind dark blue streaks of clouds, the sky was bathed in a deep red glow, promising dry roads for the day ahead.

11

SUSPICIONS

ADAM FELT CHILLED. He had already been checked out by the police and been asked to join the singing by a couple of kids who had made themselves at home beside him, one even handed him the guitar.

When they finally left, Adam stood up, a bottle of beer in each hand, intending to fetch a sweater from the car. Then he saw Michael in a car's headlights, he was carrying a suitcase.

Adam ran toward him. "Well, finally!"

"Where are the other two?" Michael's voice sounded dry, almost brittle.

"They're asleep in my car." Adam opened the second beer and handed it to him. "Was it nasty?"

"They stripped me down to my shorts."

"The two cuties?"

"They even looked up my ass."

"That's standard procedure with traffickers. Prosit!"

"Why didn't you wait?"

"I thought, better for one of us to get here instead of no one. So prosit again!" They clinked bottles. Adam thrust his chin toward his parking spot farther down the square—"Just a few steps."

"But we'd agreed that you'd wait."

"Then the two of them would still be sitting here, thinking you'd had an accident or been arrested because of the gym bag."

"I was almost in Pilsen."

"How'd you manage that?"

Michael set his suitcase down and took a gulp.

"Want me to carry it?" Adam asked.

Simone was scrunched up in the passenger seat. Evelyn had stretched out in the back, a forearm across her eyes, her legs pulled up, the open box with the turtle on her stomach.

Michael rapped on the hood. Simone banged the passenger door against the car beside them as she jumped out. Evelyn tugged her skirt down over her knees, the box with the turtle slid down against the back of the front seat. Michael held his arm out as if Adam was supposed to take his beer, bent his knees a bit, and pressed Simone to him.

"Everything okay?" she asked after a while.

"Everything okay," Michael said.

Michael didn't need to bend down to give Evelyn a hug. He gave her a little kiss at the side of her mouth.

"I'm so happy you're here," Evelyn said. "And you're not mad at me?"

"For what?"

"For giving you the bag?"

Michael ran his hand through Evelyn's hair. "They'd been tipped off, who knows who did it, at least they acted like it," he said and set his beer on the curb. "They poked a light into the gas tank."

"Wipe the grin off your face, Adam," Simone shouted. "It's revolting!"

"They unscrewed everything that could be unscrewed. A newspaper, an ancient newspaper from a couple of years ago, that was stuck in the spare tire—that's all they took. And you guys?"

"Nothing but a lot of stupid questions," Evelyn said.

"But they collared a family in the next compartment. They had to unpack everything, and I mean every stitch."

"Somebody know a hotel around here?"

"Hotel Heinrich," Adam said.

"Well then let's go," Michael said, picking up Evelyn's suitcase. "Andiamo!"

Evelyn shook out the sweater she'd been using as a pillow, threw it over her shoulders, and knotted the sleeves at her neck.

"Elfriede's out of water," she said, tucking the tent under her arm and picking up the gym bag, which she now held up briefly. "Thanks for this," she said, without looking at Adam.

"Glad to be of service, good night," he replied, and gestured as if he wanted her to go first.

"Good night," she said, "and have a safe trip home."

Simone had been waiting with her rucksack on her back, and now grabbed one strap of the gym bag. They walked quickly to keep from falling too far behind Michael. The bag fishtailed and sashayed up and down between them.

Adam stowed the turtle back in its box and then began to slink along behind them.

The three of them suddenly disappeared into the entrance of the Jalta Hotel on Wenceslas Square. Adam hung around outside for a while. When he entered the lobby it was almost empty and still pleasantly warm. Several keys were hung behind the man at the reception desk, there were passports in a few cubbyholes.

"Dobrý večer," Adam said. "How much for a single room?"

The man smiled. "Eight hundred koruny, sir."

"For one night?"

The man nodded.

"Děkuji, thanks," Adam said and left.

He walked to the top of Wenceslas Square and then turned left toward the train station. In the men's restroom a stocky man was shaving at the washbasin and humming loudly; his black chest hair spilled out over his undershirt, his belt buckle was undone. Adam squatted on the toilet. He listened to catch the melody and then to the other sounds the man emitted as he washed his face. The faucet was turned off. The man called out something, repeated it as if waiting for an answer; then suddenly he began to sing—and left the restroom singing.

When Adam stepped up to the washbasin he found a little bar of soap lying on the rim, still in its wrapper, just for him.

Michael's bottle of beer was still standing in front of the Wartburg. Adam held it up to check if it was empty, and poured what was left in the gutter.

Pulling his legs up, he lay down on the backseat and stared directly down at Evelyn's straw hat, which lay on the floor behind the driver's seat. Although he was tired, he couldn't fall asleep. He was amazed at how loud it was. Faces were constantly appearing at the windows, peering inside, "curious about an old-timer," as one of them said. And every time they jumped back, startled to see him in there.

The next morning he was awakened by a loud bang. He sat up. A street sweeper was making its way along, morning traffic was already picking up.

The hotel door was wide open. But instead of the man from last night, a young woman with wispy pale blond hair was at the reception desk. She glanced up briefly and did not return his greeting.

He sat down in one of the clunky chairs in the lobby. When the blond woman barked at him in Czech, he said, "I'm waiting for someone," and crossed his legs. He raised his head only when the elevator doors opened or people came out of the breakfast room. There was the aroma of coffee. He watched the woman water the plants in the tubs next to the reception desk and snip off dead leaves with her long white fingernails.

Adam was awakened by a bony hand on his shoulder. "I'm waiting for my wife, Evelyn Schumann," he said.

He heard the waiter pass on Evelyn's name, but the pale blond behind the counter shook her head. Adam walked over to her and asked about Michael. "Michael, Michael," he repeated. Finally the blond turned the big book on the counter around toward him and pointed to an entry where "1 + 2" had been crossed out with red diagonal lines.

"They've left," the waiter said. "You'll have to look elsewhere."

Adam stared at him. The waiter said nothing and finally shrugged.

"Hm, yes, I guess I'll have to look elsewhere then," Adam said and took his departure with a firm handshake.

12

ANOTHER WOMAN

ABOUT TWENTY KILOMETERS before Brno, Adam stopped for gas at the rest area Devět křížů. He then found a parking space not far from the cafeteria. He made for the men's toilet, his bag slung over his shoulder and containing his shaving gear, camera, and a fresh shirt. The washroom seemed designed for people like him, there was soap and a shelf mounted below the mirror. The water stayed cold, though. He carefully began to shave. He almost cut himself when a hefty man who was shaking water from his hands bumped his elbow. Their eyes met briefly in the mirror. The man, his forearm tattooed with a busty mermaid, grumbled something that Adam took for an apology. He washed his armpits, put on his fresh shirt, tied the old one around his hips.

As he entered the restaurant sultry with kitchen steam, he started to sweat. Cigarette smoke hung above people's heads, it smelled of beer. Adam reached for a tray. Although it was wet, he laid his utensils on it and waited for the line to edge forward. Standing amid occupied tables, a family rotated helplessly in a circle, overloaded trays in hand. The babble of voices was repeatedly broken by bursts of laughter, as if this were some sort of party. Adam ordered pork and dumplings, took the last two rolls with salami decorated with a blob of mayonnaise, a slice of cream cake, and a bottle of green soda. He pulled back an

empty seat he found at a window table and asked, "Možno?" When
no one replied, he sat down. Holding his tray on his lap, he pushed a
few glasses to one side and arranged his plates one by one on the table.
The soda was obnoxiously sweet.

"Could you give me a lift?" A young woman with short hair and
bright brown eyes was looking at him. "It's pretty urgent." She set a
blue backpack in a frame down beside him.

"And where to?"

"Prague?"

"I'm driving in the other direction."

"Doesn't matter."

Two tables away a bull of a man in a beige fake leather vest shouted
something to her. He held up a handbag. She walked over to him. As
she reached for it, he pulled the handbag away, but on the second try
she snatched it out of his hand. He bellowed a laugh.

"Can you give me that lift?"

Adam nodded.

"Thanks," she said and simply stood there.

It was embarrassing just to go on eating. "You want some?" he
asked, holding up the plate with the salami.

"Love it," she said and stuffed a salami roll into her mouth. Adam
also offered her the green soda and slid a little to one side of his chair.

"Aren't you going to finish the dumplings?"

She sat down, sharing his chair, and began to eat. In relation to her
athletic body, her head seemed small to him.

Suddenly the man in the vest was standing next to them. He spoke
loudly, his index finger bouncing up and down, as if explaining something. Adam could feel the young woman press against him, even
though she went on eating and pretended to hear and see nothing.
When the man finally shut up, Adam had the sense that a hush had
fallen over the whole room. He laid his right arm across the back of
the chair. The vest guy asked a question, repeated it. While Adam was

still hesitating whether he should lay his arm around her shoulder, the man beside them laughed, pulled out his wallet, slapped a bill down beside the empty plate, and walked back to his seat.

"Thank god," she whispered, pocketing the money.

Adam carried her heavy backpack to the car and stowed it on the backseat.

"Thanks. I'm Katja." They shook hands.

"Adam," he said, holding the passenger door open and waiting as she sat down, after first banging her hiking boots together to get rid of the worst of the mud from the soles.

"Ah," Katja cried when she saw the turtle. "There are three of us on this trip."

As people watched from the rest-stop windows, Adam started the engine and had no trouble putting it into reverse.

"Thanks again so much," Katja said.

"What was with the lumberjack?"

"They'd given me a ride." She coughed. "The usual misunderstanding."

"And where are you coming from?"

"Somewhere up ahead," Katja said, pointing out through the windshield.

"And where are you headed?"

"Don't know yet," Katja said, coughed, turned as best she could to one side, crammed her handbag up against the door to cushion her head, and closed her eyes.

Adam would have enjoyed a conversation with her. All the same he was happy no longer to be alone. If only for that he was willing to put up with the odor of unwashed clothes that she gave off.

13

NEGOTIATIONS

"ARE YOU CHILLY?" He reached for her left hand. "Aren't you feeling well?"

She cleared her throat, smiled, but then turned her head aside when he tried to feel her forehead.

"Where are we?"

"Not all that far from Bratislava. I needed to take a little break." He tilted his head toward the toilets next to them.

"Me too," Katja said and leaned toward him to look in the rearview mirror. "Oh god, ghastly!"

"You should change your clothes."

"Do I stink?" Katja lifted her left arm and took a whiff.

"Your clothes are all clammy. Has it been raining all that much here?"

Katja shook her head.

"I'll give you a couple of my things. How did you manage to get so wet?"

"Oh, just a stupid joke, everything fell in the water. Maybe we could wash my stuff out around here somewhere?"

"And where?"

"A campground. There's one close by here."

"Not in Hungary?"

"It's a beautiful campground, not far from the border, they even have washing machines."

"I want to make it to Lake Balaton today yet."

"I'm not feeling so well."

Adam got out. Pulled a sweater and a pair of pants from the trunk, then some underwear and socks as well.

"Here, try these on," he said. "It's really the better way to go."

Katja got out and disappeared into the restroom. The turtle had slipped and banged against its water dish. The box was already starting to get soggy. Adam spread his map out over the steering wheel.

"Fit pretty good, don't they?" he then said. The sweater was too short, the top pants button couldn't be buttoned. Katja pulled a plastic bag from her backpack and stuffed her things into it. She perched herself on the passenger seat in her stocking feet.

"Have you got anything to drink? Some tea or whatever?"

"Just sandwiches."

"No fruit. An apple?"

He pulled the string bag of provisions from the backseat. "Genuine liverwurst with good baker's bread, although it's from Saturday, or some tea wurst?" He handed her the bag.

"And where are we now?"

"Just about here," Adam gave several taps to the green line of the autobahn.

"And here," Katja said, her hand first brushing against Adam's fingertip on the map, but then moving on ahead to a blue tent symbol, "are the washing machines."

"Nothing but our license plates," Adam said as they drove onto the campground at Zlatná on the Danube, not far from Komárno.

"Straight ahead and then take a right, that's where it gets nice," Katja directed him. But when they tried to turn, two travel trailers were blocking the road.

"Out of luck. What sort of tent do you have?" Adam asked.

"A Fichtelberg, a slightly dated model."

"That's what we've got too."

They turned around and found a spot in the middle. Adam began putting up the tent. Katja wandered off to the washroom with her backpack. By the time she returned with a remnant of green plastic clothesline full of knots and a couple of old newspapers, the tent was up.

"Nobody can sleep in there," Adam said. "Guaranteed to give you rheumatism."

"We have to extend the side ropes."

"Won't help at all."

Together they gazed at the damp tent.

"I'm going to give something a try," Adam said and with no further explanation walked to the campground entrance.

When he returned he was carrying a log as thick as his arm, with a key attached. Katja began tearing up a newspaper, crumpling page after page, and stuffing her hiking boots with them. She stretched the green clothesline from the front tent pole to the passenger-side mirror.

"I managed to find a new box for the turtle," Katja said, "one that it won't slide around in so much out on the road."

"The last cabin," Adam said and gave her the log with the key. "A little present, for rest and recuperation. Paid up for two days."

"You're driving on?"

Adam nodded.

"And if I ask you," Katja said as she stepped closer, "if I ask you, please, please, to wait till tomorrow morning, just one night? We can sleep together in it, they're built for two."

"Four in a pinch," Adam said, "but that's not the issue."

"I'm as good as begging you."

"I'm expected."

"Please, one night, and you can set out in the morning first thing."

"But why?"

"Let's drop the formal pronouns, okay?"

"Fine by me."

"Let's have a look at the place," Katja said and glanced over to a woman having trouble pitching her tent and trying to push a peg deeper into the ground. "Besides, the turtle needs to recuperate too. I just gave it a bath. This'd be a great place for it, it needs to move around a little, take some nice hikes. Does it have a name?"

"Elfi," Adam said and sat down on the ground next to the turtle.

"Elfi," Katja said and knelt down beside him. "Elfi's a lovely name."

The four tables at the food kiosk were jammed. It seemed to Adam that the level of conversation died down when he showed up. They were all speaking German, even when ordering at the counter. Sausages and rye bread were all they had left. Adam bought a jar of mustard too, ordered a large beer, and ate standing.

"You sure kept your girl waitin'. Where you been hidin' all this time?" Standing in front of him was a man in his midthirties, a faded red-and-white cap on his head.

"Take your time eatin'. Wouldn't they let you across?"

Emerson Fittipaldi—Adam was able to decode the phantom letters on the hat. "Had some stuff to do," he said and swallowed the bite. He noticed that other people were listening by now.

"Hot wheels," someone behind him said.

"And what are you two gonna do now?"

"We'll see. We're on vacation."

His interrogator grinned. Adam toasted them all, put the glass to his lips, drank and drank, staring at the green splotch that began to emerge at the bottom of the glass, drank some more, could hear comments being made around him, finished it off, and set it down as carefully as if it were full.

"Now that was a thirsty man," the guy with the Fittipaldi cap said.

Adam wiped his mouth with the paper napkin and folded it up on the cardboard tray. "Well then, so long."

The counter girl pressed the two-koruny deposit into his open palm.

"Don't you want another?"

"Nope, thanks, end up peeing too much. See you," Adam said, picking up his jar of mustard and trying to walk no faster than usual.

When he entered the cabin Katja was lying with her face to the wall, a blanket pulled up to her ears. The new box with the turtle had been set between the heads of the beds.

"You're going to cut and run," he said.

Katja didn't stir.

"Doesn't matter. I can understand your not wanting to spill the beans all at once. But what's up with those folks? What did you tell them?"

He pulled off his pants and lay down on the empty bed.

"Adam," she whispered. "I don't have a penny left."

"I can lend you some money."

"I don't have anything left, not one thing. I can't pay you back. When you leave for Hungary in the morning, will you take me with you?"

"Yes, sure—"

"In the trunk, I mean. I won't get across otherwise."

Adam was silent. He looked at her hand dangling motionless from the edge of the bed.

"Which means those people out there aren't allowed to cross into Hungary either? And you're all waiting here? What are you waiting for?"

"You can ask me for a favor too," Katja said. "I've already tried it once, by way of the Danube. There were three of us."

"And the other two?"

"No idea. They disappeared, were just gone."

Adam slowly stretched out his hand, but even when he touched her, Katja didn't roll over toward him.

14

RISKING IT

"DO YOU REALLY want to try it?" Katja asked when Adam opened his eyes. Lying there staring at him, one hand under her cheek, she looked like a child. He rolled over to hide his erection. He had slept almost nine hours. The turtle was nibbling at breadcrumbs.

"Feeling better?" he asked.

"I think so."

"Why can't you get into Hungary?"

"I never applied. Nobody I know ever got a visa, except for one person. And they came and took it away from her the next day. Sitting at home, the doorbell rings, and poof! it's gone, no reason given."

"How about where there's no official crossing?"

"That's called the Danube."

"How about where there's woods or fields, isn't that the longer section?"

"It's difficult there because it's guarded better, fences everywhere, nobody knows the territory. Why do you think they're all here? But they're all scared shitless of the Danube."

"And if they nab us?"

"They won't." Like Adam, Katja had now propped herself up on one elbow.

"The Hungarians are no problem, they just wave you through. And the Czechoslovaks only look at your papers. They're not ransacking cars anymore."

"How do you know that?"

"Everybody here will tell you that. If there's one thing they know here, it's that."

Adam got up and opened the door. The sky was clouded over. He could hear kids' voices coming from a tent. A man in rubber boots was carrying a full jerrican of water back to his trailer.

"Am I the first person you've asked?"

"Yes."

Adam went to the washroom. On the way back he bought two bottles of milk, six *hörnchen*, and a jar of strawberry jam. Katja took the jar from him. The turtle lumbered through the sparse grass.

"Go get washed up, I'll take care of the rest."

"There's no rush. This early is not a good idea."

"I thought they only check your papers?"

"By ten o'clock there's usually a line, they aren't paying that much attention. People have been watching from this side, through binoculars." Adam sat down beside her on the wooden bench at the front of the cabin.

"Cheers," he said. They toasted with milk bottles.

"I want to thank you."

"Let's not talk about it. Best thing'd be just to forget it."

"Forget it?" Katja stared at him.

"Keep your voice down," Adam hissed. "That's not what I meant. I've already stopped thinking about it. That's the best way. They can tell if you're thinking about anything like that."

"We can wait till tomorrow."

"For your laundry? It's almost dry."

"To prepare ourselves."

"But not here, not with this bunch of jackasses. That's even riskier."

"There are idiots everywhere."

Adam dipped his *hörnchen* in the jar. The jam fell off the tip. He gave it a second try, hunching over to take a quick bite.

Katja opened the big blade of a Swiss Army knife and took the *hörnchen* away from him.

"Oh, so the lady's got her contacts in the West?"

"A friend."

"Swiss?"

"No, Japanese."

"Japanese? Aren't those guys a little small for you?"

"What do you mean?"

"There's got to be something of a fit. And when you're a head taller, for most men that's always—"

"Baloney. My friend is about your size, a little taller in fact."

Katja had slit the doughy roll open, spread it with jam, and handed him half.

"Do you want to go to Japan?"

"Have to wait and see."

"Can't he just marry you? Wouldn't that be easier?"

"He's already married."

"Well, congratulations. And it's because of him you want to leave?"

"You don't?"

"Not me. I'm on vacation."

Katja laughed. "An A-plus in conspiracy." She stretched out one leg, the tips of her toes looming up right in front of the turtle. "Don't run away," Katja said.

"I don't want to cut and run," Adam said. "Wouldn't work anyway. Do you think the Hungarians are going to open their border?"

"They already have, they all ran right across."

"Who ran across?"

"Our guys. Don't you know about that? They opened the border, and a couple hundred people ran and ran and they were gone."

"When's this supposed to have happened?"

"Saturday, three days ago."

"The border isn't open!"

"At any rate it *was* open. What's wrong? Does that upset you? The ones in the embassy, they've all left now too."

Adam shook his head and drank his bottle of milk down to the last swallow or two.

"Why the West—or Japan?"

"What sort of question is that! A better life. To be able to live, period."

"So you haven't lived till now?"

"I've had it, had it with being nailed inside a coffin until retirement. Nothing—you can't do one damn thing."

"Is that how you see it?"

Katja stared at the ground. "There's something I have to tell you."

"That's always a great starter."

"I was alone in the Danube."

"You mean, the other two—nobody disappeared, is that it?"

Katja nodded. "I just thought . . ."

"What?"

"I wasn't even thinking—I don't know myself why I said that."

"Have you got anybody over there who can help you out?"

"All our relatives are over there. I want to study. And I'll find some kind of job while I do. . . . What's so funny?"

"Well, see, when you invite somebody to climb into your trunk—it's good to know if it's just a spur-of-the-moment, crackpot idea."

"And you, have you got somewhere to stay in Hungary?"

"Yes, in Badacsony, on Lake Balaton, friends of Evi's."

"Your wife?"

"One way to put it."

"And where is she?" Katja held out the other half of the *hörnchen* to him.

"She's waiting for me there."

"So you actually are on vacation?"

"Yeah, sure. Evi has to go back to work in September. And I still had lots to take care of. So she and a girlfriend took off."

"Got it."

After they'd been eating in silence for a while, Adam asked, "What makes you trust me?"

"I didn't give it much thought. I didn't have a choice."

"Sure you did."

"I spotted you. Everybody was looking outside, at your Wartburg. Spies never drive up in an old heap like that."

"Just the opposite. Never heard of camouflage, of mimicry?"

"Oh, please, I'm not quite that stupid. And then there's Elfi—that's pretty wacky, you must admit."

"Just like I said, mimicry."

"And why do you believe me? Maybe I'm the spy. Young woman latches on to man traveling alone and pushes him straight into the knife as a trafficker. You see? That caught your attention."

"What a load of crap."

"Why? Who spoke to who first?"

"You mean the old maiden-in-distress trick—"

Katja shrugged. "Why not?"

Adam screwed the lid back on the jar, drank the last of his milk, wiped his mouth, and looked at Katja.

"I know what's really going on here. We're both from the Stasi and are checking up on the trustworthiness of a coworker."

"That doesn't change a thing."

"Does it ever. Nothing can happen to us either way. I take you across because I want to find out how it develops from there, who your contacts are once you're over the border, while you—"

"Oh, stop it. Right now." Katja ran after the turtle and put it back in its box.

"Well then, just think about Lake Balaton or Kilimanjaro."

"Kilimanjaro?"

"What's the name of that mountain, the one with the snow on top?"

"You mean Fuji?"

"Yeah, think of Fuji."

"Are you going to take care of the tent? I'll go fetch my laundry. They need to refund your money, half of it at least."

"I'll give them the message," Adam said and watched her go, watched her walk off in his sweater and pants and her hiking boots.

After a few kilometers, right after the village of Nová Stráž, they stopped beside a country road lined with high grass and bushes. Adam drove in reverse as far as a slight curve. Then he opened the trunk, took out the two jerricans, and stored them up against the backseat, laying them lengthwise and draping them with air mattresses, sleeping bags, the suitcase, and some sacks, so that they were no longer recognizable as jerricans.

Katja folded the blanket in half and spread it between the semicircles of the two wheel housings. She made herself a pillow out of the two plastic bags with her laundry in them, but stuffed some of it along the sides as if caulking the trunk.

"So, think of Fuji." He held out a hand to help her climb in.

"I need to go first," she said and walked up the road a little farther. "You have to turn around."

Adam walked into the high grass and took a pee himself as he watched what few cars were passing by.

When he came back Katja was already lying in the trunk with her knees pulled up. She first rolled on her back and then on her other side. "Roomier than I thought," she said.

"It'll get smaller," he said, and handed her the blue backpack in its frame.

Katja banged her chin as she tried to press the backpack tighter to her.

"That's not going to work," he said.

Adam set the backpack down beside the car, covered Katja with underwear from one of the bags, and as a finishing touch laid a raincoat over her shoes. "Nobody 'll find you here," he said.

"Adam, I'll say it now, ahead of time. Thank you!"

"No singing, no yowling, no rocking the boat. Okay? And no fear—it's gonna get dark now." He closed the trunk. The car was tilted down over the rear axle. "You've got to slide farther forward," he said when he opened the trunk. "As far as you can, up in here."

"Like this?" Katja asked, pressing her back and shoulders farther into the trunk.

"Can I give you Elfi for company?"

Katja pulled the T-shirt away from her face and nodded. "Give her to me, that's a great idea."

Adam added the open box with the turtle. Katja pressed it to herself.

"Adam?" She blinked a little. "If something goes wrong, tell the truth. Truth is always the best."

"The truth and nothing but the truth."

"You got it."

"See you soon," Adam said. He slipped behind the wheel and started the engine. "Can you hear me?"

"What?"

"Can you understand me?"

"Let's get a move on!" Katja shouted. Adam nodded and drove off.

15

HANDS HALF OPEN

BOTH LANES for the border control at Komárno were about the same length. At the last moment Adam changed to the one on the right when he spotted two travel trailers up ahead. His watch had stopped. He rolled down the window and asked the time from the woman in the passenger seat in the neighboring car. The man at the wheel raised his left arm, the woman grabbed it, turned it a bit, and called out: "Eight after ten! Closer to nine."

Adam thanked her, set his watch for ten after ten, and wound it. Most of the cars had GDR plates.

In front of him were two elderly people in a Trabant from Hungary, who sat there stiff as dummies, on the left a squarish skull with protruding ears, the woman with a headscarf. The couple seemed to him the embodiment of rectitude and harmlessness. Maybe something of that impression would flow back his way, or would the total disparity be his undoing? The family in the Škoda behind him was likewise inert, staring straight ahead. He probably didn't look all that much different himself.

If he could have had just one wish: The car right behind him would have been the red Passat, with Evelyn as an eyewitness. When they ordered him to open the trunk, he wouldn't bat an eye. Even as they led him and Katja away, his gaze would be stubbornly fixed on the ground.

It comforted him that the Trabant in front of him was also hanging low on its rear axle.

The right lane did in fact start edging forward a little faster, so that Adam now found himself waiting next to a Dutch VW bus, just as the Hungarians in front of him handed over their papers. They appeared to be paying no attention at all to the border guard. They didn't even turn their engine off, were asked no questions, and put-putted on their way.

The border guard waved for Adam to hurry it up. Bending his knees slightly, he pointed his thumb up with a "Jeden?" Adam nodded and handed him his papers. And before he could even stop smiling, he watched as the wide metal stamp was placed above a back page in his papers and came down with a clatter.

"Dovidenia," the border guard said.

"Dovidenia," Adam replied, started his engine, and drove ahead slowly, just in case a customs agent should pop up.

Before him stretched the bridge; he drove over the Danube. He would have loved to let out a roar of some sort.

"What year is the manufacture of your Wartburg?" the shorter, and older, of the two Hungarian border guards asked.

"Nineteen sixty-one."

"They have become seldom. No one drives this today anymore, am I not correct?" the other one said as he stamped his papers.

"Yes, you are," Adam said, "but it drives well, still the first motor, everything original."

Both men looked into the car. They were especially intrigued by the steering wheel, whose lower half was smaller in diameter than the upper, and by the small gearshift beside it.

"Will you open the hood, please?"

"Yes," Adam said. But when he started to get out, the border guard waved him back.

"Just open," he said. "Start engine." The two vanished behind the hood. Adam gave it gas a few times, so they could hear how the motor sounded. Three cars were already lining up behind him. When the two closed the hood again, the VW bus was trundling up. Adam signaled the guards that they needed to close the hood tighter, but the short one just called out, "Viszontlátásra."

Adam put the car in gear and drove slowly out of the border station and onto the road. He rolled up the window. After a couple hundred yards he shouted: "Made it! Made it!"

It wasn't long before Adam pulled over to the shoulder. He opened the trunk. Katja pushed the T-shirt away and looked up at him, blinking. She was lying in the same position as before. "Come on, quick, no one needs to see this." He lifted out the box with the turtle. Katja, however, moved as if in slow motion.

"My arm's fallen asleep," she said softly and tried to sit up. As if she had suddenly lost all her strength, she toppled against Adam, who, when he heard a car coming, simply lifted her out and held her tight. "Congratulations!" He gave her cheek a peck.

Katja said nothing. She walked ahead stiff-legged and sat down in the passenger seat. He set the box on the backseat and pushed the hood down securely.

"A hearty welcome to the People's Republic of Hungary. Did you hear any of that? They were interested in the motor, a pair of real cutups."

Adam honked the horn, Katja winced. He drove off. When he checked the rearview mirror he recognized the VW bus and lifted his foot from the accelerator.

"You know what? I'd love to be an amateur trafficker. It might even be a fun career! You can get across like a hot knife through butter."

Adam gave another honk as the Dutchmen passed him.

"Look at them gawk at us!" Adam waved to them. "What's wrong? What's the problem?"

Tears were running down her cheeks and dripping from her chin onto her sweater. Adam held out his blue checkered handkerchief. But when she didn't take it, didn't even seem to notice it, he let it fall to her lap, between her hands—palms up, half open.

16

HERO'S LIFE

"I'M SORRY," Adam said. "I had no idea."

Katja blew her nose in the handkerchief. She kept her head lowered, as if she were inspecting the round table or the empty coffee cups still on it.

"But it can't be all that easy to drown."

"That's what you think. Rivers are different—and then when it's pitch dark and you've got something like that on your back. And the first time your head goes under, when it pulls you down, you panic. All you know is: It's stronger than you."

"I wouldn't have gone in. I would have let them nab me."

"When you stand there looking across, staring at the far bank, the river gets smaller and smaller, and you think, Let's go, dive in, best do it right now, don't even stop and think. You're only afraid of border guards and dogs."

Adam tried to touch her hands. People at the next table glanced across. He slid closer to Katja.

"There's nothing you can do to fight back, nothing at all. It grabs you and spins you around, like some evil angel, you're powerless—"

"But you made it."

"I was lucky, that's all." She wiped her tears and sniffed hard. Suddenly she was leaning against him, her head on his shoulder. He slid closer still and laid an arm around her. He stroked her hair, the back of her head. He looked at the nape, the clasp of a thin silver chain. If the waiter had arrived a second later, he probably would have kissed her at that spot just under the clasp, where that little vertebra stuck out—the one he always used for measuring his clients.

The waiter laid the knives and forks, wrapped in white napkins, beside their plates, opened the lid of the mustard jar, and, as if the other guests weren't supposed to see, slipped two little packages of ketchup under the rim of Adam's plate. He departed again without a word.

Katja sat up.

"Here," Adam said, pushing a glass of mineral water over to her. Katja took a sip, held the glass in her hand for a moment, only to drink it down in one gulp. She blew her nose again and stuck the handkerchief in her pants pocket. Adam unwrapped the utensils and passed her a set.

"First you need to get your strength back."

"Where are you going from here?"

"Where do you want to go?"

"To the embassy, and I mean the right one, in Budapest."

"I'll take you."

Adam tried to open one of the red and white packages. He laid it down again, wiped his hands, and tried once more. Finally he put it between his teeth and yanked.

"I can't even watch this," Katja said, grabbing the other package, and opened it with ease.

Adam pressed the ketchup through the tiny opening onto his wurst. A couple of squirts landed on the table.

"What sort of work do you do?"

"I'm a tailor, a ladies' custom tailor."

"I'd expect you to know tricks like that."

"If you want, I'll dress you up shiny and new."

"Is that what that callus comes from?" She pointed to his right thumb. "I thought maybe you play guitar."

They ate in silence. Adam was glad he hadn't kissed Katja on the nape of her neck.

"Do you think they might have some chocolate here too?" she asked.

Adam turned around toward the buffet. They both got up. Katja pressed both index fingers against the glass of the vitrine beside the cash register.

"Kinderschokolade? Kinderschokolade!" he said, and directed the waiter's hand with shakes and nods of his head.

"Kettő." Adam spread two fingers. He bought four more bottles of water and paid.

Outside they sat down on a bench, each with a bar of Kinderschokolade in their hands, and pushed the little squares out. Pulling back the wrapper after each one, they stuck them into their mouths—Adam devouring one whole piece at a time, Katja biting them in half.

"What's up?" Adam asked, when Katja stopped chewing to stare at the paving stones.

"Wouldn't have taken much and the film would've started playing over again."

Adam waited for her to continue. "You mean, if you'd been drowning?" he finally asked.

"That I could touch bottom was dumb luck, nothing else. And the rest was just a matter of having trained for a long time."

"Swimming?"

"Rowing. First single scull. Then coxless pair, then fourman, until I was seventeen, and then I'd had enough."

"You just trained in the wrong sport."

"I pedaled and thrashed like an idiot, trying to get out again."

"Where do you come from?"

"From Potsdam. I was gasping for air till I thought my lungs would fall out. And then almost froze to death. Everything drenched. My neck pouch gone—no money, no papers, everything gone!"

"And all for a married Japanese guy?"

"What do you mean?"

"That's what you said."

"No I didn't."

"Of course that's what you said."

"Oh! I've always wanted to get out."

Adam gave her his last bar of Kinderschokolade.

"Thanks, I'll save it, for a very rainy day. So you're going to go on to Budapest now?"

"Have to I'd think."

"You don't have to."

"You saw what happens when you're left unattended."

Katja stuffed the wrapper into the empty box. "I feel so stupid for acting the way I did yesterday. Can I tell you something?"

"Fire away. Betray any secret you want."

"The whole time Elfi made sounds as if trying to calm me. You don't believe that, do you?"

"Sure, sure I do," Adam said. "Come on, let's go. If you want I'll even carry you."

"That'd be lovely, at least part of the way."

They stood up, each grabbing two bottles of water, left the empty boxes lying on the bench, and walked to the car.

17

PREPARATIONS FOR A FAREWELL

THEY HAD FOLLOWED the traffic signs for the center of the city and found a parking place along the Danube between the Chain Bridge and the Elisabeth Bridge. On Váci utca they lined up at an ice-cream cart. Adam watched the server pull down on the lever of the machine. The ice cream coiled into the cone, creeping upward and quickly achieving daredevil heights, till the peak curled over and froze in place.

Katja's lips encircled the tip of the ice cream, and from there her mouth automatically moved down the spiral as if she were prayerfully screwing it in. Adam, his shoulder bag under his arm, kept glancing at the circular scar on her left biceps. His sleeveless black T-shirt with the faded Brazilian flag looked good on her.

"Twist my arm and I'd have another," she said.

The server gave her a smile when she appeared before him a second time.

"He piled on a little extra this time around," Adam said as they strolled down Váci utca in the direction of Vörösmarty tér. He zeroed in on a souvenir shop. Katja inspected the display window while Adam bought a map of the city.

"Look what they have here," she said, tapping at the windowpane.

"The snow globe?"

"No, there."

"The pipe?"

"The Rubik's Cube, the magic cube you can twist and turn."

Adam went back inside and returned with the cube. Katja gave him a quick hug. Her shoulders were hot from the sun.

"I'm sorry," Katja said. "I'm not really this childish. I do have better manners. Do you want it?"

"No big deal. It's my pleasure. Now here's a practical item, so you'll have something in that handbag of yours." Adam gave her a little wallet.

"There's money inside. Way too much!"

"Just three hundred, in case you want another ice-cream cone."

He walked ahead to a bench that had just been vacated. He first placed his shoulder bag on his lap and then spread out the map.

"Oh Adam, thank you." Katja sat down beside him, shoved the last tip of the cone into her mouth, and twisted at the Rubik's Cube.

"What was the name of the street?"

"Something like Népstadion, but it's the street parallel to it, otherwise we'll end up at the wrong embassy. I've been picturing this for weeks, sitting here and eating ice cream."

"Not with a view to Fuji?"

"It's almost the same thing."

"I want to take a picture."

"No, don't."

"Why not, just for me." Adam unsnapped the leather case of his camera.

"But I don't want you to!" Katja turned to one side.

"What's wrong with that? One shot, for me."

Katja shook her head.

Not until Adam was sitting beside her again and thumbing through the street index did she finally turn around.

"If only I knew the Hungarian word for 'embassy.' "

"Should I ask?"

"No," Adam said and returned to the souvenir shop. He watched Katja through the window. She pulled her legs up, raised both feet onto the bench, and embraced her shins. When someone sat down beside her, she ambled back and stopped at the open shop door.

" 'Embassy' sounds something like"—Adam looked at the slip of paper that the salesgirl had handed him—"nagykövet." He jingled his change.

Katja followed him to the phone booth. Adam picked up the receiver and hung up again. "It works."

He reached down for the phone book dangling in its hard binder, opened it, thumbed through it for a long time with both hands, constantly flipping pages back and forth.

"Shit!" he suddenly cried, and let the phone book drop on its chain. "Some idiots have torn out the page—Katja?"

Adam stepped out of the booth and looked around. He stood there for a while. Then he started walking back in the direction they had come from.

Katja was sitting at the edge of the fountain under the statue of Mercury, next to a young couple wearing the same suede hiking boots she had on, their framed backpacks set before them.

"Hello," Adam said.

"My friend," Katja said. The young woman with a thick braid and cut-off jeans wrote a phone number on the back of Katja's hand.

"The embassy's closed," Katja explained. "They're not letting anyone in. We have to go to the Maltese Charity, up in the hills."

"Why isn't the embassy letting anyone in? They can't just turn people away, can they?" Adam asked.

"You've got to go across to Buda, to the Zugliget district, they have tents in the church garden. They'll look after you," said the young man, tugging at his sparse reddish beard. "Kozma is the priest's name. You need to ask for the way to Szarvas Gábor út, that's where the church and this Father Kozma are, everybody knows him, or so I've heard."

"And you two?" Adam asked.

"We're sleeping out on Margaret Island," the woman said, and took her friend's hand. "It's nicer there."

"We're on vacation until our cash runs out," he said. "At the end of the day everything's real cheap at the market hall. Sometimes they just give us stuff, because they know what's going on here."

"Weirdos," Adam said after good-byes were exchanged.

"Why? They were perfectly okay."

"Well, maybe. But when they don't even look at you, I mean at me."

"They looked at you."

"No they didn't, it was as if I wasn't even there. And if there's something I can't stand it's cut-off jeans, braids, and childish beards like his."

"Look where Mercury's pointing—that's west, isn't it?"

"Yes," Adam said. "That's Buda over there."

"Will you take me to this priest?"

They walked back down Váci utca.

"Do I get a good-bye ice cream?"

"If I can take your picture."

"Nope, then I guess not."

The line was longer than before. Katja dropped her Rubik's Cube into Adam's shoulder bag, laid both hands on his right shoulder and buried her head in them, as if to fall asleep there.

"By the way, Adam," she said softly. "It's really not important. But is it possible that you forgot my backpack, left it there just before the border?"

Adam didn't answer.

"It wasn't on the backseat," Katja continued. "And not in the trunk either."

"Could be," Adam said, without turning his head. "Could be you're right."

"It's nothing horrible, really it isn't—like I said, absolutely not."

"You can have my sleeping bag, and the air mattress," Adam said and stood up very straight. When he started moving, it was with tiny steps, so that Katja could follow without taking her hands from his shoulder. They kept close together like that until they were at the head of the line.

18

FAILED FAREWELL

ADAM HELD THE MAP in place on the roof of the car. The wind had folded the top half over. The evening sun stood above the hills of Buda. At the dock was an excursion boat, its railings decorated with garlands of tiny lights. A waiting crowd had gathered before a chain that blocked the entrance to the gangway. Gulls screeched. The facades of the buildings along the Pest side of the river suddenly seemed to have taken on color, to be glowing from the inside.

"For some reason I don't like the idea," Adam said as he tried to fold the map smaller. "We should have asked at the embassy anyway. Who knows what kind of tent camp this is."

Katja was still licking at her ice cream.

"Did they speak to you first or the other way around?"

"It just happened somehow."

"Don't say 'somehow.' Did you ask them?"

"They could only be some of our bunch. They were headed for Bulgaria and then got wind of what's happening here, and went to the embassy."

"So you spoke to them first?"

"It doesn't matter! Do you think I wouldn't notice if there was something fishy about it?"

"I didn't like them, looked like plants to me, and it worked perfectly."

"I still have your handkerchief."

"Keep it. As a memento."

"You couldn't use it anyway now." She wiped her hands on it. "You'll get it back laundered and ironed and blue checked, word of honor."

"Registered mail from Tokyo."

"We'll make a ceremony of it. On top of Fuji. I'll pay for your flight."

Adam had folded the map so small that only two adjoining squares were left.

They drove across the Chain Bridge. Katja had taken the turtle out of its box. "What we'd love to do right now is go on one of those boat rides, right, Elfi?"

A Wartburg passed them and honked.

"I asked them for the time while you were curled up in the trunk."

"Follow them."

"You think they're going to the same place?"

"Anybody driving that fast knows what they're doing."

On the other side of the bridge they followed them into the tunnel.

"It'd be helpful if you kept an eye on the map."

"He's just saying that out of jealousy, Elfi," Katja said, knelt backward in her seat, and let the turtle slide from the palm of her hand into the box. Once they were out of the tunnel Adam gave her the map and tapped at it with his index finger.

"Somewhere here. I drew a circle around it, that's where we need to go."

"They're going to have to turn right at some point, in fact just up ahead."

"But they're not."

"Turn right, the next right."

Ten minutes later they left the major artery and started up into the hills. The houses here had large front gardens. Behind the trees and bushes you could see villas, alternating with new structures and multifamily homes. The street was lined with parked Trabants and Wartburgs.

"Guess who's puttering along behind us?" Adam said. "Our speedster."

The trees along Szarvas Gábor út stood so close together that Katja didn't see the steeple on their left until they had stopped right in front of it. The church's garden was teeming with people. It was on a steep slope, but farther up were large tents.

Katja pulled out her last bar of Kinderschokolade, unwrapped it, and broke it in half.

"So this is the very rainy day?" Adam asked, and put his half in his mouth. The family in the Wartburg behind them was also hesitant about getting out.

"Wait," Adam said, taking hold of Katja's arm, although she had already opened the door. "I'll take a look around first." The posts at the foot of the stairway looked like chess figures. A long table had been set up in the garden, with large pots and laundry baskets full of bread. Adam climbed up to the church.

"Hello, I'm looking for Herr Kozma—" But the woman who had been coming toward him ran right by him and down the steps into the garden, where she joined the rapidly growing line waiting for food to be dished out.

Adam stepped into the church, a bright cruciform space. Except for a ciborium in gingerbread style, with a miniature Jesus on the cross, it was almost bare of ornamentation.

"We got your address from the embassy," Adam said to a woman who looked like a gatekeeper and was sitting at a little table to the left of the entrance. She pointed to a door, which led him down a hallway lined with bookcases. You could smell food even in here.

"And you're looking for . . .?" a short balding man asked.

"I'm looking for Herr Kozma."

"That's me."

"Is it possible to spend the night here?"

"If you like."

"Not me. But I have someone in the car who would like to. She swam the Danube—"

"Let her come," Kozma said.

At that moment the man from the other Wartburg entered, two license plates in his hand.

"There are five of us," he said, looking back and forth between Kozma and Adam.

"Please come in," Kozma said.

"May I take a look around?" Adam asked.

"Please do," Kozma said. His hand was resting on the end of a pew, his thumb rubbing along its carvings—a cross encircled by an omega.

Children were sitting on the steps leading down to the garden. Two older girls were playing badminton. People who hadn't gone to get what was being offered to eat stood clustered in little groups. Higher up the slope a woman in a tracksuit was hanging out wash.

As Adam was leaving, the whole Wartburg family was coming toward him—the parents with suitcases, the children with small camping bags on their backs and stuffed animals in their hands.

"Good luck," Adam said, but apparently they didn't notice him at all. The woman just glanced briefly over her shoulder, as if afraid someone was following her.

"I think it's on the up-and-up," Adam said. "They have tents, big tents, they look new."

Adam opened the trunk. He took out the Fichtelberg tent and the two sacks with whatever things of hers hadn't been stored in the backpack.

Two men approached them in the church vestibule. They were walking across the tiles barefoot, they stared at Katja and went on outside. Kozma was nowhere in sight.

"Let's hope I don't end up with them," Katja whispered. "This place smells like a school camp."

"Well then, take care," Adam said. "You've got my address."

"Don't you want to spend the night here and then head out tomorrow morning?" Adam shook his head. They extended hands. Then Katja threw herself around his neck. She said something, but so softly that he couldn't understand her.

Adam had already set the turtle's box on the passenger seat and started the engine when he noticed the Rubik's Cube.

As he was climbing the stairs, Katja appeared up top. "Adam," she called, "Adam!" and ran, tent and bags pressed to her like stolen goods, down the steps to him.

19

OFF-LIMITS CAMPING

ADAM CROSSED the intersection and pulled to a stop. "Can you read it? What's it say?"

Katja bent forward. In her left hand she was holding the Budapest map that Adam had folded up, in her right the cube, on her lap lay the road map of Hungary.

"Somehow I can't find this road, it's not on here. Turn around," she said. "We made a wrong turn somewhere. Just turn around and drive back to those traffic signs."

" 'Somehow,' 'somewhere,' " Adam said, opening the back door and hauling out one of the two twenty-liter jerricans. He unscrewed the gas-tank cap and fed the funnel in. He had to lift the can almost to his chest, the first slosh spilled.

"Can I help?" Katja called.

"Stay put," Adam managed to gasp, his face distorted with exertion. His upper body moved in rhythm with the can's glug-glugging and whenever a rapid boom-boom-boom echoed inside the can. In time, however, these hollow thuds grew softer, until the gasoline was flowing almost soundlessly into the funnel and Adam's face relaxed. Even when only drops were coming out, Adam went on holding the can at vertical. A cricket chirped.

"And?" Adam asked as he got back in the car. His hands gave off the odor of gasoline.

"You can take me back, you know."

Adam started the engine and made a U-turn.

"It was childish of me," Katja said. "I don't know myself why I panicked like that."

Adam glanced at his watch.

"You can let me out right here, I'll find my way back."

"Stop it now."

"I can't always be tagging along behind you, hoping you'll buy me more ice cream."

"And what if those people there send you away?"

"Then even great big Lake Balaton won't be much help either."

"Maybe there'll be another miracle."

"Have you got enough money?"

Adam shrugged.

"Can you lend me some? I'll pay you back, in Westmarks, one to one, as soon as I can."

"You don't need to pay me back. I'd rather you tell me where I'm supposed to be going."

They stopped at an intersection, the car behind them honked.

"Take a right here, we have to circle around to the right, there's the sign. No money, no paper, no nothing—up the creek."

"I don't have all that much, just the forints they allow—and you know how far that goes."

"I'm sorry."

"We're going to drive to Lake Balaton now, and tomorrow we'll see. We know some people there. You won't starve. You don't need to worry, not on that account."

"I don't need much."

"I've got another two hundred Westmarks. Once we've tanked up and take off for home, you get whatever is left."

"Just let me out here somewhere, Adam. You don't need to be afraid I'll make any trouble for you. Your wife won't so much as see my face, if that's what's bothering you."

"Now stop it, once and for all! What's left to eat?"

"*Hörnchen* and jam and a jar of mustard."

"Well, fork it over!"

"I'm not hungry."

"Sure you are," Adam said. "You need to eat something, by way of precaution."

They left the city just as the sun vanished below the horizon.

Around eleven they pulled in at the campground at Badacsony. The barrier was down, no gatekeeper in sight.

"Whoa, look at those prices!" Katja exclaimed. "They want thirty marks a night."

"West German marks," Adam said, nodding in the direction of a little group just returning to their tents. "They're the ones driving prices up."

"I'll just walk in," Katja said. "We'll meet again then tomorrow, okay?"

"Tomorrow?"

"Or the day after?"

"Let's go a little farther, we'll find something yet."

"Aren't you going to go meet your wife?"

"It's too late now."

"What do you mean too late?"

Adam got back into the car. "So what's up? Do you want to come along or don't you?"

Katja hesitated. "Do you know your way around here?"

"Come on."

They drove on, until Adam stopped and made a careful turn off the road.

"So have a look," he said and turned on his brights, revealing a meadow and the water. "Now that looks like it's been made for us." He turned the headlights off and opened the door. "How about a swim? Or not your kind of thing?"

"Sure, of course," Katja said. "It's just so dark here."

"Not a soul, just crickets."

"Let me get used to the idea first."

Adam at once began blowing up an air mattress. Katja unrolled the tent and put the poles together by light from the car interior. Adam helped her set it up. "Listen, frogs," he said.

When they were finished he undressed and walked out into the water.

"Don't you want to come in? The water's fine, not too cold, not too warm."

It got deeper only gradually. "Katja? Are you there?" When he got no answer, he glided into the water and swam off. He tried to move as soundlessly as possible. Everything else sounded far away. The lake was circled with light. It was dark only directly behind him.

"Now that's what I call a puddle! Now I smell like water instead of gasoline," he said. Katja handed him a towel. Adam walked around to the other side of the car, dried himself off, and fetched fresh clothes from his suitcase. "Shall we go find a beer somewhere?"

"Not for me."

"I'll sleep in the car."

"Are you still going out somewhere?"

"No," he said. "Have you taken care of Elfi?"

"I gave her a little softened-up bread."

"Anything wrong?"

"Good night," Katja said, disappeared into the tent, and pulled the zipper shut.

20

FIRST REUNION

"HELLO, GOOD MORNING." Katja was holding two tent pegs, banged them together, and scraped off the rest of the dirt clinging to them. She was wearing the Brazilian T-shirt over her bikini. "We need to get out of here."

Adam sat up. Several families had already spread towels and blankets in the general area, there was an odor of suntan lotion in the air.

"The Young Pioneer loves and protects nature," Adam said. "Did I ever dream a lot of crap." He rubbed his face with both hands, as if washing it.

"How late is it?"

"You're the one with the watch."

"Let's at least take a swim," Adam said after they had loaded everything into the car.

"You're a gutsy guy." Katja pulled off her T-shirt. Some kids were playing on the shore.

"Ugh, slimy!" Katja yelled and backpedaled.

"Elephant poop, genuine Hungarian elephant poop. You have to wade through it, if you want to get to the West, all the way to the far shore," he said in a low voice.

"That's not the West over there!"

"I'll carry you through the elephant poop and collect the bounty money."

"Bounty money?"

"Well, what you've cost the state so far, which is what they've saved on you over there."

"How much does it come to?"

"Twenty thousand, maybe?"

"That's all?"

"Or fifty. I'll buy fabric with it. Nothing but the finest. Come on, let's go."

"I don't want to."

"Once you're in—"

"I can't."

"What do you mean can't? You having your period?"

"Lower your voice."

"Well then, what is it?"

"I've told you already. I just can't."

Adam waded back to the shore. "Come on," he said, holding a hand out to her. "Once you start in with that kind of hocus-pocus, you can never shake it off. Come on, hold tight."

Taking reluctant, tiny steps, Katja entered the water, pulled her hand away and ran back.

"I'll carry you."

"No, I'm way too heavy for you."

"Come on, one arm around my neck, and now alley-oop!" Adam staggered briefly, but then walked sturdily into the water. Katja held tight with both arms.

"Don't be afraid," he panted, getting a better grip. "I won't drop you."

"Go back, Adam, please, take me back."

"Nyet," he said and waded ahead as quickly as he could.

"Please, I'm scared!"

"No need to be. Everything's fine, everything's fi-hine." Adam was almost running when the water reached his trunks. "Think of Fuji or of Elfi—it'll be a little cold at first."

Katja screamed but at the same moment flipped onto her stomach and went into a crawl. Adam slipped into the water. Katja swam in a curve around him.

"It's not so bad, is it?" he shouted and did a few quick strokes. "Everything okay?"

Instead of answering she took off. Adam swam back and forth a little, then stood up, in water to his belly button, and watched her swim away.

Hands on his hips, he sunned himself. Once in a while he opened his eyes, but Katja had disappeared beyond the sailboats.

When he finally saw her swimming back toward him, he set out to meet her.

"It's not so icky this far out."

"Not all that pleasant either," she said, turning briefly to one side and adjusting her top.

"Can I ask you something?"

"What is it?" She ran a hand over her short hair.

"Was there something wrong yesterday? Something I said?"

"No, not exactly."

"So there was?"

"Think about it. You'll come up with it."

"What am I supposed to come up with?"

"Do I have to tell you?"

"No, you don't have to. Except all sorts of stuff is running through my head now."

"I thought, Your wife is around here somewhere, and suddenly you want to camp out with a girl who promised you a favor."

"Promised?"

"Don't tell me you've forgotten."

"You thought I wanted to cash in my reward."

"That's about it. What's so strange about that? It is pretty weird after all, keeping your wife waiting."

"What does that have to do with my wife?"

"I thought she was here already?"

Katja slowly swam toward the shore. Adam waded beside her.

"It's more complicated than that," he said. "It's not an easy story to tell all at once."

"I can see how it might look stupid for you to show up with me attached."

"Evelyn isn't alone. She's here with her girlfriend."

"I see, a woman-woman thing?"

"Oh no, nothing like that."

"Can happen."

"She's bad company for her, she really is."

"That's what my father used to say sometimes—'bad company.' "

"A woman she used to work with, always the big mouth, blowing nothing but hot air. It was her fault that Evi dropped out of university."

"So what's she doing now?"

"Training as a waitress. When she really wanted to be a teacher."

"Education science?"

"German and geography, but mainly German."

"They wanted me to be a teacher, too. But I didn't go along with it."

"And so what did you do?"

"Carpentry, even completed my apprenticeship."

"Evi reads a lot. Whenever she's got the time, she's reading."

"A teacher has to work at softening up the boys, so they'll become professional military or officers or at least put in three years with the army. You don't have time left to do any reading."

"She could at least have finished her studies."

"And what does any of that have to do with you two now?"

"She doesn't even know I'm here."

"A surprise?"

"You might call it that too."

"Are you spying on her?"

"We had a fight. She took something the wrong way, and now I'm afraid she's about to screw things up."

"Cut and run for good?"

"No, not that, I don't think. But at twenty-one—"

"I'm twenty-one myself! And you're?"

"I'll be thirty-three in December."

"Well preserved."

"Would I have been way out of line?"

"Out of line how?"

"Well, last night?"

"That's not the issue."

"What is?"

"Maybe that I just wasn't in the mood."

"Hm." Although the water was now barely to his knees, he still couldn't see his feet.

"If you have to know. My pills are gone, they were in my neck pouch, and I have no real interest right now in getting pregnant, not even by you," she said. But now stood up straight. "What's she up to there? Do you know her?"

A young woman was leaning against the driver's side of the Wartburg, her arms stretched out along the roofline, her face to the sun.

"Holy shit," Adam whispered.

"Your wife?"

"Nope."

"The truth, Adam, nothing but the truth."

21

AN INVITATION OF SORTS

AN HOUR LATER Adam and Katja were sitting at a kiosk on the camp-ground, they were eating langos and drinking coffee and cola. Katja was wearing the straw hat, the box with the turtle had been set between their chairs.

"Are you mad at me?"

"You shouldn't have told her about that. She doesn't believe us anyway."

"About what a hero you are?"

"I don't trust her. She doesn't need to know stuff like that. Besides, it sounded made up."

"But she was so nice, so friendly."

"Friendly like a cat—you need to be careful."

"I didn't catch on—that she's the 'bad company.' I really thought she was your friend."

"I don't know why she's so goddamn friendly all of a sudden."

"And Michael? Who's he?"

"Her cousin, her cousin from the West. She claims that he's her marriage ticket out. At any rate they've invited us to the wedding."

"When?"

"Ah, it's all a lot of hot air."

Over the loudspeaker Bobby McFerrin announced: "Don't worry, be happy." The people at the next table snapped their fingers in time.

"Is he good looking?"

"He's old, midforties maybe. Has a big mouth, plays the big shot if the service is a little slow, gives women perfume, and if he's pissed off, he says 'Merde.' If it weren't for him, this whole mess would never have happened."

"What mess?"

"They stole the perfume from Evi, from her locker or wherever she'd put it—eh, it's a long story."

"I don't get it."

"Me either. She quit her job, on the spot, and then, because I still had stuff to do and was waiting for my new car, she took off with him—with her and with him."

"And you right behind them?"

"Me right behind them."

"And why didn't she want to wait?"

"I told you, she took something the wrong way."

"And now all three of them are staying with people you know here?"

"Actually they're friends of Evi's, I've never been here before. She got to know Pepi in Jena, the first year she studied there, and Pepi spent two weeks with us last year."

Katja stared into her cup. "This stuff used to be called mocha."

"You want another one?"

"Sure, but this time if possible with milk. And a little more of it."

Adam went to the counter. The woman in front of him had very fair skin, except for red shoulders and ears. He ordered coffee and bought some bread, cold cuts, cheese, and water.

When he came back two teenagers with freckles and coppery hair were sitting at their table. They were eating ice cream.

"You shouldn't buy that stuff here," the one with tight curls said. "You need to drive into town, get it at the super. Damn expensive even there. But here, no sirree. Wurst used to cost a little under four forints, that was socialism. Now they want three times that!"

"There are still tents here from people who took off over the border last Saturday," Katja said.

"Every once in a while we use that Trabi there, the key's in the ignition. We always park it back in front of the tent, but nobody ever shows up, and it's getting pretty grungy in there!"

"We broke into one car because of a bird inside," said the other kid, who blushed when he spoke.

"It would have died of thirst otherwise," the curly-haired one said.

"I'm going to be on my way," Adam said, once Katja had finished her coffee. He picked up the box with the turtle. "I'll be back tomorrow."

"I'll walk with you part way," Katja said and picked up the groceries from the table. "Bye, guys," she said to the two boys.

"So long," they said, stood up, and would have shaken hands with Katja if she hadn't had both hands full.

"Think your money will last you?" Adam asked.

"We'll see how close a check they keep. I can pay one night for now."

"I'll look in tomorrow about this time."

"You'll see. When I have to be, I'm a goat—I can get along on nothin'."

Adam placed the bottle of water, which he had held for her, back on top of the pile.

"I'll miss you, Elfi," Katja said.

"She'll miss you too," Adam said.

Simone had sketched a map on the back of his note with the address. He drove back to the main road, first turned left, and at the church took another hard left onto Római út.

Even from a good distance, he recognized Evelyn's white poplin skirt with the red polkadots, the one he'd made for her last Easter. Actually it was meant to be worn with a matching headband. It was fabric left over from Desdemona. Michael was walking alongside Evelyn. Adam passed them but didn't turn around. He now found the

green arrow with an 8 on it, took a right, and drove up the long driveway lined with bushes and trees and a shed.

Adam stopped in front of the house and got out. He watched the
two of them approach him. They weren't saying a word. Evelyn was
walking a little faster now. When Adam tried to give her a hug, she
went stiff and backed away.

"Hello," Adam said. "Simone said I could have our tent, and her
sleeping bag and air mattress, since you all have rooms."

"Yes, sure. You want them right now?"

"I was planning to set it up here in the garden—"

"Here?"

Michael had arrived by now. Adam shook the hand extended
to him.

"The campground is way too expensive."

"You can't be serious."

"Why not?"

"You still don't get it, do you? That I want to be left alone and not
be constantly afraid that you're lurking round the next corner?"

"And so what should I do, in your opinion?"

"You," Evelyn said, stressing every word, "should just go away!" She
left him standing there and disappeared behind the house. Michael
stared at the ground, gave him a quick nod, and followed her with
their beach bag.

Adam got into the car. He turned around and drove back slowly.
There was already a short line at the gas station. A Shell tanker was
parked between the pumps. Adam pulled in behind the last car. He
rolled down the window, took a deep breath, and rubbed his chest. At
least he knew how he'd be spending the next hour.

22

ANOTHER ATTEMPT

ADAM STOPPED EVEN with the shed and walked up the last part of the driveway. The lid on the mailbox shone in the evening sun. On the right was a metal plate with the number 8, there was no name under the doorbell. A path of small flagstones led around to the back of the house. Adam tugged at his shirt, which despite the breeze from the lake was stuck to his back again. The sunburn on his shoulders stung. He would have loved to have waited until some of the sweaty patches were dry. But he thought he had already been seen, so that his waiting like that would appear odd. He pushed the bell a second longer than necessary.

The windows were closed, except for a canted cellar hatch. He had already stuck his finger out to ring a second time when a woman in a green apron dress came hurrying toward him from around the corner of the house. The motion of her arms seemed to propel her small slippered feet. She laughed and, just before extending him her hand, wiped her nose with her forearm.

"Herr Adam," she said before he could even introduce himself. "Come along, I am Pepi's mother, I thought that it was you. Walk on, walk on."

"Is Pepi here?"

"No, you see, she is in Pécs, with her aunt and her cousins, but you can move into the room. She said that you and Frau Evelyn can move into her room—"

"That's very generous, Frau Angyal, but I just wanted to talk with Pepi—"

"Pepi comes next week, but until then you are welcome to her room. Walk on, walk on."

Behind the house the lot sloped upward. Opposite a doorway hung with colorful strips of plastic stood a large table under a pergola, its trellis overgrown with grapevine. On a small lawn beside it clothes-poles propped up lines hung with shirts and towels billowing in the breeze.

"Sit down, sit down please," Frau Angyal said and pointed to the table. She then vanished into the house. She spoke with someone, but the voice answering her was barely audible. There was a smell of laundry detergent and Palatschinken and coffee.

Adam got up to help Frau Angyal when she came out again, carrying two bottles and two glasses and several picture frames clamped under one arm.

"Please, please, Herr Adam, drink, in this heat you must drink. I drink all day." She filled one glass with water, another with white wine so cold that the glass immediately beaded with moisture—cause enough for Adam to reach first for it and toast Frau Angyal. Then he picked up the other glass and downed the water.

"Ah, our Pepi," Frau Angyal said as she stacked the framed photographs in front of him. "She had told us so much about you. And believe me, Herr Adam, that suit that you made for her, your present, that suit is her favorite—how do you say it?—favorite outfitting. Look at her, here she is speaking in her seminar. That was last October. And you know, with that suit she doesn't ever become fat. No joke, no joke, no, no. Our Pepi says if she must alter it, then it is all over, then it is no longer the stitch of Herr Adam. I would rather eat nothing, that is what our Pepi says."

Adam held the picture in both hands. Frau Angyal poured him more wine and water. "Drink, please drink," Frau Angyal cried—and at that very moment Evelyn came around the corner and walked toward them with a smile.

"Yes, Frau Evelyn, why did you tell me nothing?"

Frau Angyal hurried into the house to fetch more glasses.

"Hello, Adam," Evelyn said. "You seem to be doing fine." She sat down across from him.

"I came to get the tent, then I'm out of here."

"That won't work, Adam, you know very well it won't. You can't run off again now."

"Why not?"

"Thanks," Evelyn said with a smile to Frau Angyal, who set down two glasses in front of her. She had brought out a green bottle and a liqueur glass for herself.

"Here's to a lovely vacation, my dear Herr Adam, Frau Evelyn. Prosit!"

"Prosit!" they both replied and drank.

After the glasses had been set back on the table, they fell silent. Frau Angyal poured more wine and water.

"You can sleep in Pepi's room, we can lay another mattress in there—"

"No, no," Adam said. "Please don't go to any trouble. I just wanted to ask if I could pitch a tent here in the garden, that had been the plan, that was how it was arranged with Pepi."

Frau Angyal pulled a face and shook her head.

"Please, Frau Angyal," Evelyn said. "I don't want to leave Mona by herself, we came here together, we didn't know if Adam would have the time. I can't simply desert her . . ."

Frau Angyal first stared straight ahead and then filled her glass with liqueur. "You make as you like," she said, "make as you like, Frau Evelyn, but as long as Pepi is not here—" With that she stood up and went into the house as if she didn't want to hear another word.

"Shit," Evelyn whispered, "and congratulations!"

"You just said that I should leave. What do you want?"

"I told her that you had a lot of work to do, that you wouldn't be coming—presumably."

Evelyn got up. She fetched the tent from the house. She unzipped the bag it came in and dumped the parts on the ground. "Your little scam is enough to make me puke!"

"We don't have to turn this into a big spectacle," Adam said.

"Then I don't know what it is you're after here."

"You, only you."

"Where's Elfriede?"

"Can't we at least talk?"

"Dinner's at seven thirty, bathroom and toilet are shared by all. Did you leave Elfriede in the car? Is she still alive?"

Adam laid the car keys on the table.

When he had set up the tent, he unzipped the zipper and crept inside. In one corner he found a few pine needles. He brushed them up with his hands, smelled them, and stuck them in his shirt pocket.

23

FIRST DAY'S REPORT

THE NEXT MORNING Adam found Katja's tent closed and was about to head for the water, when he noticed a large pair of flip-flops out in front.

"Katja?" He heard a soft clearing of the throat. "Katja, are you in there?"

A hand or an elbow made a bulge in the tent roof—something rustled, and the zipper went down just far enough for her head to fit through.

"Hi. How late is it?"

"Half past ten."

"Just a sec." She vanished. Adam tried to see through the opening but caught only a quick glimpse of her naked shoulders. She kept her voice low. Adam stepped away just in time, as Katja, in a T-shirt and skirt, untwisted herself out of the tent. She stretched and made a sound somewhere between a yawn and a crow. The sky was blue, just a few clouds that looked more like white smoke drifting above the lake.

"Found your pills, did you?" Adam asked.

Katja pulled the straw hat out of the tent and put it on. "It was a late night. How'd it go?"

Adam shrugged. "Nothing special. And at this end?"

"Everybody wants to leave, almost everybody, but they don't talk about it. Anyway, it's like one big family."

"Know one, know 'em all."

"Want to have coffee? My treat. I looked after five kids yesterday evening, up at the front, they're from Ulm—five Westmarks an hour. And for the whole week."

"I don't get it."

"For a Westmark they'll give you twenty-five forints, sometimes more."

"I mean these Ulmers, they don't even know you. And they leave you alone with their kids?"

"They're real *easy*."

" '*Easy*'? That's English, isn't it?"

"Yep, they say '*easy*' a lot. I don't have to do a thing. The kids were already asleep, but just in case they wake up, I have to be there."

"But they don't know you."

"We went swimming and had supper together."

"And how are the rest managing? Are they all baby-sitting too?"

"No idea. We'll just stick around here for as long as we can, and then—"

"Who's we?"

"Everybody. Some of them have been here since June. They're waiting to see what happens. And if they can't manage here, they want to move to a Pioneer camp named Zánka, the Maltese Charity is there too. Tomorrow or the day after I can give you your money back."

"No rush. The cans and the tank are full. I'll get home on that."

"You want to go back?"

"Why not?"

"And your wife?"

"I'll take her along."

"You'll take her along?"

"Sure, what else?"

"So you've made up?"

"Almost."

"Do you love her?"

"Wouldn't be here otherwise."

"I thought I might be able to persuade you."

"You've already persuaded one guy." Adam pointed a thumb at the tent.

"You mean Susanne? We wouldn't let her drive, she was already tanked."

"Those are a woman's flip-flops?"

"Her flip-flops?"

"Must be one giant of a lady."

They lined up at the kiosk.

"And how did it go with the Hungarian girl?"

"Pepi isn't even there, but her mother keeps loading up the table, last night, this morning, and as I drove off she was back in the kitchen. The others even have their lunch there."

"The bad company plus the cousin?"

"He spent half an hour on the john this morning and then fumigated himself. The whole house stinks of Mister Superbrain's perfume and poop."

"Is he a superbrain?"

"A researcher of some sort, even gives courses at the university."

"Is he waiting it out too?"

"Not really. He's gonna have to leave in a few days. Tomorrow they want to drive to the border, to the place where the others went across."

"They can forget it, nobody's getting across there now."

"He thinks the Hungarians will look the other way."

"I wouldn't be so sure."

"He claims to have heard it on the radio, that was all he could talk about last night."

"About what?"

"About some woman who got across. 'Is this Austria?' she asked. The Austrians thought she was crazy. 'No, it's the moon,' they told her. And she starts screaming and jumping around like she really was nuts."

"I would have done the same," Katja said.

"Our turn."

Adam carried the tray with the yogurt cups and the coffee to the same table beside the low wall where they had sat the day before.

"Think maybe the two kissin' cousins will cut and run too?"

"Now wouldn't that be something."

"They keep telling stories like that here. You have no idea where you'll end up, in Austria or a Stasi hotel."

"Oh, get over it. Just try to enjoy a nice vacation here."

"You'll laugh, but part of me wouldn't mind that at all," Katja said.

"That's not how you sound."

"It really is bizarre, isn't it?"

"I'm just trying to enjoy a nice vacation here too."

Katja burst into laughter. "I thought that's why you're here!"

"How am I supposed to enjoy my vacation when I'm constantly having to assist 'deserters of the republic' in word and deed?"

"Prost!" Katja said and raised her yogurt cup.

"We forgot spoons."

"Don't need them." Katja put the yogurt to her lips and drank. Then she said, "Vacation. Here's to vacation!"

"It's almost as good as the West, isn't it?"

"I'll tell you something, Adam. We'll meet again on the other side, in Vienna or Berlin or Tokyo—I'll bet you anything on it."

"I don't think so. I truly don't think so."

Katja extended a hand to him.

"Come on. Let's shake on it."

"Cut the crap. I'm not a betting man."

"Come on, don't be chicken. It's not for money. But I'm damn sure we will."

Adam shook his head. "Like I said, a lot of crap." But he shook hands.

Katja kept a firm grasp on his hand. "Prost!" she said, raising her yogurt again.

"Prost!" Adam said. They looked each other in the eye and drank. Even after the cups were drained, she didn't let go of Adam's hand, and instead bent forward, laying her left hand on his, as if about to share a secret with him.

24

TREASURES

"HEY, DID YOU hear me? We're leaving."

Adam was startled awake.

"Did you fall asleep?"

"Guess so." He pulled on his pants and took his watch out of the pocket. "It's only four o'clock, right?"

"Almost six thirty."

"Wait just a sec, Evi, please."

She stood there without looking at him but then waved the others on ahead.

Adam folded the blanket and slipped into his sandals.

"That skirt looks good on you. But it needs the headband."

They walked across the meadow, where there was almost no one but couples, Adam staying half a step behind her. Simone and Michael were waiting beside the road.

"Could we have maybe ten minutes to ourselves?"

"What for?"

"I'd like to know whether we still belong together. When I have to watch you rubbing suntan lotion onto some other man's back—"

"Adam, for the hundredth time. It's not my fault. And I didn't ask you to follow me."

"Fine, it's my fault, we've established that. I've said I'm sorry, more than once, over and over."

Evelyn shook her head with a laugh and turned to go.

"Evi, please, why are you carrying on like this?"

"Do you know what's the worst part?" She turned back to him. "That you don't have a clue what this is all about. That you even dare to still look me in the eye. You behind the cupboard! What if it had been me standing there, with some fat guy in the tub? What would you do, would you still trust me?"

"I only know that I love you, you and no one else."

"You found some quick consolation."

"I helped her, that's all. I got her over the border in my trunk. That is the truth."

"And I'm supposed to buy that?"

"It's how it is, ask her. If I didn't love you I wouldn't be here."

"I wanted to get away from that nowhere town, and that nowhere job in the rathskeller, get away from you, period. And just be on my own for once."

"With Mona and Michael?"

"That's a whole different thing."

"Am I keeping you from collecting your thoughts?"

"If you're determined not to understand me—" Evelyn shrugged. She quickened her pace now. Simone and Michael had crossed the road and were taking a shortcut to Római út.

Adam ran after her, the blanket under his arm.

"So you've put on your big show—now what else can I expect?"

"You can leave anytime, Adam, anytime you like!"

"How about you? When are you leaving?"

They were standing side by side on the shoulder, but the line of traffic wouldn't let up.

"I don't know."

"Why not?"

"It doesn't matter when I get back. I quit my job, or did you forget already?"

"Are you planning to live off Pepi's parents?"

"No."

"You'll all be chowing down again in just a bit."

"Michael's paying for all that. He paid for two weeks' room and board, for him and Mona. I was invited to be their guest, and you invited yourself."

"What?"

"You didn't know?"

"I haven't invited myself as anybody's guest."

"So I'll be here two weeks anyway."

"And then? How are you getting back?"

"Maybe I don't want to go back?"

"Do you want to cut and run?"

"Louder! Why don't you shout louder!"

"You can't be serious?"

"Ask a stupid question, get a stupid answer."

Evelyn stepped into the road and waited on the median strip.

"Come on, come on."

"I'm not coming along," Adam said once he was across the road.

"Not coming along where?"

"To supper."

"Don't be childish, there's too much food as it is."

"And who's financing this? Not you!"

"Pepi spent two weeks with us, look at it as the generosity of a host."

"You mean of the Angyals?"

"You sewed for her for free."

Together they walked up the narrow path between houses and gardens, took a left on Római út, and then followed the curve up to the house with the green door.

Simone and Michael were standing in the driveway, beside the shed. At first it looked as if they were in the middle of a conversation. But Simone was the only one talking. As Adam and Evelyn drew closer, she fell silent. Michael smiled at Evelyn. Suddenly Simone marched off toward the road, without a word to Evelyn and Adam as she passed them, her handbag swinging.

"Mona?" Evelyn called. "What's wrong? Mona?"

Simone halted as if she were about to turn around and say something. But she just fished out her sunglasses and walked on.

"Mona!"

"She doesn't know herself what she wants," Michael said and walked around to the back of the house.

"I've got something else for you," Adam said softly, "something really nice."

"I don't want anything from you."

"Sure you do, you just have to take a seat in the car."

"I won't do it."

"Then you don't get your present."

"I told you I don't want anything."

Adam opened the trunk and took out the jewelry box.

"Last summer somebody broke in at the Findeisens'," he said, sitting down on the backseat. "And I thought if our little place is standing empty and somebody happens by, this would be easy pickings. So I brought it along."

"My jewelry?"

"Actually I shouldn't give it to you just like that."

"Are you crazy? It belongs to me!"

"Come here for a minute, just one minute."

Adam opened the far door from the inside.

"So here you are—your treasure."

Evelyn sat beside him, turned the little key, and opened the box.

"Take your time, make sure it's all there."

"You're a gutsy guy, Adam, smuggling this across the border and then leaving it in the trunk of a car. More luck than sense."

"And that's all you have to say?"

"What were you thinking?"

"I thought it would be a way of luring you into my car."

Evelyn lifted the top tray.

"It's all there. No fear."

She laid a short glittering gold chain around her neck and added a pair of ruby teardrop earrings.

"It's truly lovely having you so close beside me again," Adam said.

The table under the trellised arbor was already set. Michael and Herr Angyal, his glasses shoved up on his forehead, were sitting there, waiting.

"Adam just happened to find these in his trunk," Evelyn said, pushing her hair away and tossing her head back and forth.

Into the silence that followed her announcement, Adam said, "Yep, that's right."

25

BLOWUP

"HERR ADAM, good morning, did you sleep well, Herr Adam?"

"Wonderful. Like in the bosom of Abraham. And Elfi is enjoying Lake Balaton too."

Adam walked over to the little pen that Herr Angyal had built for the turtle.

"I gave Elfi some carrot."

"Well, she's polished that off," Adam said and sat down at the table.

"Would you like coffee, please?" Frau Angyal tipped the pitcher of warm milk and set the whisk whirling. Adam lifted the lid of the sugar bowl and shoveled three teaspoons into his cup.

"I thought today for once I'd be the last." He reached into a soup bowl for a handful of small dark grapes.

"What day of the week is it?"

Frau Angyal didn't hear him. Her whole upper body was now in motion, her face flushed. She moaned softly, gasped a quick breath, and in the brief pauses she allowed herself, blew strands of hair out of her eyes.

"Ready!" Frau Angyal exclaimed, picking up a spoon and pushing the foaming milk over the spout, from which it ran in a thin stream into Adam's cup. As she brushed his shoulder, her upper arm was sticky and hot.

"Is your husband already at work?"

"He has gone to get our Pepi, they will be here tomorrow."

"The coffee's so good, your spoon stands straight up in it."

"You are very kind, Herr Adam, always kind," said Frau Angyal with a sigh.

"You take such good care of us—it's how I picture paradise."

"May I show you something? No, remain seated, I shall bring it, keep your place."

Frau Angyal hurried into the house. Adam opened the bowl again and strewed sugar evenly across the foamy milk, then dunked his *hörnchen*. Stillness—a cricket, a lark above the vineyard, and except for the rustling of leaves, he would never have noticed the breeze.

"Look here, Herr Adam, is it not splendid? Just feel it." Frau Angyal was holding a roll of burgundy fabric in her arms, cradling it with pride and joy.

"Where did you get that?"

"It belongs to a friend. She got it from Switzerland, from her brother. Please, here."

Adam wiped his hands on his napkin and felt the fabric. "Crepe de chine? This is really marvelous crepe de chine. I once had something like it, but not of this quality, and not so much and not this color. How many meters are there, ten, twelve?"

"A dozen is what she told me, that would do for us all, she said."

"And what is to be made of it?"

"Something festive, for the wedding of her son, a dress for her. Here, please."

Adam gave his lips an appreciative twist and accepted the roll.

"Herr Adam, I do not dare, but I should ask, although you are on vacation, if you would want to. It would be wonderful if you could sew for her, because she promised if something is left over, I can use it, but only if you want to, although it is vacation, which is why—"

"Do you have a sewing machine?"

"Yes, yes, yes. Magda has an electric, and it's a Textima."

"If you really think I'm the right person—gladly."

"Really, Herr Adam, really? You are not angry with me?"

"No, I'm happy to be useful, so have her come here, or we'll go there, just as you like."

"What a joy, Herr Adam, what a joy! I shall call at once, I shall call her."

Frau Angyal disappeared behind the curtain of plastic strips, Adam was left sitting there with the roll of fabric. He hesitated to lay it down beside him.

"Whose baby is that?" Simone asked.

"Good morning," Adam said and pressed the roll to his chest so that Simone could squeeze past him to her spot. "Hope you enjoy your breakfast."

"I'm not in the mood for enjoyment," she said.

"Bonjour," Michael said without looking at Adam. He, along with Evelyn, sat down across from them.

"And a good morning to you, lady and gent." Adam took the fabric back into the house, as if to bring it to safety. He rapped at a half-open door, behind which Frau Angyal was talking excitedly. She waved him in, he bowed with the fabric, like a peddler presenting his wares. Frau Angyal pointed to the table. He laid the roll next to an empty crystal vase on the crocheted tablecloth.

"Tomorrow morning?" Frau Angyal asked, covered the speaker with her hand, and whispered, "She is very, very happy, Herr Adam."

The threesome outside sat across from one another in silence.

"You waiting for me? Dig in, dig in," Adam said. "Or have you all got upset tummies?"

"You might put it that way," Simone said. "Do you two want to, or shall I?"

"Can't we discuss this again a little later?" Evelyn asked.

"Later? Sure, for all I care. I already know what's up."

"It's not that simple, Mona."

"Oh, but it's very simple. Where's this from? Czech jam? And mustard? For breakfast?"

Adam sat down and dunked his half-eaten *hörnchen* in his cup.

"He still finds all this very yummy, our Herr Adam does," Simone said.

"Let's not make a big tragedy out of this!"

"It was a simple statement of fact, nothing more."

"Don't be ridiculous, Mona," Michael said, "you're acting utterly ridiculous."

"They evidently don't want to tell you themselves, Adam. It's going to take a while, I probably won't be here to lend an ear." She poured herself some coffee. Then Michael poured coffee for himself and Evelyn.

"Want some too?" he asked, holding the pitcher out to Adam.

"Beg pardon, beg pardon," Frau Angyal cried as she hurried from the house. With her forearm she tested to see if the pitcher of milk was still warm, picked up the whisk, pressed the pitcher to her breast, and began beating the milk. "I am very happy, Herr Adam," she managed to say without missing a beat. "Very happy!"

"Well at least someone is," Simone sighed. "Can you take me to the train, Adam? I don't want to disturb the lucky couple."

"When?" Adam asked.

He received no answer, and appeared to expect none. Like the others he was staring straight ahead, chewing slowly, listening to the beat of the whisk and Frau Angyal's moans.

"PEPI, AND HERR ADAM, come!" Frau Angyal's voice reverberated from the hallway. "Herr Adam, Pepi!"

"Good morning, lady and gent."

Michael nodded, went on chewing. "Hi," Evelyn said.

Frau Angyal's arms preceded her through the colorful plastic strips in the open doorway. "Good morning! When did you come in, Herr Adam? We didn't hear you."

"Around midnight, maybe? What time is it now?"

"Ten oh three," Michael said.

"Pepi!" Frau Angyal hurried back into the house.

"So how did it go?"

"She left on the Saxonia, at 16:25. She's getting off in Leipzig as we speak. The whole train was reserved, down to the last seat. But there was hardly anybody on it, she had an entire compartment to herself."

"Did she have anything else to say?"

Adam rubbed his eyes with thumb and index finger and suppressed a yawn. "Nothing I'm supposed to pass on, at least."

"Was she still—we were hoping you'd bring her back with you."

"That suggestion comes a little late," Adam said and turned around. Someone was thundering down the stairs.

"There she is," Evelyn said as Pepi emerged through the plastic strips. Adam walked over to greet her, they exchanged kisses on the cheek.

"Prettier and prettier," he said.

"How wonderful that you're both here," Pepi said.

"Yes," Adam said softly, "I'm happy to be here too."

"I think," Evelyn said, "that suit looks better on her now than last year. Can that be?"

Adam looked at Pepi, who obviously didn't know what to do or say.

"Have you eaten yet?" he asked.

Pepi nodded. "But may I join you?"

"Certainly not," Adam said, taking her by the hand and leading her to the table.

"I'll fetch another cup," Pepi said.

"There's one here," Michael exclaimed. "I've already poured the coffee."

Pepi sat down beside Adam.

"I'm so embarrassed that my mother has incommoded you with Magda László—now, on your vacation, it's outrageous, really it—"

"No it's not, not at all!"

"You have no choice but to say that, you're too polite—"

"No," Adam said with his mouth full. "Just the opposite. For me it's fun."

Pepi shook her head.

"Believe him, Pepi. Adam doesn't know how to take a real vacation. If he doesn't have work to do, he's an unhappy man, you saw that yourself."

"But here? It shouldn't be like that here. Do you still smoke cigars?"

"Sure."

"I finally had to send it to the cleaners. Now it no longer smells like you, like your house. How about an egg, Adam? Fresh from the coop, four and a half minutes? I haven't forgotten, four and a half. And there's pastry, Mama's been baking. She's even playing hooky from church on your account." Pepi picked up the empty milk pitcher and went into the house.

"Pastry too? You don't say," Michael said and held up the coffeepot.

"Thanks," Adam said. "Is there still milk?"

"I think it's being worked on." Evelyn pushed the sugar bowl his way. "You shouldn't believe everything Mona says."

"What shouldn't I believe?"

"That doesn't matter. Main thing is, she doesn't carry on at home the way she did here."

"Not to worry."

"Did she say that?"

"At any rate it has nothing to do with you."

"Nothing to do with me? That's not how it sounded."

"Can't you find some other topic of conversation?" Michael said as he buttered his *hörnchen*. "She's gone, thank God! I've had enough of her bitching and moaning."

"Mona was setting her hopes too high. She said that herself at least."

"Really?" Evelyn asked.

"You're asking me? You should know, I'd think. But that Michael— I mean, that you were intending to marry her . . . I knew that much myself."

"Really, Adam, you don't need to—"

"He's right," Michael said. "That much I promised her. I promised to be her marriage ticket out. But if she's going to blow that up into a lot of other demands, telling me what I can and can't do, and even threatens to turn me in—that's way over the top, it's a no-go."

"Did she?" Adam asked. "Did she threaten you?"

"Eve—Evelyn was there too." Michael lit a cigarette.

"Your new girlfriend evidently didn't tell you about that. And that's why I was hoping that you'd both come back. She's capable of anything. Even Frau Gabriel is afraid of Mona—just think of that, the boss afraid of a waitress."

Adam topped a piece of white bread with salami and a slice of cheese.

"Anyhow I'm glad Heinrich kept up his end. I can always depend on him."

"Heinrich?"

"Adam's Wartburg. He kept the name his father gave it."

"You call your car Heinrich?"

"Why the big grin?"

"Learn something new every day."

"You guys buy a new model every couple of years, and the old one gets junked. For us it's a member of the family."

"Mine's got three hundred thousand on it, and I—"

"Three hundred thousand kilometers?"

"That's what I said." Michael flicked his ashes into the eggshell on his plate.

"Well then it's earned a name too. How about Gabriela, that'd be a good fit, Gabriela the redhead? We once had an Isabella, our first Trabi, gray with a gray roof liner, you'd probably call it more of an ivory."

"Jó napot!" A woman was standing at the head of the table, a lady with a small picture hat and shiny bright red lips. Her houndstooth suit was too tight on her.

She asked something in Hungarian. As she said the name "Erzsi" and pointed toward the open door, a pile of magazines slipped out from under her arm and fell to the flagstones.

"Quite an entrance," Adam said and jumped up to help her.

"Köszönöm, köszönöm szépen," she wailed, half laughing, half in distress, and didn't stop until all the magazines had been picked up and Pepi and Frau Angyal had greeted her. "Köszönöm."

"This is Magda," Pepi said. "Our friend."

Magda extended a hand to each of them, they made room for her to sit down, Frau Angyal brought her a cup too. Pepi set the egg cup, egg included, on the table. Still in charge of the magazines, Adam had remained on his feet and was now paging through the top one, glancing back and forth at Magda. In adjusting her hat, she had let it slip too far to the right, which lent her a bold and sassy look.

Michael picked up the coffeepot, filled her cup, blew out the tea candle on the warmer, and lifted the lid of the sugar bowl.

Magda beamed at Michael and said something to Pepi. "Frau László says that she's very happy that you are here."

"Goes for me too. Such a marvelous place to be!" He smiled at Evelyn.

Pepi translated. Then they all fell silent, until Magda leaned toward Pepi again and whispered in her ear. The longer she whispered the worse her giggles got. Whereas Pepi, who had also leaned toward her at first, was now sitting up ramrod straight, staring earnestly ahead. Magda ended her whisperings with gurgling laughter.

"Frau László says that she's heard a lot about you," Pepi said.

"Well hopefully just the good stuff," Michael exclaimed, and laughed along with Frau László. "Hopefully just the good stuff," he repeated, but cast Pepi a questioning glance, since she didn't seem about to translate his reply.

"Frau László thinks," Pepi said—raising her eyes as if searching the heavens—"she thinks that you are the person who is going to sew her dress."

27

ADAM AT WORK

"AH, MAGDA IS HAPPY. I don't need to translate, just take a look at Magda!"

"She only hopes," Pepi added, "that she can also afford to pay the artist. It worries her."

Adam smiled at Magda—who wouldn't stop talking—held the fabric up and kept looking back and forth between the open magazine and his own sketch.

"I haven't started yet, and you act as if I had it all done."

"But Herr Adam, from the way you talk about it, the things you say, we already know that it will be special, something very, very special."

"It's a good thing you talked her out of that dress."

"It would just hang in the closet afterward," Adam replied. She can combine other things with this skirt."

"Should I translate for her?"

"Tell her that she has a good figure."

"A good figure?" Pepi asked. And Frau Angyal gave him a surprised look too. Magda turned around and gawked, at a total loss, from one to the other.

"Go ahead and tell her. She's a little full figured, but the proportions are right, and that's what counts—the same as with you, Frau Angyal, right?"

Pepi and Frau Angyal traded glances, then both started talking at once. Frau Angyal traced a serpentine curve in the air and a similar line along her own body. Magda stared in the mirror as if checking out this information, lifted her chin, and didn't stir a muscle.

"And now tell her, please, that you are paying me, that my work is a present, otherwise she'll leave and take the fabric with her—"

"A present?" Both Angyals stared at him.

"She couldn't pay me anyway. But you, as her friends, you were able to persuade me. . . . What's the problem? That's what it would've cost me to pitch my tent."

"You're doing it for free?"

"She's to leave the rest of the fabric to you—it's first-class goods! We'll not get our hands on anything like this for a long while."

"But Herr Adam—"

He sat down on the windowsill, pulled a cigar from his shirt pocket, gave its trimmed end a quick check, and lit it. As he blew the first smoke out the window, the three women had already lined up in front of him.

"She is happy," said Frau Angyal. "And, it goes without saying, she immediately accepted your offer. That upsets me, Herr Adam, that was wrong, you shouldn't have done that."

"Does she really not understand a word?" Adam asked, nodding at Magda.

"She's a cheapskate."

"A tightwad," Pepi said, turning toward Magda.

Adam waved his hand to drive the smoke away. He took another draw on his cigar and leaned out the window.

"No need, Herr Adam, we like the smell. It's part of your world, so Pepi says—"

"It's a deal, it's a deal," Pepi whispered. "Whatever's left over is ours to keep."

"I've already got an idea."

"We're so lucky to have you here," Pepi said. "You can smoke in the room, let the whole house smell like cigar smoke."

"What's your mother busy telling her?"

"She's explaining to Magda that she really can't accept the left-over fabric. If Mama's not careful she'll have convinced Magda she means it."

"Tell her to come back in three days for the first fitting. Take a look at that woman!"

Magda had pulled in her tummy and sucked in her cheeks, set her arms akimbo, and turned one side to the mirror. Her half-closed eye-lids made her look a little dopey.

She seemed embarrassed when it came time to say good-bye and made a hint of a curtsy. Pepi was going to drive Magda home. Frau Angyal put together a shopping list for Pepi and accompanied her to the door.

With the cigar in his mouth, Adam unrolled the fabric across the extension table with one hand—it flowed in gentle waves.

"We really can't complain," he said when Frau Angyal reappeared. "Even if I make her a blouse as well, there'll be more than half left for us. With enough for Pepi besides."

"Really? I'm ashamed of saying such bad things in front of you, Herr Adam. But Magda really is a cheapskate."

"I've already thought of something very beautiful," Adam said. "Shall we begin?"

"Right here, right now?"

He nodded and blew a cloud of smoke toward the ceiling lamp. He carefully laid his cigar on the edge of the windowsill and pulled the tape measure from around his neck. "Don't you want to?"

Frau Angyal sat down on the edge of a chair she had pulled away from the table. "How can it go on like this, Herr Adam, this is terrible. Tell me what is to come of it? Frau Evi is such a beautiful woman, pretty as a picture, but tell me, what does she see in him? Why does she do this?"

Adam's mouth twisted. "I don't know," he said. "I figure another ten days, then I'll drive home with her."

"Do you think so? You are willing to take her back?"

Adam shrugged. "It's just a lot of foolishness."

"Really? I don't know."

"We'll see. But my main concern is whether I can stay on here."

"You can stay here, of course you can stay on here, as long as you like, always, for as long as you—"

"Thanks a lot, the—"

"But you know this—there will always be a place to stay here for you."

"Thanks," Adam said, taking the tape measure in both hands and looking at Frau Angyal, who appeared to be inspecting her polished toenails.

"Pepi told me all about it," she suddenly said. "And I can assure you that we would have taken care of the baby. Pepi hoped that she was pregnant."

"How's that? What did Pepi say?"

"It was not to be, back then. But she's always talking about you. For Pepi those days she spent with you in your garden were the loveliest ever."

"I thought it was a very lovely time myself," Adam said. "Doesn't Pepi have a boyfriend? She did have one, didn't she?"

"No, he was no good for her, she was always the loser with him. When she returned home it was all over. I was so very glad."

"Pepi hoped she was pregnant?"

Frau Angyal nodded. "Yes, that was so, that was so. But only I know that—and now you."

Adam wrapped the tape measure around his left index finger. From somewhere outside came the sound of a buzz saw.

"Shall we?" Adam asked.

"Yes, yes, but what?" Frau Angyal stood up from her chair.

"I need your measurements anyway."

"What do you want me to do, take this off?"

"There's no need."

Frau Angyal turned to one side and unbuttoned her apron dress. She stood there in front of him in a white slip with a wide lace hem. "Should I leave my sandals on?"

"Absolutely," Adam said. He walked around behind her, held the tape measure to that particular neckbone and drew it along the shoulder and down to the wrist. Then he measured her hips, her waist, her chest. "I think I know what I want to do," he said as he put his pencil and notebook away. "But maybe you'll want something totally different? . . . Frau Angyal?"

"Herr Adam, would you please embrace me? Just once. Or may I embrace you?"

Adam cleared his throat. "Yes," he said, stuffing the tape measure into his pants pocket.

Frau Angyal stepped up to him and wrapped her arms around his neck. When his hands touched her back, she pressed against him. "Silk, genuine silk," Adam whispered. His fingertips traced across her shoulderblades, wandered downward, and reached Frau Angyal's rear end. She stood on tiptoes, pressed tight against him, and let out a brief lusty sound that made it clear to Adam in a flash—he was alone with her.

28

SHADOWS AT PLAY

"STAY, ANOTHER FIVE MINUTES, please, I want to look at you."

"You are looking at me, you've been looking at me the whole time."

"But not really, come here."

"Don't! And close that window too."

"Why?"

"You can hear for yourself, the awful squeaks this bed makes."

"Wasn't it wonderful?"

"Yes, it was," Evelyn said, and kissed him on the mouth. "Very wonderful, I'd say."

"Why should I close the window?"

"You should close it for me, because I want you to."

He pushed himself between her legs, clasped both arms around her waist, and laid his head on her breasts. "Do you know what you looked like when you came in just now? Like a mummy, wrapped up like a mummy."

"I can't run around the house naked."

"I first thought they had given us sheets instead of towels. They smell so marvelously old-fashioned, fresh from the ironing board."

"Yes, they do smell good," Evelyn said and ran both hands through his hair.

"Do you know why you make me so *horny*?"

" 'Horny'? What does 'horny' mean?"

"You turn me on, make me *horny*."

"What an ugly word."

Michael pushed himself up a bit higher and tugged at her armpit hair with his lips. "This patch of hair drives me stark raving crazy. Do you like that better?"

"Yes."

"Don't you ever shave?"

"Should I?" Evelyn crossed her hands behind her head. The streetlamp from Római út cast the shadow of a cherry tree on the wall. A very gentle breeze must have been moving through its branches. "Maybe you can close the window now?"

"And who's eavesdropping on us?"

"Why won't you understand?"

"And I don't understand why you want to go back to your room either."

"We're guests here—"

"I'm a perfectly normal paying guest, like anywhere else, Herr Basic Tourist."

"I know all these people, and Adam is lying there out back."

"How do you know where he is right now?"

"And what if he hears us."

"What if he does? Soldier, sailor, tinker, tailor. Let him!"

"You're nuts."

"Did we invite him? He's cheated on you for years, and now we're supposed to hold our breath because he's sawing logs out there?" Michael rolled over on his back beside her.

"Don't get your nose out of joint, you're the one who's got me." Evelyn propped herself up and ran her hand across his chest.

"It's like playing hide-and-seek—"

"Don't be angry."

"I'm not 'angry,' I just don't get it. Why do you want to stay on here with the Angyals?"

"I've just got to get used to this."

"Get used to what?"

"To you, to the whole situation."

"But what's there to get used to?"

"Being here together with you on Lake Balaton."

" 'Get used to'! I've been thinking of you for a good year now."

"I don't believe that."

"No? At Mona's birthday party last year, you wore this kind of wraparound thing that crossed up front. I've seen you in it ever since, I've never stopped thinking of it the whole time."

"Never stopped?"

"Didn't matter in what situation."

"Even when you were with other women?"

"There wasn't much happening with other women. Once you're sure you've found the right one—"

"You were thinking of me when you were with them?"

"Yes."

"Really?"

"Yes. You know I've had to get used to some things too."

"Oh, so all of a sudden?"

" 'Stick it in'—no woman has ever said that to me, just 'stick it in.' "

Evelyn tried to cover his mouth, but Michael grabbed her hand. "Stick it in," he said again. "Stick it in."

Evelyn struggled, Michael held her hand tight.

"Nobody can say that quite as innocently as you. Lie on top of me. Come on, lie on top of me."

"You numbskull, let me go."

"Come on, I want to show you something."

"Let me go, please, enough!"

Michael pressed her hand lower and lower, until it reached his penis. "Please," he said. "At least your hand, just with your hand."

Evelyn pulled her hand away.

"Come on, before you go, just a little."

Evelyn brushed the hair from her face. "You're pretty aggressive, did you know that?"

"There's nothing wrong with that."

"It wasn't meant as a compliment, not at all."

"Okay, fine, do what you want."

"You bet I will."

"Well then, go—girls and boys in separate sleeping quarters."

"Girls and boys are to sleep separately until further notice, that's right," she said and passed her hand over his penis and testicles. "This guy's asleep already as it is."

"Just you wait."

"Can you feel that?"

"What?"

"Your balls, they're wandering."

" 'Wandering'?"

"Don't you feel that? They're moving."

"Haven't a clue what they're up to."

"You see, I have to tell you what they're doing."

Evelyn kissed his chest. "Lie still, just like that," she said and tugged at his armpit hair with her lips. "Does that feel good?"

"Hm. First we'll take a couple of trips, by Christmas at the latest we'll be on our way to New York, to the Big Apple. Or if you'd rather, we'll fly to Rio, to the beach at Ipanema, you can swim there at Christmas, and waves like you've never seen. Or Mexico, I have some friends in Mexico."

"Does it snow in Hamburg sometimes?"

"Why not? Not like in the mountains, but it's all white sometimes."

"The most beautiful part is Christmas shopping in the snow."

"Whatever you like."

"It's enough just for me to picture it. All I want is just to be able to picture it."

"It's all much more beautiful than you can imagine."

"You have no idea how I picture it."

"But you don't know how beautiful it is, really beautiful! On our side you live better and longer."

"That may well be. But I'd rather hear about the King of Spheres and those machines that can think up stories."

"It just takes a little courage. You've heard yourself, people make it across every day."

"But I don't want to take the risk. I don't want to be hauled away."

"You see, now that guy's awake. I told you so. You just have to be nice."

"Show-off," Evelyn said, grabbed her towel, and stood up.

"Hey! What's up?"

Evelyn walked to the window and closed it quietly. Then she spread the towel out on the bed runner, lay down on her back, crossed her hands behind her head, and smiled. Michael pushed himself from the bed, slid down to her, and nuzzled up against her. Evelyn twisted and turned under his caresses, but kept her eyes on the shadows at play on the wall, even now with the window closed.

29

DAMN WOMEN

"DO YOU WANT to come along, Pepi?" Evelyn asked. "We're going down to the lake."

Pepi was sitting beside Adam and browsing through the magazines.

Frau Angyal was sitting across from them. "Pepi, Evelyn asked you a question."

"Are you coming with us?"

"No, I'm staying here," Pepi said and turned the page. Evelyn offered a quick wave, and with a beach bag slung over his shoulder and a blanket under his arm, Michael called out, "Later!"

"We will see you later," Frau Angyal responded, but she didn't bother to look up either.

Evelyn walked ahead, Michael followed. They walked around the house in silence and then down to the road.

Evelyn came to a sudden halt and turned around.

"I'm so sorry, I couldn't help myself, it just slipped out somehow."

"What did?"

"You're not angry with me?"

"I don't have the vaguest idea—"

"For playing along with their stupid game, for—oh, you know what I mean."

"Let's walk on ahead—not here."

"I'm just not up to this."

"It's no wonder—come on, Eve."

"That cow, that stupid cow doesn't even answer me."

"But then why did you ask her?"

"That's what I meant, it just happened somehow."

Michael nodded.

"I'm no match for that kind of hatred."

"I told you right off that we needed to—"

"In her mind now I'm just a floozy, a slut—"

"Eve, don't be so hard on yourself."

" 'Western whore,' that's what they're thinking, believe me. It wasn't enough that I walked out on their beloved Adam, but then I go and get myself a Westie!"

"A paying guest."

"That makes it even worse. They hate you for that too."

"Calm down, Eve. Nobody hates us. But it just doesn't compute for me, why you want to stay here, with the Angyals. I've been asking myself that all along."

"My stupid neediness. I really was looking forward to seeing Pepi again, her parents, the house."

"He never would have found us anywhere else."

"You don't know Adam. He would have searched till . . . And then these damn women! When they gang up on you, there's nothing more cold blooded, more patronizing!"

"We'll look for something really nice, for a place that's much, much nicer."

"Do you know what's the worst part? The worst part is that I actually feel guilty, because I think exactly the same way they do."

"Eve! He cheated on you for years, and now, when you're beginning a new life—"

"But how? Do you suppose they're going to open up the border again? The Hungarians can't afford to try that. And at some point they'll just transport them all back here, every single one of them!"

"That's not going to happen, believe me."

"Didn't you hear about it? They shot those two people, two people—"

"One, and he attacked them first—"

"Baloney—'attacked,' that's their lingo. They just picked them off, your fine Hungarians. We're in the East here, even if you do see it differently. You don't know them."

"It doesn't matter, Eve, by Christmas we'll be together."

"I've heard enough of that fairy tale. We've been here for almost two weeks now, and nothing's happened."

"You can depend on it."

"Depend on what?"

"On me."

"You can't change anything, not one damn thing!"

"The most important thing is not to be afraid. That's so important."

"But I'm not as strong as you seem to think. I'm not going to climb into a car trunk, or run between border guards, ducking real quick when they shoot."

"You don't need to be anyone else but you."

"For you I'm just the nice little waitress, and if you say jump, then I jump. That's not who I am!"

"Whatever you say you are, that's who you are—you, just as I see you right now."

"Oh! There's no way you can know who I am."

"Let's move out. At least the last few days without any Angyals or that tailor."

"No."

"And for all I care into the Budapest Hilton. I'll try to get another week of vacation, and if it's at all possible, I'll stay."

"A couple of days in the Hilton, and then I get to move to a camp, thirty people to a tent, like Palestinians. The camps are full of Stasi plants, who then later will plead to be allowed back in, into their socialist fatherland."

"We'll go to the embassy together, I'll take care of things. You'll be

able to find a place to live somewhere, I'll pay for it, and when everything's all set—"

"As an embassy refugee living outside the walls? Are you ever a
dreamer! Now that's enough to make me afraid."

"Eve, stop it, you'd wear just about anybody out."

"That's what I said, you don't know me. And if this is already too
much for you—"

"Let's take it one step at a time. We can get married, we've always
got that possibility. For now let's just find another place to stay, okay?"

"And what sort of place?"

"One where we don't have to lie on the floor and nobody's upset
that we're together."

"And Elfriede? I can't just carry her around with me."

"Then give the turtle as a present to the Angyals or Adam, he's the
one who dragged it all the way here."

"Just a moment, please. I'd be insulting them for good and all."

"What do you mean, 'insulting'? The Angyals? You really are an
angel."

"It is, or at least it was, a friendship. It's also a matter of hospitality.
I could never do it."

" 'Hospitality'?"

"You don't understand."

"They treat you, like, well, you know, like you yourself said, and
now you start in about hospitality."

"Come on, let's keep walking."

Michael tried to hold the beach bag and blanket on one side and
put his other arm around Evelyn, but the bag kept slipping off his
shoulder. They crossed the road and now started down the footpath
shaded by trees.

"Am I seeing things," Evelyn asked, "or are there really more people here every day?"

"They have to open the border, that's the only thing that will work.
Half of East Germany is camped out here."

"Maybe I *will* tell Pepi that he likes to screw his customers, how I had to see it with my own eyes the day I came home early."

"Oh, Eve. There's no reason you have to do that. She'd only think you're trying to justify yourself. That gets you nowhere, believe me, absolutely nowhere."

"What a shame. I should have taken a picture, Adam with his fat Lilli in the bathtub."

"You act as if you have to prove something to them. Why? You don't have to rely on them. In a couple of months we'll send them a pretty postcard from Rio or Paraty!"

"I feel like I've been thrown overboard. Pepi is my friend, not his. They'd never have met if it weren't for me."

There was still an open spot on the meadow close to the bulrushes. Michael spread out the blanket and arranged two rolled-up towels as side-by-side pillows. Evelyn pulled off her skirt but kept her T-shirt on. Michael began to rub lotion on her legs. "You want me to pick up the story where we left off?"

Evelyn nodded, laid her head back on her crossed hands, and closed her eyes.

"The machine painted white had told the first story, and now Trurl called for the second machine to approach, it curtsied to the king and—"

"The king was going to explain," Evelyn said softly, "why he's shaped like a sphere."

"Okay, fine," Michael said, then wiped his hands on the grass and lit a cigarette.

Genius, the king, began: "There is much in what you say. As far as our shape is concerned, I will tell you how this came about. A long, long time ago we looked altogether different, for our ancestors arose by the will of wet and spongy pale beings that fashioned them after their own image and likeness; our ancestors therefore had arms, legs, a head, and a trunk. But once they had liberated themselves from their creators, they wished to obliterate even this trace of their origin. Hence each generation in turn transformed itself, till finally the form of a perfect sphere was attained." To which Trurl, the genius constructor of the Cybernetic Age, replied, that in his view a sphere has both good and bad aspects from the standpoint of construction. "But it is always best when an intelligent being cannot alter its own form, for such freedom is truly a torment—the torment of choice. He who must be what he is may curse his fate, but cannot change it; on the other hand, he who can transform himself has no one in the world but himself to blame for his failings, no one in the world but himself to hold responsible for his dissatisfaction. However, I did not come here, O King, to give you a lecture on the General Theory of Self-Construction, but to demonstrate my storytelling machines."

"Eve, hello, Eve?" Michael whispered.

Evelyn's face was hidden by her hair. Michael bent down to her. She was snoring softly. Her legs had goose bumps. Michael spread her skirt over her thighs, stubbed his cigarette out in the grass, and lay down on his back. If he turned his head toward Evelyn, he could kiss the tips of her hair.

30

EVENING BY BLUE LIGHT

"HOW ABOUT a last swim?" Evelyn asked. "The moon's out." Michael had stopped on the restaurant terrace, where a band dressed in pleated shirts and red bow ties was still playing Abba songs. The vocalist's voice was barely audible, although her lips were touching the microphone.

"That stuff has a life of its own!" Michael bounded down the stairs, kicking his legs high.

Pretending her left fist was a mike, Evelyn sang, "You are the dancing queen," and stretched out her right arm to point at Michael. He grabbed her hand and kissed it. "Thanks," he said.

"That was fun! Where did you learn all that?"

"What?"

"All those dances. You've got to teach them to me, one by one."

"But you can already do them."

"Nah, can't either."

"You looked me right in the eye and did them."

"And the second you let go it was all over."

Michael bent down and picked Evelyn up in both arms. She threw her arms around his neck, laid her head on his shoulder. After a few yards she lost a sandal.

With Evelyn still in his arms Michael did a knee bend, snatched the sandal up with one finger, straightened up, and kept on going.

When he stopped, she kissed him on the neck. "Just a little farther, one tiny little bit farther," Evelyn whispered.

"Merde!" He tried to set Evelyn down. She held on tight. "The car," he said, and untangled himself from her.

The door on the driver's side was half open.

"Didn't you lock it?"

Michael walked around the car.

Evelyn put her hands to her mouth when she saw the smashed window. Michael sat down in the passenger seat and opened the glove compartment.

"And?" she asked.

His hands were still groping. "Gone. It's all gone."

"Everything?"

"Everything," Michael said and pulled a wad of forints from his shirt pocket. "That's all I have to my name."

"Your papers too?"

"And the credit cards, the whole works."

"You didn't leave anything back in the room?"

"The door key."

"They stole the radio!"

"They could have that as a present."

"How did they get it out?"

"I'm such an idiot. I didn't want to dance with a big bulge in my pants pocket. I figured, it's a hotel parking lot, nothing like this is going to happen."

"It's my fault. If I'd had a purse, but I'm just not a purse person, I—"

"We've got to get the police here."

"This late?"

The large glass door to the hotel was locked. Michael rang several times. A gaunt old man fingered his bundle of keys as he approached. For a good while they stood opposite each other, separated by the heavy pane. Both rattled the door—the doorman inside, Michael outside. "Goddammit, it's locked, doesn't he realize that?" The doorman vanished.

"I'm sorry, I apologize," Evelyn caressed Michael's hand.

"They may be in cahoots. He's supposed to watch the parking lot and has locked himself inside here now." Michael pounded on the door. The doorman came running back, holding a key up high.

"Are you certain that this happened to you here?" the doorman asked, with the receiver in hand as he dialed.

"Who's going to park a car here with a smashed window and leave money inside?"

Michael had to spell his name and provide his license number and the make of the car.

"They are coming to investigate," the doorman said and pointed to a sofa, framed by two floor ashtrays, their silver hemispheres overflowing with butts.

"Let's wait outside," Evelyn said.

"Be glad the car's still there," the doorman said as he held the door open for them, and then relocked it behind them.

Michael sat down on the top step and lit a cigarette. "Want one?"

Evelyn shook her head. "No matter what, it was wonderful, no one can take that away from us," she said.

"Are you chilly?"

She leaned against him. "Maybe it's a sign, maybe it means something good."

"What good could it possibly mean?"

"Maybe it says that we two should cross the border together."

"Cross the border, where there's woods and fields? Illegally?"

"Yes, sure, we don't have anything on us. And if they grab us, you say you're from Hamburg and I'm your wife."

"Who's going to buy that story?"

"They won't know any better. And in the West they'll figure out what's what, but maybe they'll catch on and say, yes, it's true."

"But why should anyone from the West cross illegally?"

"Well, because he doesn't have any papers. You yourself said it was a fifty-fifty chance."

"You must be kidding!"

"Don't you want to try it? The two of us together, hand in hand, we just run across?"

"If they nab me, I guarantee they'll think I'm a spy or whatever."

"But they don't know who you are."

"They'll figure it out. And then I land in East Berlin."

"We'd have a good excuse."

"An excuse? Because somebody stole my passport, I decided to cut and run? Not even Austies would buy that."

"Who?"

"The Austrians."

Evelyn stared straight ahead. When Michael tried to put an arm around her, she squirmed out from underneath.

"What's wrong? You mad at me?"

"I'm just trying to picture it, with you in a refugee camp, and both of us starting from scratch. And when things get tough, we'd remember running hand-in-hand over the border."

"Evelyn, you won't have to go to a refugee camp, and you don't have to cross illegally somewhere."

"But I think it'd be so beautiful to do it with you."

"Things will turn romantic enough in due time. Just wait till we're in Brazil."

"It has nothing to do with romantic."

Michael took a deep breath. "Right now at least, it's going to be plenty unromantic."

"Maybe Adam can drive us to Budapest."

"And why Adam?"

"I thought you were broke?"

"I'll borrow some money."

"From who? From the Angyals? And then with a smashed window and no driver's license all the way to Budapest?"

"I can take the train or a bus, if you like that better."

"And why just you? My papers are gone too!"

They looked at each other. Michael was about to say something when the hotel's exterior lights went off.

Before their eyes could adjust to the darkness, a blue police light pulled slowly into the parking lot. Holding hands, Evelyn and Michael groped their way down the stairs and made for the blue light.

ON THE ROAD

"I'll sit in the back," Evelyn said when Adam opened the passenger door for her.

"Then Michael should sit up front, long legs have more room up here."

Michael hesitated and cast Evelyn a questioning glance.

"We've got to pick somebody else up, come on up front," Adam said.

"Who, Pepi?"

"No, Katja, from the campground."

"Who, might I ask, is 'Katja from the Campground'?"

"The girl I gave a ride to."

"Taking a little excursion together?" Michael asked as he got in up front.

"She hasn't got her PP either, and you need your PP whether on our side or yours."

"Your what?"

"Personal papers. She doesn't have hers anymore. Otherwise our German brothers and sisters might take her for a Hungarian, or a maybe even a Russian who happens to speak very good German."

Adam started the engine and gave the dashboard three raps. "Hang in there, Heinrich. Budapest or bust."

"He always does that, don't pay any attention."

Michael watched Adam put the car into gear, release the brake, and pull away.

"Adam's superstitious. He'd like to have his horoscope done every day."

"Doesn't sound all that bad, your Heinrich. How many cylinders? Four?"

"Three. He's a sixty-one. My father pampered and coddled him. Only drove on Sundays or now and then to the theater. He wanted to go easy on him, it was always easy does it."

"It rubbed off," Evelyn said.

"Makes sense to me. An old-timer like this can be worth more now than it was new."

"This is no old-timer. I drive it like I would any other car, as you can see."

"It's earned the title after thirty years' service."

"Drives like a dream."

"Well now," Evelyn said. "Let's hope so."

"You can trust me." Their eyes met briefly in the rearview mirror. "He's never let me down so far."

Evelyn smiled a derisive smile and leaned her head against the window.

Katja was waiting beside the road.

"Whoa! Is she planning to move out?" Michael asked.

"She's wearing my hat!"

By way of greeting Katja patted the right headlight before picking up her plastic sacks, Adam's sleeping bag, the air mattress, and the tent. Adam opened the trunk and packed it all in as she handed it to him.

"That's one big girl," Michael whispered.

"Has a nice figure though," Evelyn said and smiled as the door opened and Katja sat down beside her.

"Hello. I'm Katja." She gave Evelyn her hand and reached forward to shake Michael's as well. "Thanks for letting me come along."

"We're all in Adam's hands, like it or not. Isn't that right, Adam, you have to put up with us now."

"Like it or not."

"Oh, come on, you're enjoying this."

"I'm not sure 'enjoy' is the word I'd use for having to cart you guys back and forth in this glorious weather."

"Fate has destined you to play the role of our knight in shining armor," Katja said. "But I can't think of a better one."

"Could you turn on the radio, Radio Danubius," Evelyn asked. "Or is it still on the fritz?"

"Let's have a sing-along instead," Adam said, adjusting the rearview mirror. Katja was smiling.

"Are you planning to stay on in Budapest?" Evelyn asked.

"I thought that if we don't get this taken care of today—a person's got to sleep somewhere."

"Our guys will take care of it right away," Michael said.

"Do you have passport photos?" Katja asked.

"I haven't got anything left, barely four hundred forints."

"That's not so bad, that'll last you two, three days."

"I don't even have a watch."

"That get stolen too?"

"I had to leave it at the hotel, as a deposit for all the calls I had to make."

"To your family?" Adam asked.

"To credit card companies. I needed to block the accounts."

"Two weeks ago people still needed baby-sitters, I was making twenty Westmarks an evening sometimes, that's six hundred forints. But the work's thinning out now," Katja said.

"You running short?" Adam asked.

"Around a hundred Westmarks, but the families from the West are almost all gone."

"Five evenings baby-sitting, and she has more than we're allowed to exchange," Evelyn said. "Do you really think it'll take the embassy more than one day to deal with our papers?"

"I have no idea how it'll go. The important thing is that you guys don't desert me."

"In Budapest?"

"In the embassy. I don't have a visa. If they find out that I'm actually not allowed to be here—"

"Merde," Michael said and turned around. "How did that happen?"

"Didn't Adam tell you? He smuggled me across in his trunk."

"Really?"

"I thought you all knew that."

"This may turn out to be loads of fun."

"If the three of us go in together and you don't leave me all on my own—"

"I've heard they hire taxi drivers to kidnap people. And you're going to the embassy voluntarily?" Evelyn said. "Where are your papers?"

"I tried to swim the Danube. Turned out not to be such a great idea."

"People have drowned trying it," Michael said.

"Can't say."

"If things start getting sticky for you, you tell them the truth, simply the truth and that you've since reconsidered. They'll buy you a train ticket back," Adam said.

"Suddenly they'll take good care of you," Evelyn said.

"They've always taken good care of us," Adam said.

"You sound like a Party nabob."

"What do you mean?"

" 'Taken good care'? They treat us like their property."

"I mean the train ticket. You need to get back home. They've always seen to that. Every embassy does that."

"Except that ours likes to let a few people vanish along the way," Evelyn said.

"Don't believe those fairy tales—"

"They've even disappeared some of our people," Michael said.

"And not just a couple."

"But not anymore."

"Oh yes, still happens."

"At any rate they won't make Katja disappear."

"Yes sir, comrade Adam."

"I was a comrade at one point, in fact."

"What? A Communist?" Michael said.

"For almost two years, joined before I was drafted, and right back out again on release. Meteoric career."

"Don't worry. Adam didn't even bother to show up to vote last May."

"And what happened?" Michael asked.

"Nothing, there was nothing they could do to him. Me—they would have tossed me out, from my training course."

"They didn't make any trouble for you?" Katja asked.

"Adam's got powerful girlfriends who need a good tailor."

"Bull. What are they supposed to be protecting me from?"

"No shame in admitting that a couple of nabobs' wives are among your clients."

"What do I care about their husbands?"

Evelyn laughed. "Nope, you don't care about their husbands, it's definitely not them you want to get back home for."

"When are you two leaving?" Katja asked.

Adam downshifted because he couldn't pass the truck ahead of him. The road was windy and narrow.

"Not certain yet," Adam replied. "How long are you staying?"

"Me?" Michael asked.

Adam nodded.

"Three more days. I've already used up more vacation time than I have. But I'll be back, every weekend."

"Well yes, that'll depend on the weather too," Adam said.

"Thanks to you both for thinking of those things," Evelyn said, took the straw hat from Katja's lap, and put it on.

All four stared straight ahead, as if hypnotized by the truck's anti-static strap dragging along the asphalt, bouncing at times like a hand waving.

32

WORKING FOR ETERNITY

"NORMALLY YOU JUST hold up your passport and they let you in. But in this case . . ."

"They've figured that trick out," Adam said and took a sip of his beer. Michael was having a bottle too. They were sitting on Margaret Island in Budapest, not far from the green tent—pitched close to the water but hidden by bushes—where Katja and Evelyn lay asleep.

"How late is it?"

"Somewhere between one and two, I'd say. You're the one with a watch."

"I forget to wind it sometimes, and then I can't be sure of the time."

"Mine's an automatic, self-winder."

"At home I don't need a watch. This one is a present from Evi."

"A man always needs a watch."

"Actually all I want now is my new Lada, and maybe a second garage, but otherwise . . ."

"My ex always says—"

"Who?"

"My ex, my former wife. I was married once, about as long as you were a Party member."

"And what does she say, your former wife?"

"If you love someone, she says, you always know what to give them."

"Do you believe that?"

"That's her best quote. I really couldn't think of one other thing to give her."

"Maybe she had everything."

"It used to be I'd just walk along the street and instantly see something."

"What I'd most like to give Evi is admission to a university."

"That's easy for us, you give it to yourself as a gift and can study forever."

"No limits?"

"There are people who've stretched it out for ten years and longer."

"Over here you first have to be selected for admission, and if you aren't—Evi got such a stupid evaluation her senior year, because she was the only one in her class who smoked, and showed up late sometimes, even though she lived just around the corner. Her grades were good, but she was turned down twice to study art history."

"Art history is a good way to starve."

"What do you mean? They don't earn less than anybody else."

"Maybe on your side, but you need to find a job first."

"Once you've been admitted to study, then at the end you'll get a job too. The university even has to make sure you're taken care of."

"Why the university?"

"It's better if you find a job yourself, but if you can't, they have to find something for you, or let you continue studying."

"Now that's strange."

"Ask Evi."

"How long is your provisional whatchamacallit good for?"

"Till the thirteenth," Adam said and pulled the four-page, six-by-eight-inch document from his shoulder bag. " 'Provisional Travel Pass A 08969, for Hungary, the Czechoslovakian Socialist Republic, and the German Democratic Republic (Bad Schandau).' What do you think—could I find work on your side?"

"If you really want to, why not?"

"It can't be that easy."

"Anybody who wants to work can find work."

"But not necessarily the work you want."

"No problem. You need an idea, an idea, and elbow grease and a little luck. Sometimes all it takes is being friendly."

"Isn't everybody friendly over there, at least the ones who want to sell you something?"

"Any of you folks who are good at what you do will find work on our side. There's always room at the top. What makes you ask?"

"We can't live with the Angyals forever."

"They idolize you, you're the ideal son-in-law."

"Erszi isn't all that bad either."

"Her mother? Are you serious?"

"Why not? She might be even younger than you?"

"Well, I certainly wouldn't put it past you." Michael held his beer out to him, Adam tapped the bottle with his own.

"Were you ever here before?"

"No, the East never interested me much. It got left behind twenty years ago."

"You mean in terms of economics."

"Any manufacturer who calls his bus the Icarus," Michael said with a laugh. "How do you think that's going to turn out? Progress is at home in the West."

"I don't live badly."

"If your nabobs would release the cancer statistics, you wouldn't say that. Take Rositz, just a few miles from your doorstep, spews filth that would be forbidden in the West. Inconceivable! Mona showed me that tar pit once. A plague pit. It's criminal."

"What is it you do actually?"

"Cellular biology."

"Okay, and?"

Michael smiled. "We're trying to figure out why we get old and die, so that someday we won't get old and die."

"And why do we get old and die?"

"Do you really want to know?"

"Yes, of course."

"When cells multiply, when chromosomes are copied, a little something always gets lost, a piece gets lopped off every time. At some point so much information is missing that the cell goes bad, that's after about fifty cycles. But that doesn't have to be the case. If cells could reproduce without any loss, we would continue to live, which is to say, we don't have to die."

Michael flipped his cigarette away like a firefly and lit another.

"Inhale deep, go quick."

"That doesn't have anything to do with it, or not a lot. There's a clock inside each one of us, and when it runs down, that's it, the end, unless you keep winding it up again. In principle we're already able to calculate how long you'll live, fairly precisely in fact."

"So you mean that it's feasible, rewinding the clock?"

"Yes, sure, just a matter of time. In forty or fifty years we'll have the knack of it, for the most part."

"In forty years?"

"Approximately. At least you'll be able to wind it up so that you'll live to be two hundred or maybe longer."

"And you're looking for the wind-up key?"

"Have you ever heard of telomeres?"

"Some kind of little animal?"

"Telomeres are the ends of the chromosomes, a kind of overlap, like the plastic tip on your shoelaces. Each time a copy is made they get shorter, if you want to picture it that way—that's the ticking clock. We're pretty close to it with pinworms."

"And you guys are gonna pull this off."

"More likely the Americans."

"You say that as if it was the most natural thing in the world. But doesn't that mean we've had the rotten luck of being the last people who are going to die?"

"Or the good luck; depends, I suppose. Maybe we're the next to the last, or the next to the next, but in a hundred years we'll have done it."

"And why don't we hear anything about this, if you're so close?"

"It's not all that simple either, but take cancer cells for example. Cancer cells are immortal, they don't come to an end, they keep on copying without any loss. We have to transfer what cancer cells can do to healthy cells. We've got the model, so to speak."

"For immortality." Adam massaged his chest. "So people who get themselves pickled or frozen—they've got the right idea."

"Might be, may well be."

"I'd be satisfied to grow as old as Elfi."

"As your turtle? As pets they never get older than fifty, life's too stressful living with us."

"No older?"

"In the wild they can live to a hundred or more, but Elfriede definitely won't. Didn't you know that?"

"No."

"If I could still be alive at the moment when we turn off the death switch . . . that'd be something!"

"I don't know. If you've got some who are going to die and others who won't, or at least will live five times as long—"

"It's already that way. Fear isn't going to get you anywhere. We have to free ourselves from life's brevity, from mortality. That's the only categorical imperative—escape from your own self-inflicted mortality."

"Sounds strange somehow."

"It's like a drug, once you've been up there with it, you never want to come down."

"Do you live to work, or do you work to live?"

"That's not a legitimate question."

"Yes it is. You're spending your whole life working for eternity."

"For me work is life. Isn't it for you?"

"Yes, but we don't mean the same thing."

"Why not? What you do is great work."

"Precisely because I can do what I want."

"But if she wants a dress, you can't make her a pantsuit."

"Sure I can, if she looks better in a pantsuit."

"You're sure sure of yourself, I'll give you that."

"Do you love Evi?"

"Do I love Evelyn?"

"Yes."

"I wouldn't be here otherwise. I ought to have been in Hamburg long before now."

"Are three weeks too long?"

"Do you have any idea what it means to disappear for that long? Three weeks can mean letting go of everything, the whole shootin' match—not just your own existence, but that of the others, and of the project."

"Or of immortality."

"Right, of immortality too."

They both nodded, as if they were finally in agreement.

33

LADIES' CHOICE

"I WAS SO TIRED," Katja said, "but now I can't fall asleep. I might as well get up."

"Maybe the men would like to sleep."

"And we'll stand guard? Sounds like they've got quite a conversation going."

"Could you catch any of it?"

"Nope. But Adam has a lovely voice. Damn, when he told me his real name, it was like the end of the world."

"You thought he'd been jerking you around the whole time?"

"For a moment—yes."

"I'd already moved in with him, and I didn't know even then. Everything had just his last name on it."

"Is it because it sticks out so far?" Katja tapped her larynx.

"He had to have been embarrassed as a kid, with that thin neck and then that huge Adam's apple. Somehow he was always Adam."

"It looks very masculine."

"Hm, I thought so too."

"But not anymore?"

"Oh, sure."

"And Michael?"

"That's totally different. Adam's a child in comparison."

"You think so?"

"Michael knows what he wants, keeps moving on. With him something's always happening, he's a searcher, a researcher. Been everywhere, speaks umpteen languages, there's a wide-openness there, he breathes a lot freer—it's not the same thing year after year."

"He has beautiful hands."

"Hm. But he's got some crazy stuff inside his head too. He's read everything by Lem. Lem's the reason he started learning Polish once."

"The science-fiction guy?"

"Yeah, with all the robots and machines. Michael thinks he's the greatest writer there is."

"His stuff is available to us too, isn't it?" Katja propped herself up so that she could see Evelyn. "Is he a good lover?"

Evelyn nodded.

"Was there a spark right from the start?"

"It didn't even occur to me. He was supposed to marry my girlfriend, his cousin."

"Mona?"

"Oh, right, you know her."

"The bad company."

"Is that what Adam called her?"

"It just slipped out. Why did you take off without him?"

"Adam didn't tell you about that, of course." In propping herself up too, Evelyn touched the roof of the tent. "It's damp," she said and pushed back her hair.

"You have to be careful in the morning. You bump against it and there's a sudden downpour," Katja said.

"We've got one like it, or almost the same."

"And so what was it?"

"I knew what was going on for a long time, or at least I had a pretty good idea. Mona said everybody knew except me."

"Knew what?"

"That he was screwing them, his women."

"His women?"

"His clients, his creations. He even gives them names. At first he said they were the names of the designs he created. But they're more like the nicknames guys give easy girls. He photographs them in their new outfits. You only need to look at their eyes, so hot to trot it's as if they're only taking a quick break. The last one was a silk blouse, nothing underneath of course—you could've put out your eyes with those nipples."

"Younger than you?"

"Ah, anything but! If you saw them on the street, nobody would ever think of turning around for a second look. Well past their prime."

"Really?"

"But when he custom-tailors something for them, and can he ever, they look really sharp, and that turns him on."

"Is it maybe a dressing-undressing thing?"

"Nah, it's not that simple. I caught them at it, I saw them, even though I truly didn't want to know."

"Ouch, damn! That hurts."

"I don't think I'm all that vain, I don't, but if you had seen that woman." Evelyn's hand touched the roof again. "Sorry. You wouldn't believe, I swear you wouldn't. Naked she was just an old biddy."

"And Adam?"

"I still see him standing there, behind the cupboard, not a stitch on—"

"Adam without his fig leaf. Has he a got a thing for women like that?"

"No, that's not it. They're not all that way. But theoretically it could be any one of them, of his clients, just about any woman."

"I don't know whether this is of any interest to you or not, but he was always perfectly proper with me—I mean it, a real angel."

"I believe it, I believe you."

"I'd said something stupid about how I'd fulfill his every wish, or whatever—and I was even thinking of that. I just wanted him to take me along with him, all the rest didn't matter. But there was never even a remark or a stupid move. I was beginning to think he was gay—"

"Adam?"

"Well, he's a tailor. I know a gay hairdresser, and tailors and hairdressers, they're not all that different."

"A tailor is a whole different thing."

"Doesn't matter, what I wanted to say was that he was either gay or truly loved his wife."

"Maybe he did once."

"If a man would be willing to follow me in an old heap like that, even though I was with somebody else—that counts for something."

"Yes, but what?"

Katja was lying on her back now, one hand under her head. "Do you really want to go back?"

"The awful part is I change my mind every couple of hours," Evelyn said.

"Do you have anybody over there?"

"No, no one. Adam has an aunt—well, not a real aunt, but she came to visit now and then. Her husband fled at some point, didn't want to live in the East anymore or wasn't allowed to. He's some sort of big shot now."

"All our relatives are over there. We're the only ones who haven't done it."

"Once you start thinking about it, and it suddenly becomes a real possibility, and you suddenly ask yourself what your life's about, where it goes from here—"

"And from that point on, there's no peace of mind. I even think a person has a duty to get out. We have no idea what life can mean."

"Adam is so undemanding. Sits there in the garden of an evening, with a beer and a cigar, and the neighbor comes to the fence—he even gets along with his neighbors. That always fascinated me, he was so independent, you know—it showed character. The guys at university were so cautious and well behaved. Adam was like breathing free. He never minced his words, always spoke his mind. And yet, if he's just going to sit there in his garden—"

"Have you never gone on trips together?"

"We were in Bulgaria once. He's got money. Money to burn, at least to my mind. Adam even wanted children. But . . . I . . ." Evelyn rolled over to face the side of the tent.

"What's wrong? Hey, Evi?"

Katja carefully began to stroke Evelyn's hair and shoulders.

"What's wrong? Are you crying?"

"I had them get rid of one."

"I've got that behind me too. But he was such a son of a bitch, a real thug."

"Adam doesn't even know. And don't you dare tell him, never ever. Promise?"

"Sure, I promise."

"You had a reason at least. But I, I just thought I wanted to wait. And now I'm thinking it was a good thing I didn't have it. What would I do with a baby in the West?"

"I didn't want to be tied to that guy my whole life long—all the same it crosses my mind way too often."

"Are they still out there?" Evelyn raised her head.

"Your men?"

"My men?"

"Well yes, that's true, you have two, and I don't have even one."

Evelyn blew her nose. "You can have one, that'd simplify things somehow."

"Then I'll ask in the morning if one of them wants me."

"And who are you going to ask first?"

"Adam, of course."

"But he doesn't want to go to the West!"

"All the same, if it doesn't matter to you?"

"Listen—what's that?"

"It's a mob of some sort."

"Can you make anything out?"

"The West German national anthem?"

"No, it's ours, it's our anthem!"

34

A FAIRY TALE

EVELYN, KATJA, AND ADAM were sitting in a little corner café on Nép-stadion út, about halfway between the embassies of the GDR and the Federal Republic.

Katja pushed her empty cup away. "All this coffee is putting me to sleep."

"I think it's funny we're sitting here guzzling coffee at their expense," Evelyn said.

"What do you mean? I have to pay the embassy back," Adam said.

"Damn, and here I thought you'd finally stopped footing my bill," Katja said.

"That's what money's for, to spend."

"No reason to throw it out the window, Adam. We can't even pay for a night at a hotel or a decent meal."

"Anything you guys are doing without? I don't feel like I'm having to cut corners. We couldn't have it much better than this."

"You don't even notice anymore just how degrading it is."

"If you'd be happier at the Hilton, go ahead. But you won't experience anything like last night, that's for sure."

"You mean our soused countrymen? I can do without them."

"They're all just standing and waiting in the exit line, as you yourself heard."

The waiter arrived, exchanged ashtrays, and removed empty plates.

"I'm ashamed to say it," Katja remarked, "but I feel better with papers."

"Perfectly normal." Adam pulled out another cigar. "Will this bother you?"

"Not me."

"Wait till we're outside. Shall we pay?"

"I wouldn't mind something else to drink. Some juice maybe."

"But the really awful thing is . . ." Katja propped her elbows on the table and hid her face in her hands.

"What?" Adam asked, the cigar already in his mouth, and shook the box of matches.

"You'll think I've lost all my marbles, but once I was outside again, I was on the verge of tears—"

"What amazed me," Evelyn said, "was that you were even willing to give it a try."

"I thought I might need diapers."

"That close to fudgin' your undies?" Adam said and lit his cigar.

"Well, the main thing is it went all right," Evelyn said.

"I was on the verge of tears—that same old familiar smell." Katja shook her head. "I'm sorry."

"You're right, somehow it reminded me of . . . school or something."

"Lunchboxes," Katja said. "As if they'd all just opened their lunch-boxes. And then the way they tried to buck us up."

"They weren't unpleasant," Adam said.

"No wonder, now that everybody's running away from them. They're tickled pink if somebody says they want to go back. Wait and see, once you're home, just how nice they are to you. For twenty years now they've forbidden you to sing the words to their own national anthem."

"Good God, I don't want to go back!" Katja said.

"I didn't mean you."

"And then all at once that smell. Suddenly it seemed I'd been away for years."

Adam laughed and then had to cough. "I could sell my provisional travel pass. To the highest bidder."

"Nobody can ever take you seriously, Adam."

"Just wait. I bet there's a pack of people who'd be interested. Like those guys who were counting out their dollar bills for everybody to see. If I asked them—"

"That was Michael!" Katja jumped up and ran outside.

"Do me a favor, Evi? On the way back, sit up front with me?"

"But you'll have to put that thing out."

Adam laid the cigar in the ashtray and looked around for the waiter. Katja appeared at the door.

"We need to come outside, he's got something he has to say to us, something's happened."

"Bad?"

"I don't think so."

Evelyn followed Katja. Adam took the cigar from the ashtray, puffed until it was glowing again, and walked to the counter. He watched the waiter's ballpoint move across the pad, and then stared at the amount, underlined twice. He counted out the currency and laid it on the bill with a soft "Viszontlátásra." The waiter thanked him with a slight bow.

As he reached the door Adam took another puff on his cigar and blew the smoke into the milky blue September sky.

"He's arranged pleasant quarters for you in the embassy, has he?" Adam asked, as Katja and Evelyn finally stopped hugging.

"Make all the jokes you want, but in a few days the border will be open," Michael said. "That's certain."

"As certain as immortality."

"They're opening the border!" Michael said.

"Bull," Adam said. "Who's been telling you fairy tales?"

"It may not suit you, but in a couple of days—"

"Why shouldn't it suit me? I may actually make some money on my travel pass."

"From here on, I'm footing the bill for everything," Michael said. "And this evening we're going to live it up."

Adam blew one little cloud of smoke after another into the air and led the way to the car. He unlocked it and opened the doors from inside. Michael held the door open first for Katja, then for Evelyn.

"Can I sit up front?" Evelyn asked.

Michael nodded and stepped aside so she could get in.

It took them three-quarters of an hour to find their way out of Budapest. Adam had given Evelyn the map, but she very quickly fell asleep. And Katja had closed her eyes too. Only Michael was sitting up and staring out the window as if not to miss a detail.

They left the autobahn at Székesfehérvár. In Veszprém Adam didn't take the exit for Balatonfüred, but instead, hoping to see something of the landscape, drove parallel to the north shore of the lake in the direction of Tapolca. But only a few kilometers beyond the bypass around Veszprém, the motor had started to stutter—and now at last it fell silent. Suddenly everyone was wide awake.

"No problem," Adam said, letting the car roll onto the shoulder, "it's just the spark plugs."

He took out the tools stored in the trunk, released the hood, and smiled. He reminded Evelyn of a magician about to begin his act. He raised the hood. He had shown her a couple of times before how to pull the plug caps, unscrew the plugs, and clean them with a wire brush. But when Evelyn got out of the car, she saw that he wasn't doing anything, just standing there with his hands on the fender and his eyes closed.

"Adam," she said softly. "Is something wrong?"

35

TOWED

IT WAS EARLY afternoon before Adam could finally be persuaded not to undertake further repairs of his own and to be towed instead. Evelyn and Katja were able to get several cars to stop. But either they were not going to Lake Balaton or didn't have towing gear or gave them some explanation they couldn't understand. Finally Evelyn and Katja hitched a ride to the next village and called the Angyals.

Around five o'clock Herr Angyal stepped out of his white Trabant. Stretched out on a blanket beside the road, Michael and the two women had nodded off. "Cylinder-head gasket," Adam called to Herr Angyal as he was pulling a large bowl from the passenger side. After Evelyn had taken over the potato salad, Herr Angyal pushed his glasses up on his forehead and bent down over the engine. Katja handed out utensils and plates, and Michael poured white wine from a large bottle. But neither Adam nor Herr Angyal would join in the picnic.

When they had finally got the towline attached to the Wartburg, they wiped their hands off on the grass and sat down with the others. Adam ate his potato salad straight from the bowl and popped the few remaining meatballs into his mouth.

"Do you think your car can handle us all?" Michael asked.

"We could hitchhike," Katja said.

"You all get in with him," Adam said. "Two long honks mean stop. Two short ones—you're going too fast."

"Three shorts," Michael said as he stood up, "you're passing us." He reached out a hand to Adam, who held his out and let himself be pulled to his feet.

Once they were all in the Trabant, Herr Angyal rolled down his window, pushed his glasses back into place like goggles, and held his arm up as he slowly pulled away.

"What an incredible racket," Michael said. "You get to hear the whole works all at once."

Katja turned around and waved to Adam, who, however, was concentrating on glancing back and forth between the Trabant's rear end and his own rearview mirror.

"It did feel as if I was in a fairy tale," Michael said. "I can't begin to describe how happy I am. When he told me I didn't need to worry, it'll all be over in a few days—I'm so glad I don't have to leave you behind alone." Michael turned around halfway and laid a hand on Evelyn's knee. "It really is like a fairy tale, isn't it?"

"Please," Evelyn said. "Keep your eyes on the road."

"I won't believe it until I'm across," Katja said.

"You can lay money on it. Normally you can't get zilch out of an embassy staff. So that when they voluntarily open their mouths and—"

"Maybe they were just trying to get rid of you," Katja said.

"The Hungarians have signed the international refugee convention and canceled their agreement with your lunkheads—they won't repatriate anybody back to the GDR. That's what they told me. And in Bavaria they're opening up one camp after the next. They're expecting a huge stampede. And that's not just in tabloids like *Bild*."

"And we can just drive right across?" Katja asked.

"We're blasting off as soon as the border's open, and we'll take you along."

"You can let me out in Munich."

"You can always come with us to Hamburg. That way you two could work on the red tape together—practical, wouldn't you say?"

"I really wasn't planning to go to Hamburg."

"Just for a couple of days. At my place you could have a room all to yourself."

"I don't know how Evelyn feels about that. Maybe you two might want—"

"No, think how fantastic that'd be for Evelyn. Just imagine, you both could head out together, to the harbor, the fish market, the Alster lakes, the museums—that'd be much more fun than all alone. And on weekends we'll do stuff, we'll take little trips—"

Michael had turned around so far that Herr Angyal had to give him a tap and point to the rearview mirror.

"So now sit up straight," Evelyn said.

"And what if it is just a fairy tale?" Katja asked.

"They knew what they were talking about."

Herr Angyal flipped his sun visor down. The sun sat atop the road and looked as if it were searing a hole in the horizon.

"If you want, Katja, you can move in with us, with the Angyals, there's still an empty bed in my room," Evelyn said.

"You mean I can do it, just like that?"

"Sure, why not?"

"It'll be funny not to see Adam in the rearview mirror anymore," Michael said and turned to look back through the rear window.

Evelyn and Katja turned around too. Adam appeared to be intently focused on the tow line and the Trabant's brake lights. They could make out two vertical lines between his eyebrows. He blinked a lot.

"He should put his sun visor down," Katja said, turning around again and fishing the Rubik's Cube from her purse.

"Yes, he should," Evelyn said and signaled Adam to do it. But he didn't notice her.

36

A SUNDAY

"LET THAT BE, PLEASE," Frau Angyal said, edging Evelyn away when she started to clear the breakfast things from the table. "Off to the hills, everybody! Adam, please, the weather's supposed to be lovely."

"We used to make the climb a lot," Pepi said, "it's such a beautiful spot."

No one thought of anything better to say. And even Michael and Katja, who were once again sitting in front of the television, vanished to their rooms like obedient children. Adam took the loafers that he hadn't worn since early summer out of the trunk and exchanged his sandals for them.

They had to wait for Pepi, who was searching for her rucksack. Frau Angyal had made tea and, despite protests, some sandwiches too.

It was so quiet you could hear every car and every moped for miles around. Only the occasional cries and shouts of children drifted up from the lake. Sometimes there was what sounded like the pop of a gun in the distance.

"Poor starlings," Evelyn said.

Just as the church bells began chiming, Pepi appeared with her rucksack, which she was unwilling to hand over to either Adam or Michael.

They walked down to the end of the driveway and turned left, along

Római út, as if heading for the lake. But at Saint Anne's Chapel they turned left again.

"I never noticed that before," Adam said. He had stopped in front of the chapel.

"Noticed what?" Michael asked.

"Why, there—1798!" Adam pointed to the date above the door. "Everybody stand underneath it. Come on, we haven't taken any pictures. Misha and Evi on the left and right, you two in the middle."

Nobody objected to Adam's directions. He took his time and kept changing the stop.

"When I say 'Go,' then you start walking, you take one step forward."

"Why?" Michael asked.

"Believe him, it's a great effect, really," Evelyn said.

"Go!" Adam said and pressed the shutter release. And now one more."

All four resumed their position under "Anno Domini 1798."

"And—Go!" Adam shouted. "Very good!"

"Now you." Evelyn took the camera from his hand. "Katja on the outside, you next to her," she said.

Adam flinched as he touched Michael's arm, which lay on Pepi's shoulder. He cautiously put his arm around Pepi's waist.

"That doesn't work," Evelyn said. "Just stand there."

"And Go!" Adam commanded. They took a step ahead one more time. And then Pepi led the way up the path, which meandered past vineyards and open plots, till it joined the upper road. From there they soon turned off again, following signs for the Róza-Szegedy House. "This is definitely older than two hundred years," Pepi said as they stood before it.

A dozen people were waiting for the restaurant terrace across the way to open.

"We'll come here later for lunch," Michael said. "I have to invite you all at least once."

Here the woods began. They moved along the stony path Indian file, Pepi and her rucksack in the lead, behind her Evelyn, with Michael bringing up the rear.

After about fifteen minutes the path grew less steep and led across the higher vineyards.

"Are they harvesting yet?" Michael asked. They heard voices and the plop of grapes landing in plastic buckets.

"Those are Zweigelt grapes," Pepi said.

Once the owner of the vineyard recognized Pepi, he cut off a few clusters and, holding them between thumb and index finger, offered them one by one across the fence, where the Germans accepted them in their cupped hands. As they walked they ate the small sweet grapes.

The day was once again as warm as in August. Before them sailboats crisscrossed the lake and the bay below. Along the edge of the path lay overripe plums, wasps buzzing around them. Coming to a narrow stone stairway, they climbed up and rested on a bench hewn out of the rocks and giving off a damp coolness. From there it wasn't far to a stone cross from 1857, whose metal Jesus had been painted with an emphasis on dripping blood. Not far from it a waste barrel filled to overflowing formed a little mound of trash.

They sat down on rocks farther down from the cross and five to ten feet back from the precipice. The region on the far southern shore of Lake Balaton was flat except for two hills. The sun was mirrored on the water, where clouds traced more definite shadows than over the land. But they never seemed to move. The vineyards below were textured, hatched surfaces, smoke marked a couple of fires. A lark hung in the air at eye level.

The thermos of tea was passed around, Pepi doled out the wrapped sandwiches. Adam spread his sweat-soaked shirt on the warm rock and took a couple of pictures.

"Down there we'll have grilled catfish with a garlic-wine sauce," Michael said.

"Are you leaving tomorrow?" Katja asked.

Michael nodded and pushed a slice of apple into his mouth.

"I thought you were going to wait for us."

"Would like nothing better, but that's a no-go."

"They lied to you, they just wanted to get rid of us."

"I promise you, it's no fairy tale."

"I can't take this any longer," Katja said. "Can't you stow me in your trunk?"

"I don't have a trunk."

"Then under some blankets or bags, it'll work. They're not checking anymore. And even if they do, they'll let us through."

"Believe me, it's just a matter of a couple more days."

"You wouldn't be risking anything," Katja said.

"And how do you picture it? Should I say I hadn't noticed you'd crept in back there?"

"For example."

"Can't you find another topic for conversation?" Adam said. "Anyhow, you're not going to find a more beautiful spot anywhere." He walked with Pepi to the monument.

They heard a sirenlike honking before the train came into view as it pulled into Badacsony. The rhythmic beat of the wheels slowed down. Once the train stopped, they could hear the station's loudspeaker.

Adam passed his hand over the pedestal of the cross, on which names and dates had been chiseled or scratched. The older the date, the more artistic the workmanship. "Pepi," Adam said, pointing to a name that stood above a semicircle of two laurel sprigs. " 'Kiss Gábor, 1889.' And here's another eighty-niner, 'Bodó József.' We could ask someone to engrave our names here, that would give people something to wonder about a hundred years from now too."

"Yes," Pepi said, nodding. "It'd have to be at night. I know somebody who could do it."

Adam went "Hm" and nodded. They walked back to the others, he put his shirt on.

Pepi led them on to a viewpoint from where they could see the peaked hill in the hinterland. She told about the Romans, for whom the Római út was named, and explained how lava, igneous soil, was good for cultivating wine. Otherwise they didn't say much. Michael put his arm around Evelyn's shoulder a couple of times, but Evelyn had only monosyllabic replies to everything he said, and the path kept forcing them to walk single file. Pepi stayed in Adam's vicinity. The last part of the way Evelyn walked between Katja and Pepi, while the two men hurried ahead in the hope of still getting a table on the terrace.

Later that afternoon they walked down to the lake, sunbathed, and drank coffee. Only Katja went into the water. She swam out so far that Pepi wanted to notify the rescue service.

That evening, shortly before seven, they were sitting at the table set for supper waiting for the Angyals to join them.

"That was a lovely day," Evelyn said.

At almost the same moment they heard Frau Angyal call from the house, her arms fumbling at the plastic strips. She was wearing the blouse Adam had made for her.

"Come in, come in."

Katja, Evelyn, and Michael raced to the television. Adam poured himself another glass. He stood up, glass in hand. But instead of going inside, he lingered at the little pen to watch the turtle, which had climbed into its shallow bowl of water.

"Adam," Pepi said.

Frau Angyal's voice could be heard inside, she was translating.

"Looks like it's happened," Pepi said.

She flinched too when both Katja and Michael let out a scream.

"Sorry," Adam said, set his glass down, and wiped his damp hand on his pants.

37

A BONFIRE

IN THE DRIVEWAY in front of the house Adam and Herr Angyal had layered twigs, branches, and logs. Adam had borrowed Michael's lighter and started the fire with a rag drenched in alcohol. The Angyals and their guests were seated in chairs around the fire.

"For him it's a victory, even though he can't stand Gyula Horn, but it's almost as important as the funeral for Imre Nagy this past June," Pepi translated.

"In fifty-six he was nineteen years old, he was part of it," Frau Angyal said. "He was involved in it all."

"And he's really never been back to Budapest since?" Katja asked.

"No. We were at the airport twice. But now, now we'll definitely make the trip, he has to make the trip now."

"No matter where you go in Budapest you can see bullet holes in almost every building. Or they've been plastered over," Pepi said.

"To the heroes of fifty-six," Michael said, raising his glass and nodding to Herr Angyal.

"If I lived here," said Adam, who had impaled a potato on a stick and was holding it in the fire, "wild horses couldn't drag me to Budapest."

"You shouldn't say that, Adam. For him Budapest was everything—friends, family, girls, cafés, theaters, movies, the baths. To give up all that—Budapest was the most wonderful city in the world."

"I admire Papa for his resolve. He wanted to go to university, but he decided it was best to give that up too."

"Why didn't he go to the West? That would have been possible, wouldn't it?" Katja asked.

"Nobody understands that, sorry to say. And that may sound strange coming from his wife, since when all is said and done I wouldn't have met András otherwise. I wonder if he would even have turned his head for a woman like me in Budapest."

"Oh, Mama, you two would have found each other anywhere. Don't say things like that."

"In Budapest there were women, very different women."

"Papa's best friend was so badly wounded that they had to amputate both legs. He put a bullet through his head then. That's why my name is Jozefa, Josephine," Pepi said.

"The depth of his resolve has always frightened me. I had never seen anything like it. I was seventeen when Pepi came. And what did he learn here? How to snap his fingers and drink wine, that's what he learned."

"Papa just remarked that they were betrayed on all sides, betrayed by everyone."

Herr Angyal went on speaking. His voice sounded brittle, as if at any moment he would have to clear his throat.

"They thought the Americans would help them at least. They didn't even send guns. A young friend of his—who had attended boarding school in Switzerland, nothing but diplomats' kids—he knew right away that no one would risk helping the Hungarians."

Herr Angyal got up and on unsteady legs disappeared behind the house.

"Stay here, Mama, let him."

"He's so difficult sometimes. We shouldn't have started with this."

"He started talking about it. And don't make such a face, he's hardly drunk anything."

"You must excuse us, please, we never talk about this. . . . My husband still believes that Europe's freedom will be decided by us Hungarians."

"Those aren't Papa's words, they come from Lajos Kossuth."

"How does that poem go?" Frau Angyal asked, " 'Abandoned the Magyar . . . abandoned . . . ' "

" 'Abandoned, and alone, forsaken by craven nations, the Magyar.' Papa was even a member of the Petőfi Club."

"What kind of club?" Katja asked.

Everyone turned around to look at Herr Angyal. Pressing something to his chest with his left hand, in his right he held a newspaper, which he gave Evelyn. Staring from the front page of a *Time* magazine dated January 1957 was a rather intellectual-looking young man, his head slightly lowered, in his hands a short rifle, fingers more patting the barrel than gripping it. Underneath it read, "Hungarian Freedom Fighter." In the upper-right-hand corner, as if on a banner, was written, "Man of the Year."

Herr Angyal stopped. He spread open a piece of cloth and held it before him with both hands. One corner had been singed.

"A flag?" Michael asked.

"Papa rescued it. If they'd caught him with it—"

"What if I tell you now—" and Frau Angyal waved for Pepi to be silent. "About the search, an official search of the house."

"What? Neither of you has ever said anything about that!"

"You had only been born. He was in the cellar, oh my, when I think about it, but they didn't open the cellar hatch, just running back and forth, back and forth. He had set fire to the flag, it did not burn. He had poured alcohol over it, but they were gone by then. I washed and washed the flag, but the smell never left, nothing I could do. It stinks for twenty years now."

"And if they had found him with it?"

"Prison, at least."

"He wanted to burn it in order to save it," Adam said.

"What do you mean by that?" Michael asked.

"Well yes, better to burn it than for it to fall into the wrong hands. There can be no greater proof of love."

"What is it?" Evelyn asked. "What are those rivers?"

"Our Kossuth coat of arms," Frau Angyal whispered. "Four rivers and three mountains." She turned to her husband with an even softer whisper. He didn't so much as glance at her. When Pepi gently prodded him, he responded with a few brusque words. And his glasses slipped from his forehead to his nose.

"Papa wants to raise the flag, someday he wants to raise it high for everyone to see."

"And who should see it here, please? The neighbors? He is drunk, once again drunk."

"My father was born in thirty-three," Adam said. "In 1945 they were too young to get involved in any of it but old enough to realize what was happening. None of them went to the West, and none of them joined the Party. No one understood that either."

Herr Angyal folded up the flag, held it in both hands, and then kissed it. He sat down in his chair, the flag in his lap, pushed his glasses back up on his forehead, and bent down to pick up his glass.

"It seems clearer and clearer to me now," Adam said. "They weren't about to be taken in by anybody. They kept their distance from all of it—if they had some character." He fingered his potato and tried to peel away the black skin.

"Maybe I don't understand, because it sounds so sad, hopeless, as if life were over right from the start. A person had to have tried at least," Katja said.

"What do you want to try? What are you supposed to want?" Adam asked.

After a pause, with everyone looking at her, Katja said, "Well, to be happy, to go someplace where things function, where you can live reasonably. I would keep on trying, over and over, or I'd throw myself out the window."

"It's not always a matter of either-or," Adam said without lifting his eyes from his potato. "You can't say that this is nothing here. And besides, it's enough that people like András or my parents didn't sell themselves, couldn't be corrupted. That's worth knowing and thinking about."

"A real philosopher, our Adam," Frau Angyal said.

"I'm not criticizing that, Adam, really I'm not. Who am I?" Katja said. "It's just a feeling that that's exactly what I don't want. I never wanted to get out as much as I do now, at this moment. I'd love to just pick up and leave this instant."

"For you it's sure to be the right thing," Pepi said.

"At least it's a good thing for Katja," Adam said.

"Papa, let's hear that snap, please!" Pepi repeated her request in Hungarian. Frau Angyal shook her head. Suddenly Herr Angyal raised his hand—a report so dry and loud it was as if his fingers were made of wood.

"Again," Pepi cried, tucking her head between her shoulders. But Herr Angyal was already bending down for his wineglass. "Gute Reise," he said in German to wish them well on their way, and toasted first Evelyn, then Katja. Except for Adam—who was tossing his hot potato from one hand to the other—they all raised their glasses. Evelyn's was empty again by now. But she set it to her lips anyway, and swallowed.

38

ON THE ROAD AGAIN

"GOOD ONE—as if I could fall asleep now."

"But in the state you're in?"

"Driving's always the last thing I can't manage, believe me, the last thing. Are you afraid?"

"Well, you don't have to step on it on my account. Besides, that's a pretty nasty draft."

"She'll be sorry! I know she's sorry! She was drunk, just plain drunk!"

"We all had a little too much to drink—"

"I mean, later in the night, she was really plastered by then. Raving like a madwoman, saying the same stuff over and over again, as if she'd totally lost it."

Katja lit a cigarette and handed it to Michael. Because of the smashed window she had pulled on his sweater and his windbreaker and wrapped a T-shirt around her head. "Turn around, turn around. I'll get across one way or another."

"I can't. No can do!" Michael banged the steering wheel so hard the car went into a brief swerve.

"Are you nuts!" Katja cried.

"Why can't any of you understand that I don't have any more vacation days, this week was pure goodwill—last week was pure goodwill.

They're all waiting for me. But none of you would know anything about that—real work, that's a totally strange concept to you."

"No it isn't," Katja said. "Except that if you love Evi, if you really love her . . . I shouldn't have come along."

"It was for her sake that I suggested it, so she wouldn't be alone, to make things simpler. And what thanks do I get? It's so damn absurd, to throw that in my face."

"So it's true."

"What's 'true'?"

"It's true that I'm to blame."

"No, it isn't."

"But it was me you were talking about."

"She admires you. She told me straight out that I should leave with you."

"With me?"

"Because of the whole thing with the trunk. That you'd do better in the West than she would and stuff like that."

"I was certain she'd be coming along."

"*You* were certain! I just have to think of all the things we'd planned. She wanted to go to university, wanted to start right away. She wanted to go to Brazil and New York, to Italy, and I said yes, we'll do it, we'll do whatever you want."

"You were a whole new world for her."

"I was, past tense, was, over and done with."

"That's not how I meant it."

"It's how I mean it."

"You need to turn around—really, turn around!"

"She came slinking across night after night. I had spotted it right off, the needs dammed up inside her. She was literally starved—"

"For sex?"

"For everything, for sex, for hugs, for caresses, for making plans, for everything. She told me how she felt in that Podunk, buried, six feet under, that's what she said, buried alive. And he doesn't get any of it. Or doesn't want to. At least I'm rid of him. That much at least."

"Adam's happy as things are—some people are undemanding."

"Undemanding! You call him undemanding? She caught him at it. I was there when she arrived sobbing her heart out because he'd been screwing around with some old biddy, and not for the first time either. She told me all about it. And then started hugging Mona and me when we said, 'Come on, we're on our way . . .' "

Michael passed a Wartburg and despite oncoming traffic stayed in the middle lane until he had overtaken a long line of East German cars.

"Don't be scared, it's as good as three lanes here."

"And then?"

"Suddenly there she was in my room. At first I thought she was just looking to play around a little. But she was so uptight, at least to start with, that I thought it was going to have to be a quickie, so that Mona wouldn't pick up on it. But she was so, I don't know—she said such beautiful things. I never dreamed that a woman with looks like that can be that way."

"Be what way?"

"The way a man actually always wants her to be. I figured that's only in the movies. Plus no kids, never divorced, and still young, but then different somehow too. That's what I thought at least. My mistake. Merde!"

Michael banged the steering wheel again.

"How you mean 'different'?"

"If somebody is suddenly willing to leave everything behind, her whole life, just for you, that's pretty incredible, don't you think?"

"Yes."

"It gave me such self-confidence, that's why I went along with the whole thing. She was constantly apologizing because the Angyals took his side, of course. For them I was the evil Westie. That really hurt Eve deeply."

"And you too."

"What's a man supposed to think when a woman like that suddenly dumps him?"

"But she hasn't dumped you."

"She wanted me to stay on, to stay another whole week."

"And then?"

"She might come with me—maybe. I told her that people are waiting for me, that I've kept them waiting for two weeks now. Waiting doesn't even come close. Without me they can't move ahead."

"So she just wanted to stay on at Lake Balaton?"

"Yeah, right."

"Nothing beyond that?"

"What do you mean, 'beyond that'?"

"Well, but maybe if she—"

"I have to work, goddammit, work! Why doesn't anybody get that?"

They hardly spoke for the rest of the way.

When they arrived at the border station at Sopron, Katja unwrapped the T-shirt from her head and fished her provisional travel pass from her purse.

"And what if they send me back now?"

"They don't care what that thing is you show them, or who stamped it."

They heard the bright putt-putt of a Trabant pulling up behind them, and some excited voices. Only when they were almost up to the barrier did they notice the people at the edge of the road. There weren't more than twenty. But they were making such a hullabaloo that Katja smiled and waved at them.

But they weren't paying any attention to the red Passat and the two people inside. They were cheering two men in a white Lada with Dresden plates and the Trabant behind them, which pulled up so close now that they could see tears running down the cheeks of the woman in the passenger seat.

"There are cameras up ahead," Michael said. "Brace yourself."

39

THE MISUNDERSTANDING

"THAT'S FOR YOU to decide," Evelyn said.

"You know very well what I want. But what if he suddenly shows up here again?"

"You don't need to trouble your head about that."

"But I do."

"He's not coming back. This has nothing to do with him."

"Aha."

"Do you move back in with me or are you staying with Pepi?"

"What do you mean, 'with Pepi'?"

"Adam, please! I have eyes in my head."

"I was with her just one time, for a fitting—"

"I don't want to hear about it. Spare me."

"Spare you is good. As if you've spared me."

"So it's time to start blaming each other? The skirt you did for Pepi turned out beautiful, I'd love to have one like that."

"It's yours. There's still fabric left." Adam reached for the bottle of water. It was empty. He held it up and waited for the waitress to look his way.

"Were you two here often?" he asked.

"Once, to dance—the time they robbed us."

"Not a pleasant memory."

"All depends. The place was jammed." Evelyn avoided looking at the man with big glasses and black hair who was sitting three tables behind Adam and constantly staring at her.

"Could you ever have imagined our guys would pull it off?" Adam asked.

"What?"

"We're going to get a real opposition."

"Forget it. Day after tomorrow it's history. You'll see just how quick they all end up in the West."

"All the same. Hungary is like a trip to the West now. And the Poles aren't playing ball anymore either."

"The less they're given to eat, the wider they're allowed to open their mouths. And pretty soon they won't be letting us into Hungary anymore." She stubbed her cigarette out.

"Have you got any money left?"

"Almost all of it. Somewhere around twenty-five hundred."

"I've exchanged the koruny, the tank is full." Adam pointed to their empty coffee cups and the bottle of water.

"Enough for this, anyway."

"Didn't you make some good money here?"

"I've got unlimited room and board, at least till Christmas."

"You wouldn't have gone home?"

"Not without you. I could have more work here than you can shake a fist at."

"Pepi asked me if I wanted to give German lessons. She knows two Russian teachers who were told they're going to have to teach German now—from one day to the next."

"How long do you want to stay?"

"A couple of days yet, as long as the weather holds. What's up with Heinrich?"

"The starter, the fact is I need a new starter. I just hope he makes it."

"Our Herr Angyal has quite a knack. Have you seen the box he built for Elfriede?"

"First-class turtle luxury is what it is. Elfi's definitely going to want to stay on here."

The waiter arrived with the bill—Evelyn handed Adam her wallet.

"Didn't you order something besides?"

"I'll get some water elsewhere," Adam said and paid.

She pushed her half-full glass his way. Adam drank it down. The black-haired man paid too. They stood up from the table and left the restaurant.

"It's pretty discouraging," Adam said, glancing down over Evelyn, "but I could never come up with a pair of pants that would look any better on you than those jeans."

"I've gotten really fat here. Maybe that's what you like?"

As she walked, Evelyn put on her straw hat. She didn't look around but she had the feeling the black-haired man was following them.

As they approached the wharf, which projected out into the lake like a jetty, an elderly man spoke to them in German. In his basket were figs, resting amid dark green leaves.

"Try them, try them," he said. "Take some, as many as you like."

Evelyn stroked a fig carefully with her fingers and took a bite. Adam took some money from his wallet.

"Very fresh, from my garden," the man said. Evelyn nodded and stared at the old man's gnarled hands circling to select the best figs in the basket. "Take them, please, take them all."

Adam paid, they walked on. The black-haired guy was in fact following them. He was a short, almost wispy man.

"Did you notice his hands, like roots," Evelyn said and laid an arm around Adam's shoulder. "And the thumb, notched like a cutting board."

"I never realized before that this is what they mean by Plattensee, the flat lake," Adam said.

"Don't look around right away," Evelyn said, "but some weird guy is slinking along behind us. Do you know him?"

A couple of people who had been watching a ship pull out were now coming toward them. There were fishermen sitting along the edge of the wharf.

"Well, good day to you," the black-haired man said, blocking their path and extending a hand to Adam. "Warnemünde didn't work out, it appears, or are we on the Baltic here?"

He's crazy, Evelyn thought when she heard his bleating laugh. Adam, with a fig in each hand, held out his forearm, which the other guy squeezed. "I didn't recognize you. Are you here on vacation too?"

"Well now, I wouldn't exactly call it vacation, more a business trip." He let out more bleats. "Just a joke. I thought, since I have a visa, I ought to make the trip too."

"Sorry, but I don't know your name," Adam said and turned toward Evelyn, "but this is the garageman, from the station down by the Polyclinic. I got that hubcap from him."

"Well, it's a small world, especially for us—ain't nothing can be done about that," the garageman said and laughed again. "Just wanted to put in an appearance. Be seeing you, be seeing you."

"Yes," Adam said. "Good luck to you. Good-bye."

Evelyn gave him a nod as well.

"Whoa," she said after they moved on a bit. "He's creepy."

"I think so too," Adam said. "Although I'd swear he's harmless."

"Were you at all afraid crossing the border?"

"Funny thing—no, I wasn't."

"Really?"

"I was thinking of you the whole time."

"Even with Katja in the trunk?"

"Yes. It was all about you. I can't give you any reasons, but that's how it was."

Evelyn laid her arm around Adam again. "I need to tell my mother—she doesn't know a thing about this."

"Luckily it's a little late to write postcards," Adam said.

"Don't give me that, we still have some time here."

"Do you want to take the ferry tomorrow? From Tihany? There's a marvelous pastry shop there. Do you know it?"

"No, I don't," Evelyn said. "Will you read to me this evening? Pepi has a book by Gustav Schwab in her room, printed in that old-fashioned Gothic."

They had reached the end of the jetty and were standing now between two fishermen. The water was dead still, except for low waves that the aft of the ship was sending out into the lake to its right and left. They ate their last two figs in silence. Then Evelyn leaned her head against Adam. Her straw hat slipped a bit to one side. For a moment it looked as if they were both wearing it.

40

BEDTIME STORY

"BUT IT MUST have dawned on you at some point, since Prague at the latest."

"Why since Prague?"

"Or even earlier, you had my gym bag after all."

"So what?" Adam laid the open book on his stomach.

"Everything was in there—my grades, birth certificate, vaccination card, even my proof of baptism."

"And how was I supposed to know that?"

"Didn't you open the gym bag?"

"No."

"And the jewelry? Why'd you bring the jewelry along?"

"I told you, it seemed too risky too leave it at home."

"But you were smiling that funny way. For me that was a clear signal."

"Because I finally had you sitting next to me again."

"And today—I said that I finally had to tell my mother."

"You wanted to call your mother because she doesn't know where you are. I thought if you're staying on here, then it was for my sake, so that we could drive back together. Do you really want to go to the West?"

"I hoped you did too." Evelyn plumped up her pillow, hugged it with both arms, and lay down atop it.

"Do you think I can just turn my back on everything—on the house, the garden, the graves, everything? How do you picture that?"

"There's not one person waiting there for you, it's really a lot easier for you."

Evelyn got up and closed the window.

"I've told you over and over that I'll be driving home. What's in the West for me?"

"But you've been acting completely different. Why did you drag all that stuff along, my documents, the jewelry, Elfriede. You can find work anywhere. And be paid a hundred times better. Why were you questioning Michael about that? I thought you were seriously considering it." Evelyn leaned against the windowsill in her nightie and crossed her arms.

"And I thought, if you're staying, then you're staying. Why didn't you go with him?"

"What a stupid question—really, that question's enough to make me want to . . . oh, just leave me alone."

Adam had got up now too and walked over to face her.

"Do you think I would have gone through all this if I didn't love you?"

"Then don't ask such dumb questions. I've gone through some things myself, you know."

"Okay fine, then we're even now."

"And what's that supposed to mean?"

"That I don't blame you for anything, and you shouldn't blame me."

"Sounds like a divorce agreement." Evelyn fell back onto the bed.

"And since when have you known that you want to leave?"

"I've only been really sure since this morning." She was staring at the ceiling.

"You can't be serious? Since he left?"

"All I know is, I'm not going back."

"And why?"

"Why didn't I know it before this morning?"

"Why do you want to head across?"

"Because I don't want to go back. I don't want to keep on playing waitress, keep on applying for university, keep on being refused, keep on looking into all those fat-ass faces that ask why you're not for peace—all that shit."

"That will change, third time's a charm, they'll accept you."

"No. There's too much freedom here already. I've got used to it."

"Used to what?" Adam sat down on the edge of the bed.

"To the idea of moving on. I want to move on."

"What sort of sense does that make?"

"I don't know myself if I'll really like it over there, but I want to give it a try."

"Give it a try—great, and when it doesn't work out? We have only one life."

"Right, you said it."

"You never talked about this before."

"Of course we've talked about it. You were always coming up with ideas about how to meet somebody in a waiting lounge and exchange boarding passes. That was your idea."

"That was just a game. We never talked about trying anything like that."

"But I was constantly thinking about it, constantly."

"I don't believe you."

"How can you say that? Mona and I talked about nothing else—Mona was already on her way!"

"And went back."

"So what? What does that prove?"

"That she loved him."

"That's not true, simply not true at all. Why do you think she stopped giving a hoot? She just laughed whenever Frau Gabriel said something, laughed in her face. For her Mike was a ticket to the West, that was the whole point."

"Then she could have stayed on here."

"What are we talking about here, exactly?"

"You quit your job too. Did that have anything to do with cutting and running?"

"In some way, sure."

"And what way was that?"

"Mona always said that these were our baby teeth, that our real teeth hadn't grown in yet."

"Now that's absurd—don't you see how absurd that is? Baby teeth—"

"It gave me a such a sense of freedom, though. I've always felt this way. They could kiss my ass, because I'm out of here."

"That's so childish, Evi."

"And why's that?"

" 'Such a sense of freedom'!"

"If freedom is childish, then I'm childish. But it's how I feel."

"Giving it all some serious thought would be better."

"I don't need to give it any more thought, I've thought about it for a long time now. Why don't you want to go across?"

"Why should I want to?"

"Then you're not thinking! I could say whoever doesn't want to go across has never done any real thinking."

"Why should I have to think about it if I don't even want to go across?"

"Why should I have to think about it if I don't even want to stay here? Do you have any idea just how arrogant you've become, how narrow-minded."

"But for me it's not even an issue. Why should I want to leave?"

"Well, you certainly did ask Michael—"

"Bull! We were just discussing it. We had to talk about something."

"Everybody thinks about it, you do too. There's nobody who doesn't think about it."

"Which means either I come with you, or it's over?"

"This just keeps getting worse and worse." Evelyn rolled over on her side and looked across at Adam. "After the fortieth anniversary, they'll really clamp down. You've always got a lot more upset than me. Have you forgotten how the Chinese handled things? Why can't you see it?"

"This'll be different. Just think of the Poles. And if the Hungarians leave the border open—"

"I'm telling you they won't let us out after this—fat lady sings, curtain falls. You can count on it!"

"They won't be able to get away with it."

"They've always been able to get away with a lot of things."

"And what happens from here on?" Adam said without looking at Evelyn. "We've asked an awful lot of them already."

"The Angyals?"

"Did he pay them, by the way?"

"Why do you ask?"

"Pepi dropped a hint. At any rate he didn't pay the whole bill."

"Well, he can't help it if we were robbed."

"Neither can the Angyals."

"If in fact he didn't pay it all, then he'll send it. They'll get their money. Is that why your conscience is bothering you?"

"What do you mean, my conscience is bothering me?"

"You don't have to help clean up—they don't want you doing that, they want to admire you, maybe even as a son-in-law, but they definitely don't want a man who helps clean up."

"What's wrong with a man who helps clean up?"

"Nothing, but you're not at home here."

"I know what I'm doing."

"Can I ask you a question? Out of pure curiosity, and I won't blame you—did you do it with Pepi's mother?"

"What makes you think that?"

"Yes or no?"

"No, but why the question?"

"Sounds a little weak."

"Evi, please. Let's not go there!"

"I just want to figure out what your type is."

"That's something you heard from your precious Mike. He thinks I'm capable of just about anything anyway."

"She's been so moody. First she was all pissed off because I showed up with him—"

"I can understand that."

"Then suddenly everything was just like before, and I was her second daughter, and now she's back to grimacing just to manage a smile."

"What do you want? What more is she supposed to do for us?"

"They'd love to keep you here."

"Is that right?"

"As a tailor, as a son-in-law, as a lover. And you can stop laughing!"

"And what do we tell them? We're going to vacation here forever?"

"Not forever."

"Are we staying till tomorrow, for three more days, another week?"

"Whatever you want. Whatever our Herr Adam wants."

"Do you have any idea what we're talking about?" Adam slammed the book shut and slipped it onto the nightstand.

"You were going to read me the Laocoön story," Evelyn said.

"Tomorrow," Adam said, turned out the light, and stretched out on his back. He pulled the blanket up to his neck and took a deep breath.

Once she got used to the dark, Evelyn could make out the silhouette of his face. She cautiously raised her head to see if his eyes were still open. By the light of the streetlamp she could see the sweep of Adam's long lashes. His right hand lay between their pillows, his left across his chest. She heard the turtle in its box.

Even when they argued, she knew her Adam only too well. She didn't want it to be like this. She deserved something better than a man who cheated on her. Nevertheless she bedded her face against Adam's right hand. She stroked his forearm, threaded her hand up the sleeve of his T-shirt, thrust her palm across his shoulder, reached his throat, and touched his Adam's apple with her fingertips—it scurried away like an animal, but in the next moment had already turned back to her.

41

FAREWELL

"WHAT WERE YOU DOING the whole time?" Adam shouted and revved the engine. The car bumped down the driveway. "I told you we needed to be on our way."

Evelyn rolled her window down and leaned out to look back. A handkerchief fluttered in her right hand. The Angyals were veiled in a cloud of exhaust—she was wearing her new blouse again, Herr Angyal waved with a tool as if about to get back to some repairs. Pepi was already walking into the house. Adam turned left on Római út.

"What was that about?"

"I had to go one last time, and they both were making sandwiches, one after the other."

"Who's going to eat all that? A week's worth of 'em."

"There's also apples and plums, cucumbers, wine, cider, water, and pastries. They even sent your jar of Czech mustard on its way again."

"Why?"

"All for her lost children, she said, and for little Elfriede. Where is she? In the trunk?"

"The box just fit."

"Well then, she won't be in a draft," Evelyn said. "The cheesecake is still warm. Will we all see each other here again sometime?"

"I'm glad just to be on our way." He gave the dashboard three raps. "Heinrich, head for home."

"I still don't know if that's a good idea, Adam. You can let me out at the train station. I've still got the connections that Katja wrote down."

"It's not out of my way."

"And what if they give you trouble?"

"You think they won't let me back in? They'll welcome me with a hand kiss and roses."

"You can always say someone kidnapped you. I slipped sleeping powder into your tea, and when you woke up you were in the West. Luckily you made your escape, back to the land where workers and peasants have for once and for all put an end to man's exploitation of man, where—I'm sorry, I'm sorry, that was silly." She gave Adam's shoulder a pat. "I just wanted to say that it might be easier if we separate sooner."

"I told you I'd take you there, and you thought that was a good idea."

"And what if I have to go?"

"You just went."

"I just mean, what if I do—or you?"

"The motor can't be turned off—or only at the top of a hill."

"Are you going to do it nonstop?"

"It's an up-and-down route. I can always stop on the hilltops."

"To be honest, I imagined our good-bye a little different."

"How? With tears and a long embrace?"

"At least not with you keeping one foot on the accelerator."

"All you have to do is stay in your seat. All I'm saying is, you can just as easily not get out. We'll be home tonight. It's your decision."

"Don't start in again. Besides, they're sure to have sealed your house by now. You won't even be able to get in."

"You think I'm going to let that bother me?"

"Nobody's ever going to bother you from here on."

"What do you mean by that?"

"Just what I said."

"Don't start in with that crap again!"

"Why crap? What's going to happen once you're home? You'll write me love letters, tell me how you love only me, just me alone, and will be true to me and wait for me?"

"Is that so strange?"

"I'll bet you anything, Adam, that by the day after tomorrow one of your creations will stop by and comfort you. Her and all the rest. They'll tear each other limb from limb to try and comfort you."

"You and Michael wouldn't have been such a bad match. He always knew everything about me too. Could even tell me the future."

"It'll be the same as it's always been."

"What do you mean, 'the same'? How can it be the same if you're gone? Nothing will be like it was."

"You'll have the run of the place now. Good-bye boredom. A harem right here on earth, a new one every day."

"But where are my eunuchs?"

"I'm serious. I've asked myself plenty of times why you need me at all. I was just in the way of your paradise. Not that you didn't like me, and I don't look all that bad either."

"But your cooking leaves something to be desired."

"Yours too. And you've had twelve years more than me to learn."

"Wasn't it lovely, though?"

"Sometimes yes, sometimes very lovely."

"Look, there's the lake."

"Will you take care of Elfriede?"

"She's yours."

"Makes no difference. She's better off with you. It'll be nice and quiet for her hibernation. Besides I can't arrive with a huge box like that." Evelyn rolled her window up.

"That wouldn't be such a bad thing right now, a little hibernation," Adam said.

They took the road in the direction of Keszthely, Zalaegerszeg, Körmend.

"Are you hungry? You didn't eat anything." Evelyn reached back for the cheesecake, set it on her lap, unwrapped it, broke off a piece, and stuck it in Adam's mouth.

Looking for some tissues, Evelyn opened the glove compartment.

"Did she forget this?" Evelyn held up the Rubik's Cube.

"She gave it to me, said she didn't need it anymore."

A new Wartburg passed them with a honk, but neither Adam nor Evelyn waved back.

At the border station near Rábafüzes the Hungarians let them through without stamping anything, the Austrians just waved them on.

"Are you happy?" Evelyn asked as they approached Fürstenfeld near Graz.

"No, why should I be." After a brief pause he said, "Funny, you can read everything, but it doesn't feel the same as it does with us. It's like I'm at a carnival, except the Ferris wheel and shooting galleries are missing."

"That's about right. It all looks as if somebody's added in the color somehow."

"Potemkin villages."

"Yes," Evelyn said, "as if it all weren't for real."

42

KNOWLEDGE

"I DON'T THINK they even expected any payment. It's a kind of special service. It's not our fault. Besides, they didn't charge for the gas, either."

"You've got some nerve. In the East you'd have had to pay for it too—would have to pay for it anywhere," Evelyn said. She held the infrared lamp so that it warmed the turtle.

"I told them I don't have any money, just a couple of schillings."

"And the two hundred Westmarks?"

"For a very rainy day."

Evelyn looked at him.

"Does that make me a cheat? A car like that is something special for them, they have fun fiddling around with it—plus they're lending a helping hand to their brothers and sisters."

"That's nasty, Adam. Without Rudolf who knows where we'd have ended up. And wouldn't have had something warm in our bellies either."

"You've forgotten the lake, we wouldn't have seen the lake."

"Don't be such a grouch."

"I'm just saying that he also pointed out the lake to us from the car window."

"Look at this! The Angyals even thought of these."

Evelyn had now clamped the infrared lamp between her knees and was unwrapping the tiny salt and pepper shakers.

"Can't you give them a hundred at least, as a kind of goodwill gesture?" She cut a few slices of cucumber.

"The repair garage?"

"And for the towing?"

"I don't even know yet if they can fix it."

Adam bit into the bread smeared with soft cheese, pushed a piece of cucumber into his mouth, uncorked the wine, and toasted Evelyn. "Here's to the Angyals!" He drank and passed her the bottle. She took a drink too.

"At least we don't have a single worry until tomorrow morning," Adam said, took another swig, and threw himself on the bed.

"Are you finished?"

"I've had enough."

"I could just go on eating and eating."

"Who knows when you'll get your next meal here."

"I really put on some weight, though, despite everything."

"What do you mean, 'despite everything'?"

"It wasn't exactly a relaxing vacation."

"At any rate we've made it this far, it's a lovely area. Isn't that a bit too warm for Elfi?"

"She loves it, I can tell. This would be a really great place for a vacation."

Adam pulled open the drawer of the nightstand. "Real wood looks a little different . . . somebody forgot something. A Bible, now that's funny."

"Think it might be intended for us?"

"Because we're some kind of refugees?"

"Well, as a way to sort of cheer us up or something. Around here they even say 'grüss Gott' as a hello. That's a lot of God-bless-yous."

"They had no idea we were coming."

"Could have put it in there while we were down by the lake."

Adam turned on his nightstand light and stuffed Evelyn's pillow behind his neck as well. "I've already forgotten the name."

"Rudolf and something ending in 'dunkel,' " Evelyn said.

"I meant the name of the lake. The famous one is the Chiemsee, but this one here, the smaller one?"

"All I can remember is Chiemsee too. And you're sure you don't want anything more to eat? The pears are good."

" 'Then the Lord God formed man of the dust from the ground, and breathed into his nostrils the breath of life; and man became a living being.' "

"Into his nostrils?"

"Did you think it would be into his mouth, like in a first-aid course?"

And the Lord God planted a garden in Eden, in the east; and there he put the man whom he had formed. And out of the ground the Lord God made to grow every tree that is pleasant to the sight and good for food, the tree of life also in the midst of the garden, and the tree of the knowledge of good and evil.

"I read all that once, because I thought they might ask me about it in Leipzig."

"For art history?"

"Yes, for the admission interview."

"Did you know about the tree-of-life part?" Adam laid the open book on his stomach.

"Not really."

"I thought it was all about the knowledge of good and evil. I've never heard anything about a tree of life."

"So you mean there are two trees?"

"I just read it to you," he said and picked the book up again.

. . . the tree of life also in the midst of the garden, and the tree of the knowledge of good and evil. A river flowed out of Eden to water the garden; and from there it divided and became four rivers. The name of the first is Pishon; it is the one that waters the whole land of Havilah, where there is gold; and the gold of that land is good; bdellium and onyx stone are there. The name of the second river is Gihon; it is the one that flows around the whole land of Cush. And the name of the third river is Tigris, which flows east of Assyria. And the fourth river is the Euphrates. . .

"Like the Kossuth coat of arms," Evelyn said. "I'm sorry, go on."

The Lord God took the man and put him into the garden of Eden to till it and keep it. And the Lord God commanded the man, saying, "You may freely eat of every tree of the garden; but of the tree of the knowledge of good and evil, you shall not eat, for in the day that you eat of it you shall die."

" 'Shall die'?"
"I thought you'd read it. Didn't you?"
"But why 'die'? I thought they just had to leave paradise?"
"Maybe it's the same thing."
"Because they can't die in paradise?"
"Yes, of course."

And the Lord God said, "It is not good that the man should be alone; I will make him a helper fit for him." So out of the ground, the Lord God formed every beast of the field, and every bird of the air; and brought them to the man to see what he would call them; and whatever the man called every living creature, that was its name. The man gave names to all cattle, and to the birds of the air, and to every beast of the field; but for the man there was not found a helper fit for him. So the Lord God caused a deep sleep to fall upon the man, and while he slept took one of his ribs and closed its place with flesh; and

the rib which the Lord God had taken from the man he made
into a woman—

"But men and women have the same number of ribs!"

. . . made into a woman, and brought her to the man. Then the
man said, "This at last is bone of my bones and flesh of my flesh;
she shall be called Woman, because she was taken out of Man.
Therefore a man leaves his father and his mother, and cleaves to
his wife, and they shall become one flesh. And the man and his
wife were both naked, and were not ashamed.

Adam had to sneeze. "Have you got a tissue?"
"In the car, all we've got here is toilet paper." Evelyn brought him
a fresh roll of toilet paper from the bathroom. "It's white and soft, not
our emery-board stuff."
"It's completely illogical," Adam said and blew his nose.
"Maybe by 'father and mother' it means God himself."
"But how does that work with 'mother'?"
"Do you know this one? God says to Eve, 'Do you want an apple?'
'Didn't you forbid me to eat them?' Eve asks. 'Go ahead, take it, tastes
wonderful, you won't be sorry.' 'You sure?' Eve asks. 'Yes,' God says,
'but us girls have to keep that to ourselves.' Katja told it to me. Good,
isn't it?"
"Katja told you jokes?"
"Maybe I'll see Katja again."
" 'Now the serpent was more subtle than any other wild creature
that the Lord God had made. He said to—' "
"Wonder if I'll see Katja again."
"How should I know?"

—said to the woman, "Did God say, 'You shall not eat of any
tree of the garden'?" And the woman said to the serpent, "We

may eat of the fruit of the trees of the garden; but God said, 'You shall not eat of the fruit of the tree which is in the midst of the garden, neither shall you touch it, lest you die.' " But the serpent said to the woman, "You will not die. For God knows that when you eat of it your eyes will be opened, and you will be like God, knowing good and evil." So when the woman saw that the tree was good for food, and a delight to the eyes, and that the tree was to be desired to—

"Does it really talk about desire?"

—and that the tree was to be desired to make one wise, she took of its fruit and ate; and she also gave some to her husband, and he ate. Then the eyes of both were opened, and they knew that they were naked; and they sewed fig leaves together, and made themselves aprons. And they heard the voice of the Lord God walking in the garden in the cool of the day; and the man and his wife hid themselves from the presence of the Lord God among the trees of the garden. And the Lord God called to the man, and said to him, "Where are you?" And he said, "I heard the sound of thee in the garden, and I was afraid, because I was naked; and I hid myself." He said, "Who told you that you were naked? Have you eaten of the tree of which I commanded you not to eat?" The man said, "The woman whom thou gavest to be with me, she gave me fruit of the tree, and I ate."

"Ha!" Adam exclaimed. "Now that's the way to shift blame."

Then the Lord God said to the woman, "What is this that you have done?" The woman said, "The serpent beguiled me, and I ate." The Lord God said to the serpent, "Because you have done this, cursed are you above all cattle, and above all wild animals; upon your belly you shall go, and dust you shall eat all the days of your life. I will put enmity between you and the woman, and between your seed and her seed; he shall bruise your head, and you shall bruise his heel." To the woman he said, "I will greatly multiply your pain in childbearing; in pain you shall"—

"Come in," Evelyn called. Adam bounced up from the bed. There was another knock. Evelyn put the infrared lamp on the chair and walked over to open the door.

"I fixed up something for you real fast," their landlady said, turning the tray to get it through the door. Evelyn shoved what was on the table toward the wall.

"This is leberkäse, help yourselves, please, and if you're hungry there's plenty of it. I wish the lady and gentleman a good appetite, and if there's anything I can do, please, let me know. Is the little fellow doing better?"

"Thanks, yes, and thanks again," Evelyn said.

"Well then, sleep well," the landlady said.

Evelyn and Adam stood at each end of the tray, which took up almost the entire table.

"That should have arrived a bit earlier," Evelyn said. "I'm stuffed." They laid the bags of sandwiches and fruit on the windowsill next to what was left of the cheesecake.

"Think she was listening?" Adam asked. He threw himself back on the bed and picked the Bible up from the floor.

"Let her. We must have been making a good impression," Evelyn said, directing the infrared lamp back on the turtle.

To the woman he said, "I will greatly multiply your pain in childbearing; in pain you shall bring forth children, yet your desire shall be for your husband and he shall rule over you." And to Adam he said, "Because you have listened to the voice of your wife, and have eaten of the tree of which I commanded you, 'You shall not eat of it,' cursed is the ground because of you; in toil you shall eat of it all the days of your life; thorns and thistles it shall bring forth to you; and you shall eat the plants of the field. In the sweat of your face you shall eat bread till you return to the ground, for out of it you were taken; you are dust, and to dust you shall return."

"Is that the end?" Evelyn asked. She had speared a piece of leberkäse and after inspecting it briefly, put it in her mouth. "So now you're deep into your favorite topic again, aren't you?" she said as she chewed. "Do you know the myth where God withdraws so that he can make room for something else to happen? We should read that together sometime."

" 'The man called his wife's name Eve, because she was the mother of all living. And the Lord God made for Adam and for his wife garments of skins, and clothed them.' "

"So God was a tailor too!" Evelyn said, interrupting him.

"Do you want to hear the rest or not?"

Evelyn nodded and turned the infrared lamp off.

Then the Lord God said, "Behold, the man has become like one of us, knowing good and evil; and now, lest he put forth his hand and take also of the tree of life, and eat, and live forever"—therefore the Lord God sent him forth from the garden of Eden, to till the ground from which he was taken. He drove out the man; and at the east of the garden of Eden he placed the cherubim, and a flaming sword which turned every way, to guard the way to the tree of life.

Adam clapped the book together with such a bang that Evelyn flinched.

"That's absolutely unbelievable, isn't it? We're not allowed back into paradise because we know what's good and what's bad and all we need to achieve perfection is eternal life. But God doesn't want anybody like him around. That's monstrous, why don't people tell you about that? And there's nothing here about an apple either, or did I miss something?"

"You want some?" Evelyn asked. "It's delicious, try it, with sweet mustard." She cut off a slice of the leberkäse crust, spread mustard on it, and sat down on the edge of the bed beside Adam.

"It's fucking vicious," Adam said.

"Why are you getting so upset? Taste this." Evelyn waited, holding a speared chunk of leberkäse to his lips.

"Doesn't it upset you?" Adam asked.

"Try this," Evelyn said, holding a hand under the fork. "It's delicious."

43

TWO PROPOSALS

"GRÜSS GOTT. Did the gentleman sleep well?"

Adam nodded. "We would like some breakfast."

"But of course, please, the buffet is in the public room. Would you like coffee or tea?"

"Is it included in the room charge?" Adam asked, as his finger traced two circles.

"Yes of course, please, have a seat, what can I bring you?"

"Then coffee, two coffees."

"Would you perhaps like an egg as well?"

"Yes, I would, thanks."

"And how would you like it, soft- or hard boiled?"

"In between."

"Four and a half minutes, would that be all right, sir?"

"Yes, please."

"And where would you like to sit?"

"Doesn't matter."

"Please, sir, the choice is yours."

"Good morning," Evelyn said as she came down the stairs.

"Grüss Gott. Did you sleep well?"

"Yes, thanks," Evelyn said.

"I'm glad to hear that. The gentleman ordered coffee for you. Is that right?"

"Yes, thanks so much."

"And an egg perhaps?"

"Yes, sure."

"Four and half minutes, like the gentleman?"

"Yes."

"Thank you," the waitress said and went into the kitchen.

"You planning on saying grace?" Adam whispered as they were standing side by side at the buffet. "Why'd you drag that along?"

"That was your idea. You wanted to give it back."

Adam clamped the Bible under one arm, handed Evelyn a plate, and removed the transparent plastic dome from the platter of cold cuts. "All this still seems a bit weird."

"Hm?"

"I keep thinking they want something in return."

"What do you think they want?"

"So damned friendly. They don't even know us."

"I want some of that too—a little more, and a couple of pieces of that red fish there."

They returned to a corner table with full plates. Adam laid the Bible beside him on the bench and slipped it under the overhanging tablecloth.

The waitress arrived carrying two bright silvery pots of coffee on a tray, and right behind her was a young man in sneakers.

"Oh, our savior!" Evelyn cried.

"Grüss Gott, Rudi," the waitress said.

"And what are the odds?" Adam asked, pushing a chair in place for Rudi.

"We've tried everything, a whole raft of starters, but none of them worked. We can jump-start it, that's no problem, but then you'll have to drive straight through."

"I was planning to do that in any case."

"I'm sorry. We've never had one of those in our garage."

"It's a sixty-one," Adam said.

"And so what do we do now?"

"Well, same as yesterday, what else?"

"But then why did we stop here for the night in the first place?"

"I'm sorry, I thought we'd be able to get it running again," Rudolf said.

"I didn't mean that the way it sounded," Evelyn said. "Except if we stall again—"

"Then I'll come and tow you. No problem." He gave her his business card.

"We're just going to have to risk it," Adam said.

"Where are you headed?"

"To Trostberg, it's not far, they say there's a camp there."

"Don't you know anyone here?"

Evelyn shot Adam a glance. "I don't know anyone here."

"In Trostberg they're putting them in tents, a thousand four hundred people, maybe more, and they're only going to send you on your way again."

"And so where should I be heading for?" Adam asked.

"If I only knew. If I were you I'd try and find some more permanent arrangement. There are just the two of you, right?"

The waitress arrived with the eggs and served Rudolf a cup of coffee. "Enjoy your breakfast."

"This was really a crazy idea," Evelyn whispered. "I'll take a train or a bus to the camp, and that'll be that."

"I don't know, maybe this is just flapdoodle," Rudolf said, looking now at one, now at the other. "And if it is, then I apologize, it's only a suggestion. I don't want to interfere in your affairs."

"What's this about?" Adam asked.

"As I said, it's just a suggestion, I don't know how much your car is worth, it's something of an old-timer, and I'm just saying—"

"It's not an old-timer."

"I might give you, I could give you three thousand for it. I don't know if that's too much or too little, just a suggestion. I like the car, it's got some style, that steering wheel, the dashboard, the fenders—some real style."

"Three thousand?" Evelyn asked.

"A suggestion, like I said—I really haven't got the foggiest—"

"But that's a car that's lived its life in a garage," Evelyn said.

"That's obvious, you can see, no rust—been really well taken care of."

"You mean three thousand Westmarks?" Adam asked.

"Yes, of course. Three thousand, cash."

"Cash?"

"You'd have it within half an hour."

"Cash in my hand?"

"Yes, a suggestion, just a suggestion. Might you be interested?"

"On the whole, yes, that'd probably be the best thing. I mean, in our situation." He glanced at Evelyn, who was glaring at him.

"Don't want you to think that I'm trying to take advantage of your situation."

"But you are," Evelyn said softly.

"Evi, that wasn't helpful."

"I'll also take you wherever you need to go, that's no problem."

"It's none of my business," Evelyn said, "but three thousand for a car like that—that's peanuts."

"Evi, it's an offer."

"I thought your car was not for sale, that's what you've always said. That car was the reason you wanted a second garage."

"We're just talking here."

"Why all of a sudden now, at the first offer that comes along?"

"I'm really very sorry, I didn't intend for you to—"

"It's a good offer."

"That's not true, Adam, you know yourself that's not true." Evelyn burst out laughing. "He's married to that thing, Rudolf. Did you know that? He belongs to it."

"Ohmymymymy, it was just an idea. I'm going to go poke my

head in the kitchen," Rudolf said, stood up, and took his coffee cup with him."

"Three thousand is damn good, Evi. I can exchange it at eight or nine to one and it'd be like getting that Lada for free."

"Does it take just three thousand Westmarks to turn you into a madman?"

"I know what I'm doing," Adam said, picking up his egg and beheading it. He cut a roll open and smeared the halves with butter and began to eat. Evelyn watched him as he swallowed and hastily took another bite.

"Do what you want. But then you do that in any case."

She lit a cigarette.

"Aren't you going to eat any more of that?"

"It's all yours."

"I'm just saying it'd be a shame to waste it."

Adam took the roll she had already bitten into and laid it on his plate. "Let's fix up a couple of sandwiches to take along—or is that something you'd rather not do."

Evelyn pulled the ashtray closer. "I should have taken the train, that would have simplified everything."

"Then they would have shoved you into some sort of tent. The nights are really cold here now."

"At least go get him," Evelyn said. "It's all embarrassing enough as it is."

"It's good coffee, almost better than at the Angyals'."

"Should I leave?" Evelyn asked.

"One step at a time," Adam said and went on eating.

Evelyn stubbed out her cigarette, grabbed a couple of grapes, reached for the room key, and stood up.

"Evi, wait a sec, please."

She turned halfway around.

"Evi," he said, then wiped his mouth with his napkin and was sliding his way out from behind the table when the Bible fell from the bench.

"So what is it?"

Adam bent down. He couldn't find the Bible right away. "I wanted to ask you . . . ," he said as he straightened up, pressing the book to his chest, "I wanted to ask you if you'll marry me." He took another step in her direction. "I'm very serious, will you?" He took hold of her right hand and rubbed his thumb across her fingers and the ruby red ring. "You are so beautiful," Adam said and smiled.

"What made you ask that?"

"Would the lady and gentleman like anything else?" the waitress asked, staring at the Bible in Adam's hand.

Evelyn and Adam shook their heads in sync. "Or wait," Adam called after her. "Maybe two more coffees, please, if that's all right? Is Rudi still here?"

44

IN THE PHONE BOOTH

"STAY HERE."

"Not enough room."

"Don't you want to listen in?"

"And it stinks in here."

"Then leave the door open."

Evelyn leaned her back against the door. Adam was holding the receiver and an address book in one hand.

"It's weird, pressing numbers."

"Why's that?"

"It goes so fast."

He laid a few one-mark coins on top of the phone and looked at Evelyn.

"Hello?" he asked, turning back to the phone. "Yes, hello, this is Lutz, Waltraud and Manfred's son. Could I speak with Gisela, please, Gisela Luppolt. Lutz, yes, we're in Bavaria—in Bavaria!—not far from Rosenheim, in Haidholzen, or I guess it's more Stephanskirchen—with Evelyn, we're here together—yes, from Hungary, with the car, and made it this far—we wanted to ask, if we could see you sometime, arrange to meet . . ."

Adam held his hand over the mouthpiece. "Her husband. Aunt Gisela? Hello, this is Lutz—Adam, yes, sure, Adam—whatever. Rosenheim, near Rosenheim—hadn't planned on it, but we just thought if they're going to open the border, we'd take advantage of it, probably won't happen again soon. No problem at all, with the car, just like that. Five days ago. We're living here with a family, in their kids' old room. Rudolf, the fellow we're staying with, has been driving us around, to Trostberg, to get our checklist of all the various offices we need to visit for registration and insurance, all sorts of stuff, and there'll be some questioning too, but only in my case, and that has to be done here. I don't know, not a clue, they want to know where I was stationed in the army and so on. No, we've been lucky, given how chilly it is at night. We've had good luck, really, a lot of good luck. Evelyn, her name's Evelyn—no, not yet, but we're together, we thought if we can manage the border we can manage the next step. Not yet, but we may get around to it."

He turned back to Evelyn to nod at her.

"I can't say yet, it happened just sort of whizbang, now or never. Work, of course, work, Evi plans to study, in Munich maybe. Twenty-one, she wasn't allowed to before, they wouldn't let her, at least not to study what she wanted—yes—would we ever—love to—no question—absolutely—hey, that doesn't matter, doesn't matter at all."

Adam put another mark in. Evelyn pressed against the door and stepped outside. She walked past the drugstore and sat down on a bus-stop bench. Two men had just emerged from a bank, gesturing and engaged in a lively conversation. They now shook hands and parted. After taking a few steps, the tall one turned around and called out something, so that the shorter one, his hands thrust into his coat pockets, likewise turned around in midstride, but instead of answering he just raised his left arm for a brief wave. Sparrows nearby rose up in a flutter, and with them several pigeons. Evelyn closed her eyes and held her face up to the sun. Then she laid her head to one side, until she could feel the collar of her quilted blue jacket against her cheek. The jacket smelled of detergent and something else, some unfamiliar scent.

"What are you up to?" Adam called. "I've been looking for you."

He had startled Evelyn. Now she leaned back again.

"Have a seat," she said and closed her eyes again.

"What's wrong?"

"What do you mean?"

"Didn't you see me?"

"There were these two men just now. At first I thought they were deaf-mutes, they were making such wild gestures."

"Why didn't you wait?"

"But I did wait."

Adam sat down beside her. "We can move in with them. They have a kind of guestroom, separate shower and toilet just for us. No charge either, we're invited guests."

"Great."

"What's with you?"

"Nothing, that's super."

"She was very cordial. I didn't have to explain anything, she just said right off that we should come."

Evelyn nodded and pulled the zipper on her jacket up as high as it would go, till her mouth vanished in the collar.

"Don't you want to now? Do you want to stay here instead?"

"Telephoning is really not your strong point."

"Are you going to start in again?"

"You wanted me there with you."

"Yes, to listen in."

"But you didn't let me listen in."

"You should have given me a signal."

"It's fine."

"I'm not doing this for the fun of it. It's a shitty situation to be in. I want to hear what you have to say too."

"It turns you into a total stranger, it's scary."

"Do you want to stay here?"

"No, of course not."

"Then don't make such a face."

"I can't help it. I've got to get used to you again."

"I thought we had all that behind us."

"I thought so too," Evelyn said. "Did you tell them we'll be bringing Elfriede?"

"That's not all that important."

"Somehow it all feels just like it used to—"

" 'Somehow'?"

"Like when school started up after summer vacation."

"I always liked those first few days of school. No need yet for a guilty conscience."

"I've been wondering the whole time if it was the right thing to do, sending Mona the second key."

"It's a good idea if somebody in town knows what's what—not just your mother."

"I would like to have told her myself."

"It's going to be a shock no matter what."

"She even signed something once, she's not allowed to have any contacts with the West."

"You're her daughter, that's a whole different thing."

"Just the opposite, it could cost her her job."

They sat there for a while, not saying anything.

"What are you thinking about?" Evelyn asked.

"Ah, nothing."

"A person's always thinking about something."

"In Dresden, on the platform, as your train was pulling out, I helped a man with two suitcases. I think he was the porter at your hotel."

"At the Jalta?"

"Yes. His suit was a kind of summer wool, very light, very unusual. You can't find it in our shops."

"And what does that mean?"

"Nothing, absolutely nothing," Adam said.

"Did you have anything to eat this morning?" Evelyn asked.

"You smell good."

"And you're stubbly," Evelyn said. She leaned against him, took hold of his arm, and held tight with both hands.

"DID YOU receive the forms?"

"No."

"That can't be, actually. Here, this is what they look like."

The man across from her, who had stood up and extended his hand to greet her, now held up several pieces of paper. "Didn't you fill these out along with the others, with someone to help you?"

"We're staying with friends. I didn't receive it."

"That can't—as I said, I'm quite certain that along with the rest you . . ."

He squared the pages of forms on his desk and wrote a couple of numbers in a dark bordered box.

"You're surely aware of what it's like around here," he said as if to himself. He looked tired, sitting there across from her. Evelyn liked him, it was as if they had met somewhere before—a man of about fifty, with a thin mustard-colored sweater, a pastel shirt underneath.

"So then, last and first names?"

"Schumann, Evelyn."

"Born?"

"May 19, 1969."

"Where?"

"In Torgau."

"Torgau? In Saxony?"

"Yes, on the Elbe, district of Leipzig."

"Your parents?"

"What do you need to know that for?" she said with a smile. He was so stiff, he needed to smile too.

"It's all a part of it. Your parents?"

"With date and place of birth? I was raised by my grandparents until my mother was finished with her studies."

"Then your mother first."

"Born November 11, 1946, in Wittenberg."

"Her profession?"

"Economist."

"Economist for what?"

"Well in general, for production. She works in Wolfen."

"And what does she do there?"

He wrote slowly, hesitating at times before setting the tip of his ballpoint to paper, as if it were a drawing.

"Your father?"

"He came from Turkey, and vanished there again too. Never contributed a penny."

"A man from Turkey, in East Germany?"

"From West Berlin. My mother studied in Berlin."

"You can provide no further information?"

"They never saw each other again."

"Siblings?"

"I have a brother, a half-brother, Sascha, he's twelve."

"Your education?"

"Graduated from high school. Three semesters of pedagogy at the University of Jena. Since 1988 I've been training as a waitress."

Evelyn lit a cigarette. "May I?" she asked, when the man scowled. She smiled.

"It's not usual here," he said and pushed an empty ashtray across. "Did you come alone?"

"No, with my life partner. We plan to get married."

"And what is your life partner's name?"

"I thought you interrogate only men who've been in the army, am I right?"

"I need it for your records. You arrived together."

"Frenzel."

"First name? You do know that . . ."

"Lutz is his name, Lutz Frenzel."

"And born?"

"In 1956, December sixth."

"And where?"

"You'll have to ask him, I don't know."

"How long have you been acquainted?"

"Since 1987."

"You were living together?"

"At his home, his parents' former home. Since his father's death he's lived there alone."

"His mother?"

"He was still very young—an accident, on a moped, if I recall correctly."

"And his profession?"

"He's a ladies' tailor, master tailor—self-employed, he could have had apprentices."

"And how long have you had a desire to leave the GDR?"

"Always."

"But you went ahead and studied pedagogy."

"That was the only subject for which I could get admitted—they wouldn't take me in art history. I would have also been willing to study German or maybe used my French somehow."

"Can you speak French?"

"The French you learn in school, from seventh grade on, I got an A on my final exams."

"You were in the Free German Youth?"

"Yes."

"Youth Consecration?"

"Yes."

"Socialist Unity Party or Block Party?"

"No."

"And you and Herr Frenzel drove to Hungary with the intention of taking advantage of the opportunity."

"I wanted to leave."

"But he didn't?"

"He arrived after me."

"You met there, then?"

"Yes."

"Were you afraid you wouldn't be allowed to make the trip together?"

"We had had an argument."

"Because he didn't want to leave?"

"I'd rather not talk about it, it was a private matter, we had a very private argument."

"Was he trying to keep you from leaving?"

"Not directly."

"And his motive was?"

"An interpersonal problem, if you like."

"Did Herr Frenzel do service?"

"Service?"

"Was he in the National People's Army?"

"Yes, sure, eighteen months."

"Are you certain?"

"That's what he's always told me, eighteen months and not a day longer."

"Do you know his rank as a reservist?"

"Soldier, if that's a rank."

"Some were discharged as corporals or noncommissioned officers."

"You'll have to ask him."

"Was he with the border patrol?"

"No, very basic, a footslogger."

"And why didn't he want to come to the free world?"

Evelyn stubbed out her cigarette. She looked straight at him and tried to smile.

"That's not the way to put it. He wanted to be together with me. And in the end that's why he came."

"Are you certain?"

"I think it will be good for him too. He has a truly golden touch. He can really make a start of things here and build a career."

"I have to ask you yet again why he didn't want to come with you? Or put another way, are you certain in the judgments you've formed about your life partner?"

"Are you suggesting that Adam's a spy of some sort?"

"Adam? Who is Adam?"

"Herr Frenzel. Everyone calls him Adam."

The man made a note on a checkered slip of paper.

"But the last name is correct?"

"Yes, Lutz Frenzel, also known as Adam."

"This line of questions is also in your interest."

"This is ridiculous, really. Adam was the only person I know who never voted. They always sent friends of his father, members of the Liberal Democratic Party, and they had to ask him why he hadn't voted. Adam just laughed at the GDR, he no longer took it seriously."

"And wanted to stay all the same?"

"He's easygoing."

"As a self-employed man? Doesn't that mean a lot of work?"

"He did work, never stopped, in fact."

"You mean 'easygoing' but not in the sense of lazy?"

"As far as he was concerned it could have gone on like that till retirement. Two weeks on the Baltic or in Bulgaria in the summer, and the rest of the time he sits and sews and sketches and does photography."

"Did he make any calls to the GDR while you were in Hungary?"

"He called two or three of his clients."

"To tell them that he wasn't coming back?"

"That he was extending his vacation a little."

"Did he have contact with anyone who did go back?"

"He drove a friend of ours to Budapest so that she could catch a train."

"So this friend took a train back to the GDR."

"Yes, for private reasons."

"Maybe not all that private?"

"It was all about a man, if you must know, a man from the West, from Hamburg."

"Do you know his name?"

"Yes, but I'm not going to tell you."

"Did Herr Frenzel have any contact with the embassy of the GDR?"

"Why would he have any contact?"

"A routine question."

"We were there once."

"You were in the embassy?"

"Our papers had been stolen, our wallets, everything."

"Stolen from you and Herr Frenzel?"

"From me and an acquaintance."

"The one from the West?"

"Yes."

"And how did Herr Frenzel react?"

"How would you expect him to react? He helped us."

"Could it be that he initiated a situation that forced you to visit the embassy of the GDR?"

"You don't really think that Adam stole our papers! That's absurd. We got out of the embassy all in one piece and were even provided a little money."

"But Herr Frenzel's papers were in fact not stolen. What was he doing in the embassy?"

"He was just making a show of it, he was accompanying us."

"And who is this 'us' now?"

"A girlfriend, who had tried to swim the Danube and lost her papers in the process."

"Did he tell you that?"

"Yes, but she told me that too."

"And what is this girlfriend's name?"

"I'd rather not say."

"An equation with a good many human unknowns, don't you think?"

"He picked her up on the autobahn—no papers, no money—and he smuggled her across."

"And how did he smuggle her across?"

"In the trunk of his car. He also brought my jewelry and our turtle over the border."

He squinched his eyes briefly, the right corner of his mouth twitched.

"So then he brought someone over the border into Hungary in his trunk?"

"Yes."

"He told you that?"

"I know about it from her as well."

"And were the gentleman from Hamburg and Herr Frenzel previously acquainted?"

"Just barely. Adam was jealous. It was a problem between two men, or maybe call it a woman problem, but nothing more."

"Between the acquaintance from Hamburg and Herr Frenzel."

"Yes."

"And how did this acquaintance come about?"

"I rode to Hungary with him and his girlfriend."

"And Herr Frenzel right behind?"

"Yes, but not for political reasons. Adam loves me, is that so hard to understand?"

"I do understand, but please, we are just doing our duty in asking certain questions."

"Adam—Herr Frenzel if you like—had no use for the GDR and got out, along with me. Those are the facts. What is he supposed to be after as a spy? Dress patterns?"

"There are simply a few particulars here, which, if we were to—"

"But as you can see, we're both here!"

"That will do for now. Thank you very much."

"Then I can go?"

"Yes, of course."

"Well, fine."

"And if you happen to find those forms, please be so kind as to drop them by, we're starting to run short."

Evelyn nodded. She stood up, pushed the chair against the table, and looked across at the man, who had also got to his feet and appeared to be searching for something in the filing cabinets behind him. She waited for him to turn around but finally left the room without saying good-bye.

46

SPIES, TAKE TWO

"THEY REALLY DO have better scenery here too," Evelyn said. The nail of her index finger touched the train window several times. She had taken off her shoes, stretched her legs to rest them on the seat across from her, and now opened the turtle's cardboard box. "What are those slabs? They smell funny." She pointed to the two books beside him.

"Our guidebooks, for birds and plants, they were always in the car, always handy."

"Elfriede definitely misses her beautiful box."

"And who was going to carry it? Besides we couldn't show up with a pen like that."

"Look, there are the Alps again, and behind them lies Italy . . ."

"Behind them lies Austria . . ."

"The Alps are Austria, but behind the Alps lies Italy. We'll take a trip there soon, Elfriede."

"But without Elfi." He folded up his newspaper.

"It could be, Elfriede, that you'll have to stay at home." Evelyn folded the cardboard flaps down. "You act as if you've seen all this!"

"Am I behaving the wrong way again?" he asked, not looking up.

"Aren't you in the least anxious to see it all?"

"Sure I'm anxious, especially whenever I do or say something wrong again."

"You don't have to take your anger out on me. He ran me through the wringer too."

"They would've found a job for him on our side too, I guarantee you."

"But he was polite. Our guys tried to scare you, you never knew if they were ever going to let you out."

"Nobody's ever tried to pump information out of me the way he did."

"Maybe not you."

"You either."

"But you're tetchy."

"And you get offended when I just ask if you've called your Mike."

"Because you don't believe me. And even if I had called him, so what? Anyhow, surely I ought to be able to expect that you'll believe me?"

"You don't believe me either."

"I simply don't believe that Michael was there in Trostberg. He would have let us know, we were registered there, after all."

"Why would he have let us know? He was wearing a uniform, was there on business."

"And I think, quite frankly, that you're mistaken. What is Michael supposed to be doing in an old barracks like that, and in uniform besides?"

"I saw him, of course I saw him. Even though he closed the door again right away, because I spooked him—"

" 'Spooked'—now that's new. You told me he had closed the door again right away, but not that he was spooked."

"He was spooked. He saw me, flinched, and beat a retreat, flinched and retreated."

"Why should he lie?"

"How should I know. Research on eternity sounds better than intelligence officer or whatever it is he does."

"We can give him a call then."

"What's that gonna prove?"

"That he lives in Hamburg."

"Don't be so naive."

"You're saying he gave me a phony number?"

"Would you know where it was ringing?"

"But why go to the trouble of putting on that whole show?"

"You think they don't have spies too? And you don't need to grin like that."

"You guys have got some screws loose."

"What do you mean, 'you guys'?"

"You, just you, have some screws loose."

"Then why did you say 'You guys'?"

"I mean people who are constantly suspecting other people."

"What do you mean 'constantly'? And specifically which people?"

"Just in general, I meant it all just in general."

"I don't suspect people in general."

"Can we drop this now, okay? Please." Evelyn leaned back and stared out the window.

"Did Michael suspect me? Tell me, did he think I was from the Stasi? Tell me yes or no, that's all."

"No," she said without turning her head. "We never talked about you, period."

"So for you two I simply didn't exist?"

"I didn't want to talk about you. He did ask about you, but I felt like it was none of his business. Can't you understand that? Did you want to talk about me with your Lillis and Desdemonas and whatever their names are? Let's hope not. I think I might resent that."

"I didn't, but then I didn't want for us to go our separate ways either."

"You wanted something totally different, but your soul was still with me. Thanks heaps."

"Go ahead and laugh, but my soul was truly and always with you."

Adam crossed his legs and, it appeared, went back to reading his newspaper.

"I'd very much like to believe that," Evelyn said.

"Then do."

"I keep trying. I've been trying for two weeks now."

"And what's keeping you from it?"

"Nothing. But I just keep on trying."

"And if you can't bring yourself to do it?"

They looked at each other.

"Somehow you're so unhappy. You were always in a good mood somehow, even in Hungary. Maybe it isn't enough for you, just being with me."

" 'Somehow,' it's always 'somehow.' "

"Is polygamy what you want?"

"Let's get married first, and then we'll see if I need one or two more."

"Don't make a joke of this. Men are like that—or at least some of them. I'd rather we talk about this than just joke around."

"I don't miss Lilli and have never missed her. Period. What more am I supposed to say."

"And Pepi?"

"Pepi is a lovely girl and will make a good university teacher, and I would love to see her again sometime, but it's not what you think it is."

"So then what is it?"

"What?"

"Well, there's something wrong with you."

"Now that's rich. We leave it all behind—lock, stock, and barrel—and I don't know how I'm going to earn my daily bread, and you ask if something's wrong."

"Do you want to go back?"

"I try to picture what it'll be like when Mona walks into our house and your mother and the rest of them, and take out whatever it is they need—it's something a man thinks about. I can't just turn off the switch."

"We don't need that stuff anymore."

"On Monday there were ten thousand of them in Leipzig. Imagine, ten thousand!"

"Adam, we've made it, we're here in the West, we have all the papers we need, we'll be given passports, we have three thousand Westmarks, I can study whatever I want, we have a roof over our heads for free, and you make a face like a prune."

"It's not been all that much fun so far."

"That's over and done with, we're on our way to Munich."

"Well yes, not exactly downtown Munich."

"You've either just been sitting in front of the tube or playing with that stupid cube."

"I find it interesting what our brothers and sisters are up to there in the East. As long as they're allowed to get away with it, we should at least watch what's happening."

"You're not curious about anything here."

"We've toured all sorts of lakes and villages and towns. And I've been reading besides, if that's any reassurance. Almost halfway through." Adam reached for the Bible beside him, and held it up. Several sheets of paper were stuck in at the middle. "I dare you to get this far."

"You might have looked in on a tailor or visited a fabric shop."

" 'Good day, my name's Adam, I come from the East.' Do you think they have anything to teach me?"

"I mean the business end of things, what you get for what, where you get a business license. It's all lost time."

"One step at a time. Besides, people here don't even know what a tailor is. They buy everything ready-made."

With her toes Evelyn fished for her shoes and slipped into them. "What a shame, we're almost there. I would love to just keep going." She stood bent at the knees for a look in the mirror to comb her hair. "Tell me, if such a question may be permitted, what are those bookmarks in the Bible? Are you copying down the wiser sayings?"

"What bookmarks? These forms? Just keeping my place with them."

"What forms?"

"Here." He handed her the pages.

"No, Adam, tell me it isn't true."

"What isn't? All this crap they wanted to know—it's just like in the East."

"But we're not in the East anymore."

"Aha."

"Why didn't you say something! We were supposed to fill these out. He wanted them back from me, he asked about them."

"Did they also ask you about me?"

"No."

"Not one thing?"

"Only if I had come alone or with someone."

"He asked me that one too. I told him he should ask you."

"That's what I told them too." Evelyn pulled on her jacket. "Come on, you need to get ready to get off."

"I'd really like to know what that was about," Adam said.

"They're looking for spies."

"If I were a spy, though, would I ever have a good story ready for them."

"I don't know what it's all about. I really don't," Evelyn said, sat back down, pulled the cardboard box with the turtle onto her lap, and gazed out the window.

47

KITCHEN TALK

"LOOKING FOR SOMETHING?" Gisela asked as Evelyn opened the door under the sink, and the garbage pail came rolling out at her and lifted its lid.

"Now that's practical," Evelyn said, "and comical too, somehow, like it's tipping its hat."

"You don't need to rinse first, just put them in, either along the side or, look, like this, in between." Gisela took the platter from her and placed it crosswise to the other plates in the dishwasher. "Cups and saucers, the smaller stuff up top, utensils here. Just not the big knife, see, it has a wooden handle. Always hand-wash wood. Hand me that bowl."

"But it's too big somehow."

"Ah, pooh, look, just on top of the rest, no problem. And the cups, too, they fit along here, on a slant. Works best when it's fully loaded. Just don't put spoons together, 'cause they fit into each other." Gisela distributed several teaspoons around the boxes of the plastic basket. "Open that again. The door under the sink, open it again, that's where the detergent and clear rinse are. The detergent here, and this is for the rinse—but it doesn't need any, there's enough there, usually good for four or five runs. And now turn it on. Right. You don't have to adjust anything else, just push the button and you're done. I keep it at fifty-five degrees. Just turn it on once it's loaded. But don't open up while it's running, it doesn't like that, it's not the youngest anymore."

"And no drying either?"

"Nope, tomorrow we'll take everything out shiny clean."

"And glasses?"

"I always run them over quick with a towel. If they're not perfectly straight up—"

"I'd love to make myself useful somehow. Maybe do some of the shopping?"

"Oh Eva, I'm just glad that you're both here. We use the car to do the real shopping, and I pick up the little things on my way home from work."

"And what about housecleaning?"

"That's Monica's job, Mondays and Fridays. I'm just happy to finally have some life in the place again. Johannes didn't even come home for Christmas, and I understand—Guatemala is more interesting than Eichenau. And when Birgit does show up, she likes to sleep in the living room anyway, so she can watch TV."

"We'll be getting a little money shortly, we can add it to your household budget—I think your husband would think that's fair."

"You can do that, sure. But you can take a lot of what he says with a grain of salt. He's a sweet man, really. Come on, let's take a load off. Want to share a little Baileys with me? Do you like liqueurs?"

"Yes, sure do."

Gisela ran a cloth over the kitchen table.

"I don't have anybody to tipple with once in a while," she said, sitting down across from Evelyn and unscrewing the cap.

"Aren't they waiting for us?"

"Let 'em be. Let them have their man-to-man talk. Eberhard is a stickler for fairness—which means anybody who works less than he does should earn less. He measures people by the work they turn out. Not even I could change that, it's a family trait. They all worked themselves to death—grouches with their noses to the grindstone, every single one."

"Adam has never been able to really enjoy a vacation either."

"Prosit, Eva, here's to you, to you both, and to your being here and to your new life."

They touched glasses and drank.

"Well, is that something or not?"

"Oh yes."

"Well then, down the hatch."

"Goes down easy," Evelyn said. "Wouldn't take much to get hooked on it."

Gisela poured another round.

"A woman needs two legs to stand on. You need to enjoy life while you're young."

"That's why I left. I knew there had to be something else to life."

"Yes, something else always comes along in life. Prosit, Eva, here's to the future."

"And to you, Aunt Gisela."

"Call me anything but aunt."

"I'm sorry, but since Adam—"

"Prosit, Eva."

"Prosit, Gisela."

They heard laughter coming from the living room.

"We're going hiking tomorrow, to the upland moors, you'd like it there. Hiking is a must in Bavaria. You're going to join us, aren't you? And once you've got the rest of the red tape behind you, it all starts up—I'll introduce Adam to the women in my sewing course. With a little luck he can take charge in no time—the woman who runs it isn't even a tailor. Gets jittery hands whenever she has to cut fabric."

"Adam's great with the shears. Is he ever! Clients tore each other limb from limb to get him."

"I'm not worried about you either. Anyone with looks like yours, my girl, as long as you don't head down the primrose path . . ." Gisela wagged a warning finger. "You'll see, they'll be tearing each other limb from limb for you, too, no matter where you go. Where did you get that hair?"

"From my father—my mother's a blonde, in fact."

"And then blue eyes to go with it—the men must fall at your feet by the thousands."

"Well, I do all right. I want to study no matter what, I want to study."

"Adam's going to have to start from scratch, but if he rolls up his sleeves . . . Prosit."

"Yep, we'll start from scratch," Evelyn said and finished her second glass.

"Another sip?"

"I'm way out of practice, I can't handle any more."

"Oh come on, three legs and a woman stands even better."

Evelyn let loose with a snort and pressed the back of her hand to her mouth. "Sorry."

"You're something else. And don't look so shocked." Gisela began to giggle. The mouth of the bottle slipped from the edge of her glass— she stared at the little puddle of Baileys. For a moment she looked completely sober, but then began to giggle again and pretended she needed to hold the bottle with both hands.

"You know, all this seems like a dream to me," Evelyn said. "When I think that next week I'll go into Munich and can pick whatever subject I want to study—it's totally incredible, you know? I can't even begin to imagine it." Evelyn gave a start. "What was that?"

"That's the dishwasher, the dispenser just opened, does it with a pop." Gisela giggled some more. "What a shame you couldn't see your face. We have to toast your little scare. And don't make a fuss, we can handle this."

Evelyn had laid her hand over her glass. "Better not," she said. "I think I'm going to be sick."

"From that little bit? What's wrong? Damn, Eva, that can't be. You're white as a sheet." Gisela held her hand to Eva's forehead. "Sweetheart, are you okay?"

Those were the last words that Evelyn could recall later. And that she had wanted to say yes.

48

AFTER THE PHONE CALL

"AREN'T YOU going to talk to me at all now? You're acting like a child," Evelyn whispered. She was sitting on her bed, folding laundry. Adam had stretched out on the other bed next to her. "If I hadn't told you, there'd be no problem."

"So now I'm to blame," he said softly.

"You turn everything into such a big deal." She snatched Adam's socks from the radiator and laid them in her lap as she sat back down on the bed.

"A big deal?"

"A colossal deal."

"You could have apologized, at least."

"For what, Adam? Because you see spooks?"

"And why didn't you tell me before? We could have made the call together."

"How would that have changed things?"

"It would have changed everything."

"Everything?"

"Yes."

"And how, if I may ask?"

"It would have been a shared operation."

" 'Shared operation'—I thought everything we're doing here is a shared operation."

"That's what I had hoped too."

"Poor little pussycat—"

Adam sat bolt upright and grabbed hold of her wrist.

"You call that blowhard up," he hissed, "I don't know how many times, give him our number, and not a peep to me. If Katja hadn't called here, I wouldn't have known about any of it. That's the picture. And now spare me your smart comebacks."

"And who told you that Katja called?" Evelyn grabbed up the socks in both hands and hurled them onto Adam's bed. After picking up the folded laundry, she walked over to the wardrobe by the door and sorted things into cubbyholes. "How can anybody be so stupid!" she whispered. "What a numbskull!"

Adam spread the socks out beside him. Evelyn slipped on a cardigan, lay down on her bed, reached across to Adam's pillow, and picked up the Bible.

"You could at least ask," he said.

"Why? This doesn't belong to you either. It was a shared theft," she said.

Evelyn opened the Bible to the spot where the forms had been stuck as a bookmark.

"What would you have done if he'd asked you for our number because Katja wanted it?"

"I don't think I would have spoken to him in the first place."

"And how are you going to go about finding out if he's an intelligence officer?"

"How did you go about it? Tell him that crazy Adam is seeing spooks?"

"I told him we'd arrived safe and sound. We'd agreed I would at least let him know that."

"You had agreed that you'd call him?"

"That's what he asked me to do."

"Great, maybe you'd like to study in Hamburg?"

"Do you want to go our separate ways?"

"No matter what it is he does, he's guaranteed to make a lot more than I ever will."

"You don't say."

"Then all our problems would be solved, in one fell swoop."

"Oh, is that so? It was Katja I was calling about."

"Katja?"

"Yes, what else? We've got so many friends here, I don't know who to drop in on first."

"I didn't know you and Katja were such bosom buddies."

"What's that supposed to mean? But, yes, I liked her right off."

"Because she failed her swimming test?"

"Because she knew what she wanted and followed through on it, all on her own."

"She once told me about some Japanese guy."

"Japanese? What Japanese guy? You're her hero. Without you—who knows where she would have landed."

"Katja would have come out all right one way or another."

"Maybe, maybe not. It was heroic anyway. You should remember that, it'd do you good."

"What good would it do me? After all, you're always telling me to think of the future."

"I only mean that the sewing course and this room and Uncle Eberhard—this isn't what it's all about. Soon this will all be a thing of the past."

"I don't think so."

"We'll find something in Munich, something in the city—"

"With a garden and hardwood floors, ideal layout, in a pleasant neighborhood."

"Even if it's small, tiny for all I care. I can wait tables again."

"You're going to study, not wait tables!"

"I'd like it much better if we could start all over again, living together, but not in a house where everything smells of your family.

My pillow doesn't even belong to me. And people in Munich are desperate to find someone like you—everybody says that."

"Is that in the Bible?"

Evelyn flipped the page. "Someone like you, who can tailor clothes
to order, tailor like you do, with such great ideas. Why shouldn't
things turn around for you? Even if you have to play second fiddle at
first, for a year or two, that's not so awful. You keep an eye on the tricks
of the trade, the business tricks, and then take over the clientele. Anyone who's used you never wants anybody else. You know that. Faith,
love, hope—that's in here somewhere. Love, that we have, and faith in
you as well, the only thing you're missing is the hope, hope, nothing
else—and for that you have me. I am hope. I'll sell my jewelry."

"Don't you touch it—no way are you going to do that."

"My grandma would say it's the right thing to do. She only wore a
couple of things, the rest just stayed in its chest. In case it should ever
be needed, and it's needed now."

"I'll find something, Evi. Just not this sewing course, not after that
scene."

"Scene? What scene?" Evelyn sat up.

"Didn't Gisela say anything?"

"No. She was a little snippy somehow, a little funny somehow."

"Enough with the 'somehow,' 'somehow' is awful."

"So what happened?"

"Nothing, I was designing it like I always do—the right way, the
better way."

"Designing what?"

"Her friend Gaby wanted two bows or ribbons, on the left and
right, incredible, like a fat bumblebee with tiny wings."

"And you told her that?"

"It was beyond belief, I thought she was joking."

Evelyn grasped the edge of the bed with both hands.

"I just told her I wouldn't do it, that I wasn't in the gewgaw business."

Evelyn took a deep breath. "But if that's what she wanted?"

"She can sew it herself, what does she need me for. Either I sew it or I don't sew it. And if I do the tailoring, I don't tailor crap like that. It's that simple."

"Oh, Adam—"

"It's how I've always done it and it worked out very well—for my clients too."

Evelyn reached for a pair of socks, turned them right side out, and coiled them in a ball. Suddenly she gasped, Adam sat frozen in place too. The front door slammed shut downstairs.

"Was that both of them?" Evelyn whispered.

"Don't think so, just Gisela. He always locks it."

"You should've done it for her sake, for Gisela's. She's been so proud of you. You should've sewn it, she would've had to see what you saw, and would've understood—"

"Two missing," Adam said.

"Two?"

"Two different socks are left over."

"Just like always."

"You mean I've always worn them like this?"

"You've only noticed just now because you're holding them side by side."

"Goes against my principles."

"Then toss them out," Evelyn said and stood up.

"And you're sure there aren't two others somewhere?"

"Somewhere, yes. But not here." Evelyn disappeared into the little bathroom next door.

When she returned, Adam was sitting on the bed. The bag of socks had been put away. But two were now hanging on the radiator as if they weren't quite dry.

49

TWO WOMEN

"SO, AND NOW we'll let that cook for seven minutes."

"I know China exists on the map, but that's about it."

"And?"

"And now I find out it's a science unto itself."

"Everything's a science."

"*China and the Search for Happiness*—you're reading this?"

"The author's one of our lecturers."

"I don't know one word of Chinese."

"I'm just a beginner myself. It's right next to the main building. And in two years we're off to China or Taiwan for a year."

"Sinology isn't exactly a fit with art history."

"It just came to me because you said maybe something with languages, and I thought we could attend lectures together."

"All those symbols—way too much for me."

"You have to memorize and cram for everything."

"All the same."

"We can get together on Wednesdays or for breakfast. Maybe you'll find a place close by."

"With hardwood floors and ornamental plaster? This kitchen would be all I need. I've never seen a kitchen as huge as this. Will the other two be joining us?"

"Michaela is in classes, and Gabriela is off taking driver's training, not exactly her strong point. Do you two need more than one room?"

"It'd be nice."

"I still can't believe Adam came with you. He must really love you."

"You've said that."

"I figured he was hopeless, a hopeless case. What's the matter?"

"You're looking so good."

"Oh, Evi, you're sweet."

"Has nothing to do with sweet."

"What do you expect me to say? You just have to look in the mirror."

"That's not how I meant it. Just look at you. I would never believe that you've been here only a couple of weeks. It's as if you belong here, are at home here. And then when you look at Adam, he's just spinning his wheels, and he hardly eats anything."

"And you?"

"I'm somewhere in the middle, between you and him."

"So not a hopeless case?" Katja laughed. "Evi, come on, it was just a joke."

"But I'm not joking."

"You worry too much."

"If I had your clan to back me up, I wouldn't have any worries either."

"My clan invites me to dinner once in a while, and Uncle Klaus helped me get this room here—but in fact I don't want them to do anything for me."

"That's just what I mean, though, without them you wouldn't have got this."

"But in exchange I'm supposed to teach them both Russian—and I've forgotten everything I knew. But I said yes, I'd give it a try."

"You see, and I would have said no. That's the difference. You have relatives here, a real family, and that's fantastic."

"And you've got Adam and a honeymoon in the West."

"If you can call that a honeymoon."

"Well, Lake Sims isn't so bad. So when are you getting married?"

Evelyn shrugged.

"But you told me you two were happy there."

"Win some, lose some."

Katja scowled.

"I'm sorry," Evelyn said. "I can only think in clichés—'no pain, no gain' and all the rest of it. I know myself how awful it sounds."

"I came close to falling in love with Adam."

"I noticed."

"When?"

"When I saw you wearing my sun hat there at the campgrounds. You were waiting for us, and I thought that might be the case. Did you two ever do it?"

"No."

"Can't say I'm convinced."

"I said I almost fell in love with him, so I can't say that there wasn't anything. But he couldn't have cared less."

"There have been times when I wished he was dead."

"Dead?"

"Haven't you ever wished somebody would just vanish from the face of the earth? That you were rid of him, that you no longer needed to think about him?"

"Nope."

"He sits there in front of the television the whole day, playing with your cube, and if he's not doing that, he's lying on his stomach beside Elfriede and watching her. And Uncle Eberhard tells him five times a day that the ones who are standing up and fighting over there now are heroes. Those are the heroes, not the ones who cut and run."

"I thought he was a cutter-and-runner himself."

"He was in prison, in Bautzen, for almost a year. As he sees it we fled only for economic reasons, and now it's time to fight, not just sit around on our butts here. And when you get down to it, Adam thinks the same way."

"Oh, baloney. It won't amount to anything. In a couple of weeks everything will be just like before. Whether it's Krenz or Honecker doesn't matter one bit."

"That's what I say too. But Adam keeps on babbling about zero hour, and how he's going to miss his zero hour."

"What zero hour? If anybody's accomplished something, then it's us. Without us there'd be nothing going on over there now." Katja stirred the spaghetti. "Wait till he's found a job."

"Nobody here needs a custom tailor, they buy everything off the rack. Even Gisela doesn't want him to make her anything, not even for free, as a kind of rent. I don't understand it either, why women here don't want clothes that really fit, fit like they should. Adam says they don't have any sense of what custom tailoring means anymore. And he's had no responses to his job applications."

"But they're looking for people all over the place. They were even handing out flyers in the camps. They're looking for skilled workers."

"But not for ladies' custom tailors."

"Sure they are, they're looking for them too."

"You should have known him before. He practically never took a vacation. He couldn't do it, he couldn't just do nothing."

"And so?"

"In his mind it wasn't actual work."

"You mean, more like an artist?"

"His women came to him, and he made them look beautiful. And once they were beautiful, he screwed them."

"Isn't that more of a rumor?"

"I caught him in the act. But we've covered this topic before."

"You think what he misses is his women?"

"If only that was it. We argue constantly, but he's as needy as a lapdog. I look at other men and ask myself why it is that I'm with Adam. I think I could get along with almost any man who's halfway decent to me."

"It'd be great if it were that easy."

"I ask myself, Why Adam, of all people?"

"Oh come on, Evi. Do you feel like you're too good for him?"

"Nonsense. That's not what I mean. And what's with Marek?"

"We'll have to wait and see. I don't have the faintest idea where that's going. You want a plate or a shallow bowl?"

Evelyn nodded.

"Well which, plate or bowl?"

"Doesn't matter. Some men have a way of talking and gesturing, they're sort of jaunty, they're so wide awake. I like the wide-awake types. You can see it just in the way they walk. I only have to see how a guy walks and I already know everything, or almost everything."

"A little luck helps too."

"And have you had good luck?"

"Have I ever! First Adam, then the both of you. Michael lent me some money, for what they call probation here."

"What? You were in prison?"

"In prison?"

"Well, you said 'probation.' "

"No, no, it's the security deposit you pay the landlord. Three months' rent up front. In case something needs to be repaired afterward."

"Three months' rent? Are they nuts?"

"Oh, you'll manage that somehow. And if worse comes to worst, you ask Michael. Adam doesn't need to know."

"Adam believes Michael is an intelligence officer, or something like it. He says he saw him in Trostberg."

"What do you mean, an officer? I stayed with him at his place."

"Before the camp?"

"He knew somebody there, who arranged things so that I didn't need to go to the camp. Other than to go and fill out forms. Give me that gorgonzola there."

"The whole piece?"

"Yes." She put the cheese in the pan. "On the drive across all Michael could talk about was you. He kept coming back to it."

"Was he angry?"

"He just couldn't fathom it. I told him, turn around, but he was too stubborn."

"If only he'd given me a little more time."

"Any regrets?"

"I don't know."

"Hey, Evi. Are those tears?" Katja took the pot off the stove and drained the spaghetti. "What's wrong? Are you sorry?"

"There's something I have to tell you."

"Oh dear, well out with it. What's up? . . . Come on, tell me."

"I'm going to have a baby."

"Holy cow, Evi!" Still holding the colander in both hands, Katja stared at her.

"I know, what a stupid thing to do."

"I never would have guessed. Is it Michael's?"

"I don't know, maybe, or maybe not."

"Can't you determine that?"

"And how do I do that?"

"And Adam?"

"Might be."

"Does he know?"

"No."

"Do you want to keep it?"

"I don't know. Do you deal with that here pretty much like with us?"

"Not a clue. But I think so. You'll come up with something—no matter what."

Katja poured the spaghetti into the pan with the gorgonzola. Then she walked around the table and gave Evelyn a hug.

"I know that perfume," Evelyn said, "I had some once too."

"From Michael?"

"Hm."

"So does that disappoint you?"

"You too, I would think."

"Oh, please, he was just trying his best. And you should tell Adam, maybe that will wake him up. He's always wanted a child. Sorry, I've got to stir." Katja walked back to the stove. "Can you hand me that pear? I'll admit, it knocks me for a loop. I thought, here comes some stuff about the Stasi or whatever."

"No, and thanks a lot."

"Well when you lead into it that way. Who would think it would be a baby?"

"It's just that when you have no one you can talk with, it just sort of blurts out."

"I'm the same way."

"Is that ready yet?" Evelyn pointed to the pan.

"First hand me that pear. Are you hungry?"

"No."

"Come on," Katja said, "at least give it a try. Or how about the pear, a piece of pear at least?"

"Yes, a small one."

Katja turned off the gas, and while she was quartering the pear, Evelyn pulled a little package from her purse.

"Here, for you," she said.

Katja looked at her, hesitated, then took the present out of Evelyn's hand, ripped the cellophane tape off, and unfolded the paper napkin.

"What—for me?"

"I have one like it." Evelyn raised her right hand with its ruby red ring.

"Evi—"

"We're such friends, almost sisters, aren't we?" Evelyn took the ring from her. "Where do you want it, right or left?"

"Doesn't matter."

"You see, perfect fit."

"You're crazy, absolutely crazy," Katja said. Then they sat down across from each other at the table and ate the pear.

AT THE EICHENAU S-Bahn stop, Evelyn got off the last car and walked toward the exit. Suddenly someone grabbed her hand, she whirled around.

"Adam! Has something happened?"

"You said you'd be back around noon."

"I said I didn't know when I'd be back. Your hand's like ice!"

Evelyn pulled the scarf from her neck and tied it under Adam's chin.

"I wanted to invite you to lunch," Adam said. "Did you eat already?"

"We had a late breakfast."

"Took longer than you expected."

"Are you feeling any better?"

"When I'm out of the house, yes. I saw the doctor. I'm now officially certified as ill."

"What's wrong?"

"Ah, just the usual 'emigration syndrome,' 'adaptation problems.' They recognize it as an illness. He told me I'll even get a little extra money." Adam tried to take Evelyn's hand. "I'm not doing anything awful, I've never played sick before. This is the first time. It doesn't change anything, except a little more money. Why shouldn't I have done it? In some way it's actually the truth. And you, how did it go?"

"Not that great."

"With Katja?"

"Oh, Katja mothered me from start to finish. She even sent along a little something." Evelyn hooked her arm under Adam's. They passed a boy who was rattling the lock on his bike and cursing softly to himself, then turned down the street leading into town.

"Katja's apartment is a dream come true, in the entryway there are mirrors and a chandelier, all very elegant—the real West."

"And how many rooms?"

"Just one, but it's huge. There are two other students in the apartment, each with her own room. The kitchen is huge, they even throw their parties in there, and there's an old-fashioned bathroom with a huge tub. Makes you realize just how dull and middle-class all this is. I bought some tissues, here."

Adam stopped to blow his nose.

"Any problems?" Evelyn asked.

"Not really."

"But really?"

"His latest maxim is 'No pain, no gain.' "

"I've heard that one."

"I can't find my house key anywhere."

"Adam . . ."

"I'm just saying that I can't find it. I thought maybe you took it by mistake."

"I did not take your key by mistake."

"Eberhard wanted me to sign up at the supermarket, they're looking for people to run the bottle return, part-time."

"At the Tengelmann?"

"Something like that."

"And?"

" 'And' what?"

"Were you there?"

Adam stopped in his tracks. "You think I should be sorting bottles?"

"I'd do it."

"That's easy to say."

"I really would do it."

"And I won't. Were you at the university?"

"I first have to get a document notarized."

"What?"

"My graduation exams."

"Why would they need to be notarized?"

"I don't know, but that's the way it is. And then I'll be majoring in art history and Romance languages."

"And in the afternoons you'll work the bottle return."

"Everybody wants a security deposit. You can't rent anything without a deposit. I was at the jeweler's."

Adam stopped in his tracks. "You promised me—"

"He didn't want them."

"What?"

"He flat-out didn't want them."

"What do you mean, 'he didn't want them'?"

"He says they're not genuine."

"Is he crazy?'

"He said none of the stones is real."

"He just wanted to haggle."

"No, not at all. He just shoved them back at me—no interest, period."

"I told you you shouldn't. And this is your punishment. You hold on to family things."

"You sold Heinrich for the first offer that came along."

"Family jewels are only for a very rainy day."

"Well, it looks like it's pouring down. I don't want to be a beggar forever."

"That's one for Uncle Eberhard. 'You don't roll up your sleeves, you land in the garbage dump.' "

"Stop it now."

"Did you show the jewelry to anyone else?"

"No, that was enough for me."

"Well, they're still beautiful. In my eyes it's all genuine."

"I wonder if she knew."

"Of course she had to know."

"My mother didn't. She blew her top because I got them instead of her. I gave Katja one of the rings."

"You're a generous soul."

"But how does that make me look now?"

"So you think she ran off to the pawnshop with it?"

" 'Course not. But all the same—"

"How did she find a place to live so fast?"

"Through her relatives. They're taking care of everything for her. Besides, she has a boyfriend, a Polish guy."

"She could have come by one of those with a lot less trouble."

"He's been here a good while. He studied landscape gardening and something else, and is going to get his diploma soon. He and Katja are going to Zurich in two weeks, they'd like for us to come along."

"Do you think that's a good idea?"

"It would be nice. He has some business to take care of there, and we could take a look at the city. Leave in the morning, back the same evening."

A bell rang behind them. The boy they'd seen before now went around them on his bike. Once he was past he called out something they couldn't understand.

"I saw the doctor, too," Evelyn said.

"The gynecologist?"

"Yes."

"And? Everything okay?"

"Yes."

"What was it Katja sent along?"

"Marble cake."

Adam tugged at Evelyn to sit down on the bus-stop bench. "Come on, let's have a little picnic."

"Not here, it's too cold. You've already got a cold."

"You have something against picnics?"

"Are you trying to catch more cold?" Evelyn walked a few steps farther and then turned around to Adam. "Where's your winter jacket?"

"It's not my jacket, I won't wear it."

"Then we'll buy you one, but you can't go without one. Come on, let's do it now."

"No."

"You put up with Eberhard's little maxims, you can put up with his jacket."

"Yesterday there were two hundred thousand people in Leipzig, and there's to be a huge demonstration in Berlin, a legal one."

"What does that have to do with your jacket?"

"Which means, we have to hope they don't pull it off, right?"

"Cut that crap."

"But we do, we hope they won't pull it off, and Eberhard hopes they will—that's how it looks to me."

"Well, I in fact have other problems. Come on, please!"

"Saint Eberhard would be happy to give his jacket to our sisters and brothers in the East."

"Come on now!"

Adam turned around. She watched him walk away. When he got to the bus stop, he pulled a newspaper from the trash can, spread it out on the bench, stretched out his legs, and pursed his lips as if he were about to start whistling.

Slowly, very slowly, Evelyn walked back to the bench. With each step she covered a vast distance. Just a few more breaths and she would be standing before him, look him in the eye, and say those familiar words, words so familiar that it suddenly seemed pointless to speak them.

51

LAKE ZURICH AND GREEN LIGHT

"WE SHOULDN'T have separated. I knew it wouldn't work."

"Marek hasn't showed up yet either."

"We should've just boarded and that'd be that. Now we're standing around here cooling our heels and looking silly."

"We've seen a lot, though. And as punishment for our mistake, let's finish these off."

"What are they called again?"

Katja had opened the little white cardboard box and now held it up so she could read the blue printing: "Lux-em-bur-ger-li, Sprüng-li."

"Is that who makes them, or what they're called?"

"Probably Sprüngli because they spring right up into your mouth."

"The pink ones are the best."

"Have another."

"Should we save at least one for each of them?"

"Oh, we'll buy some more."

"Do you have that much money?"

"They only cost a couple of francs. We're not going to think about money today."

"Funny, isn't it?"

"What?"

"That we've got the kind of money now that will get you anything? Does that already feel normal to you?"

"These Sprüngli here," Katja said as she chewed, "are beyond description—ice cold inside and melting, and suddenly you think it's done its thing, and then you bite into something hard, that's the wildest experience."

"And the mountain peaks, snowcapped, and that glow as if heaven were peeking through. I sometimes think Adam lives on another planet. I stand here looking at them and I'm happy—and him, he doesn't see a thing."

"Well, you did give him a hard nut to crack."

"He acts like he's the first and only person on earth."

"And you really haven't spoken to each other since?"

"Nope."

"Not a word?"

"Nothing, zilch."

"Does he want the baby? He must have said something, didn't he?"

"He asked who the father is. And then he said he'd have to think about it."

"Dead silence for ten days now?"

"Five. I couldn't bring myself to do it, couldn't get the words out."

"I can't imagine how you can go five days without talking to each other. He was cheerful enough earlier today, him and Marek."

"It wasn't exactly the perfect moment, maybe. He had been writing job applications, a slew of applications. But everyone tells him that doesn't do the trick. You have to appear in person, present yourself, get acquainted with people. I told him he's got to try harder, to make the extra effort—because we're expecting a baby. The baby part was the last straw."

"What a shame, I'd hoped—"

"He takes off somewhere every night, or almost every night. The stairs creak something awful—by the time he's at the bottom, our fine hosts are sitting bolt upright of course in their pillows and asking themselves what's happened now. Eberhard was even convinced Adam was going to set the house on fire. Twice I woke up, and there he stood in his pajamas at the foot of my bed. Oh, dammit, it's so beautiful here, and he manages to louse this up for me too."

"It's really incredible. Have you ever heard about the green light? It's the rarest light there is, it's only when the air is very very pure and you watch the sun sink into the lake, and suddenly there's a burst of turquoise-green, a brief supernatural glow. Let's link arms, maybe something will happen now."

"And if Marek shows up, and he's still not here?"

"Then we'll come up with a plan. You need to tie your scarf, you look frozen to death. I think Adam was truly shocked when he saw the bill."

"He needed that feeling again that lunch was on him."

"But then he chose that Terrasse place or however you pronounce it. We could have gone Dutch."

"Let him be, it's okay. You guys paid for the trip. That's his car money. The sooner he spends it, the better. Best thing would be we're completely broke, maybe he'll catch on then."

"His hands were a little clammy."

"He smells different somehow too. I'm not allowed to say 'somehow' when he's around, but it's the case all the same."

"That's your pregnancy nose."

"No, he really smells different."

"Adam's been given a tough role to play."

"Stop it. He should take an example from Marek, who just forged on ahead—he even had to learn German, and now he'll soon have his diploma in his pocket. Marek is a treasure—I'd turn Catholic for him."

"I don't think he's Catholic, at least I haven't noticed any telltale signs yet."

"Adam can't get his nose out of some ancient bird and plant guides he found in the car. Of late he's been visiting the zoo. And if I ask him what he does there, he says he's 'taking a walk.' He could at least sew something for me, maternity things, dresses, pants. The water's so clear here."

"You just have to have an idea, and then you'll make it, *easy*. Marek has a friend who buys the chicest clothes at Zurich flea-markets, and then she marks them up and resells them in Munich—it's evidently going very well."

"I thought everything was more expensive here?"

"They wear things here twice and then give them to their cleaning lady, who turns them over for a few quick francs."

"Ah, I just want everything to be normal again, so that it's perfectly natural to go into shops here and buy Sprüngli. Will we ever get to the point where we can stroll along here and say: 'That hat there, that's mine now.' "

Katja unlinked and ran toward the bridge. Marek spread his arms wide. Evelyn turned her head away. The bus to Küsnacht opened its doors a second time to let a woman board. Then she looked out over the lake. The bluish clouds were threaded with narrow orange veins. She heard Katja laugh. Katja called her over.

"Marek has something to tell us, come here!"

Evelyn's steps slowed as the two of them went into another hug.

"Have you heard?" Marek asked. "You really haven't? You didn't notice the newspaper headlines? Everybody's talking about—that's all they can talk about."

"Okay, but what is it?" Katja asked. "Spit it out."

"Have you seen Adam?" Evelyn asked.

"I thought you were going to do the boat ride together."

"We've been waiting here for forty-five minutes."

"Look, it reads: 'These are to be enjoyed on the spot'—and that's what we did. You're too late." Katja split open the empty Sprüngli box.

"The wall is gone," Marek said.

"Who's been spreading that nonsense?" Evelyn asked.

"Everyone. On TV they're showing nothing but Berlin, how every-one's running across, it started late last night. You're the last ones to know! I swear it's true." Marek raised one hand. "Wait a sec!"

"Marek, no, please."

Marek walked over to an elderly couple. "Excuse me, my girlfriend here doesn't believe that the wall has been torn down in Berlin."

"Oh, indeed it has," the man said. The woman nodded. The man touched the brim of his hat. They walked on.

"So then," Marek called across. "Do you believe me now?"

Evelyn and Katja had already turned away. They were gazing across the water to the mountains and the sunset, whose colors now filled the entire sky.

52

BROTHER AND SISTER

THE RADIO MUSIC helped calm her a little. Half past—she gave herself another twenty-eight minutes. If Adam still wasn't back she would go to the phone booth and call Katja. She'd leave at ten on the dot, ten o'clock wasn't too late. Is he there with you? she would ask Katja. Why Adam, who else? He's taken off again. Since last night, without one word, left in the middle of the night. He doesn't tell me anything, he only talks to you guys. How should I know where he is? Evelyn knew what Katja's voice sounded like in those huge rooms, where everything was lovely and well thought-out, everything in its place. Katja was her friend, her only friend, but she wouldn't hear a word said against him. She would do anything, Katja had said, for Adam. But she had also said that Adam shouldn't treat her like a doormat, that he had no right to simply take off and not say anything. Evelyn pictured Adam there with her, standing at the window, without moving, without breathing, as if even that was too much for him, and when he did breathe, take a deep breath and let it out again like a sigh, he would massage his chest. She could see his larynx, his Adam's apple, like something was stuck in his throat and he was choking on it. Maybe that's why he'd been certified ill. She knew no one like him, no one who kept trying to get used to his own death. But she would never say anything about that to anyone, wouldn't talk about it even to Katja, that would be a betrayal. But she would tell her what happened yesterday evening, when they had gone out together again, to get away from Uncle Eberhard, that ogre, that Bautzen prisoner of 1957 who hadn't fled but was a political refugee, who hadn't run away from his responsibilities. Eberhard the Ogre claimed Adam broke the dishwasher. They had just wanted to have a beer at the Blue Angel, where Adam could play pool. She would tell Katja about the painter who had joined them at their table, a painter from Dresden. They had instantly recognized he didn't really belong here, here in Bavaria, sitting there by himself. But he had no regrets about having left, having cut and run four or five years ago now. But now he was afraid they would all be coming here, that he'd have to see people he had hoped never to see again. She had no fear of that, but the fact that everything had just fallen into their laps over there, without their having to flee or risking anything, just like that, while they sat on their butts at home—there was something unjust in that. They could talk with him. His name was Frank, and not all that unknown a painter either, Frank, but she'd forgotten his last name. Frank had invited them to stop by and have a look at his studio, have a drink, talk and eat—most painters, he had said, are good cooks. He issued us a real invitation, his address on the beer coaster. And do you know what Adam said? Not what you think, nobody would ever guess. Thanks, Adam said, would love to, love to—and here it comes—would love to stop by sometime with my sister. With his sister! Can you imagine! He meant me. He was trying to fix me up with him. What could I have said? It would only have exposed him. And of course the painter reacted instantly, new person, new role—bang!—knee to knee, the whole routine. I would have taken a look at his work, but now I'm not going to play along. Besides, Adam wouldn't come with me anyway. His head's in a muddle, in a fog. And then his breathing. I keep thinking he's just lying out there somewhere. I don't cry, I've done enough sobbing by now. I don't even know why I cry, I really don't. He loves me. Yes, he loves me, he loves me and hates me. Ever since he fell in love with me, he's hated me too. Because he wouldn't be here otherwise. That's the truth, there's no denying it. Evelyn blew her nose. Five times a day I think we ought to separate. But then—Do you know where he was that day in Zurich, where he really was? I couldn't believe it. But then he didn't let on either. On the way back from Villa Wesendonck, he left his camera on the streetcar, on the tram. So he ran off trying to track down his camera, back to the stop where he got off, to the police, the lost-and-found. And the only reason I caught on was because Adam was making all these calls to Switzerland. At first I thought he had some business contact, because he'd been very impressed by the way the Swiss dress—Switzerland, that was his West. And I thought maybe he'll be able to make it in Switzerland. But it was always just talking with the lost-and-found. All gone, not just the camera, but the pictures from Lake Balaton and Lake Sims, too, they were all still on the roll of film inside, all of it down the drain, gone, gone, as if it never was. He was embarrassed, he was furious with himself, desperate, yes, desperate. Suddenly Adam's like a little boy. But in the next moment out he comes with his maxims, à la Eberhard the Ogre, but turned around. For him there's too much of everything. Too many words, too many dresses, too many pants, too much chocolate, too many cars—instead of being glad that there is finally enough of everything, he says: Too much, too many, an inflation of stuff that buries everything else, the essential things, the real things. That's how he talks. Once he even started in about original sin. No kidding, original sin! He said original sin is what drives people to want more and more money, and that ruins everything. Not just in Switzerland, but in a fundamental way. Because everybody always wants more and more and nobody knows any better anymore, just more and more And when I said that if there really is such a thing as original sin then it's God's fault, because people have too little. And if you have too little . . . But that just ticked him off. He thought I was joking. Bu all the same he wants a new car. Or at any rate he wants his Heinrich back. Maybe he's been reading the Bible too much. I've had it with him! I can't listen to any more of his speeches. If I could I'd move in with you. The moment it's available, a room next to yours, beautiful, just like yours. You don't have to worry that I'll come bawling to you or talking your ear off, no, that's not it, but just not to be here alone anymore and always to have to pass by Eberhard when you want to get out. Or you could come here, that'd be lovely too, but if you say you're coming, then come, come here, or I'll come to you, just for one night, but do come, do come, if only for a few hours. Come here, it's quiet here, good for sleeping, just twenty minutes now, just nineteen. . . .

53

FAILED RETURN

"MY GOD," KATJA SAID, pointing to the little folding table, "what's all this?"

"That's not all—there, the whole bed's full, and there's another box of them too."

"And who did this?"

"Some crazies maybe or the Stasi, not a clue. Didn't Marek come along?"

"He's meeting with his professor, can't get away. Did they tear up all the photographs?"

"You can see for yourself. Take your coat?"

"Are you two taping them back together?"

"That's all we've been doing for two days now."

Evelyn took Katja's coat and hooked the hanger on the top edge of the wardrobe.

"If you put them in an album maybe it won't be so apparent to people."

"That's what I'm doing right now, an album with all of his creations, at least those that are halfway useable. He can make a presentation when he applies for a job."

"You're nothing short of heroic."

"If you'd ever told me I'd be restoring my enemies to their glory—"

"Well, at least pictures of them."

"Those are my enemies, you know, the women and the photographs, maybe their pictures even more so."

"Are they all black-and-white?"

"He's always photographed just in black-and-white."

"So tell me," Katja paged through the album. "Attractive woman. Is she here too?"

"You mean—"

Evelyn nodded, took the album from Katja, and thumbed through it. "This one here, Lilli I and Lilli II, and she's at the back again in an off-the-shoulder item." She handed the album back.

Katja smiled. "Funny to picture it. Does he have a thing for pudgy ones?"

"They're not all like that."

"She's not the youngest anymore either."

"Doesn't bother him."

"He's a talented fellow, your Adam," Katja said, clapping the album closed.

"Want something to drink?"

"Hey, now this is wild." Katja bent down over a photograph that was missing its lower half. "Did you ever see him like that, with long hair and a beard?"

"Before my time. He'll be right back, a quick trip to the supermarket."

"How awful!" Katja said, sat down on the edge of the bed, and slid a photograph, reassembled with cellophane tape on the back, from the table into the palm of her hand. "Barbarians!"

"You can say that again."

"Are these his parents?"

"I think so."

"Are you two talking again?"

"Now and then, the bare necessities. Want some tea?" Evelyn pulled a large tile from under her mattress and placed it on the carpeted floor just beneath the outlet. She filled a pot with water and set it on the tile. Then she took an immersion heating coil from a hook beside the washbasin.

"Aren't you allowed in the kitchen anymore?"

"Yes, we still are, but I'd rather be up here."

"I've ordered an extra key for you. The security deposit just passes from me to you. Michael's completely all right with that."

"Except that Adam won't go along with it."

"Doesn't need to know, you can tell him that Marek or my family is paying it."

"Adam still has his car money."

"He'd do better to use that for a new camera. Say! Is that still our jar of mustard, from the campgrounds?"

"The Angyals wanted to send it along with him."

"Can I have it once it's empty?"

Evelyn nodded. "Don't you dare say a word to Michael about the baby, okay?"

"Wouldn't think of it. But he's going to find out at some point. And what if it's his?"

"Let's not, not right now. An alteration shop has responded. Adam can start with them, half days at first."

"That was sure a throwaway line."

"Let's wait and see."

"And? Is he going to take it?"

"With him, that'd make three of them, and the boss comes from Tehran, a Persian."

"Adam needs to get out among people. Does he still play with it?"

She was looking at the windowsill, on which lay the two socks and the Rubik's Cube.

"He keeps trying, over and over. Did you ever solve it?"

"No. But I never tried that hard. Where's Elfi, by the way?"

"Under the radiator. Elfriede doesn't like it here either."

Katja edged three parts of a photo closer together.

"Adam is a very handsome man, short, but handsome."

"Except he hardly eats anything now."

"What I don't get is that they let Adam back in."

"They thought he had left that first night for the West and was only now coming back. All the people in his compartment wanted to know what it had been like."

"When the wall came down?"

"Yes, where was he and what had he done."

"Marek says that they could close things up tight again very quickly."

"I told Adam that too. They're going to lose all control."

"And what did it look like?"

"Everything in shambles, just look at it."

"I mean in the East, in general."

"Not much different, nothing special."

"Did he bring some books back with him?"

"Why books?"

"Well, I thought, since you're such a bookworm."

"He just packed up the photographs, a notice that his new Lada was ready to be picked up on September twenty-ninth, and my headband that goes with the summer skirt with the red polka dots. Not one pair of shoes, no coats, nothing."

Katja stood up when Adam entered the room. They shared a brief hug.

"Am I interrupting something?" he asked.

"We're not about to let anything interrupt us, right, Evi? Here, a little present, supposed to be good."

"Cigarillos? Look like luxury goods."

"Marek was in Amsterdam, bought them for you there. And from me you get your handkerchief, laundered and ironed, as promised."

"And still blue checked, too," Adam said.

"Katja wanted to know what it was like." Evelyn removed the glue and cellophane tape from the shopping bag.

"Behold the mess," he said.

"Did they break in?"

"You could call it that too. Some through the door, some through the window. Must have been quite a lively coming-and-going."

"Those bastards," Katja said. "Well, at least you can laugh at it."

"I don't know," Evelyn said, "if that's what I'd call laughing."

Adam edged his way between the bed and folding table to the window and opened it. "Any objections?" He carefully opened the package and took a whiff of the cigarillos. "Nothing like going out in style," he said. "I'll be sure to offer Uncle Eberhard one. We'll see if he knows a good thing when he smokes it."

"At least Mona was able to deal with the mailbox, even without a key," Evelyn said and pulled the plug on the immersion coil.

"I don't get it," Katja said.

"She claims she never got our letter with the key. At least that's what she told Adam."

"And your mother?"

"She won't answer the phone. I don't know what's up there." Evelyn took the butter and the shrink-wrapped cold cuts from the bag and laid them on the tray.

"And how did it look?"

"Beautiful, a blanket of leaves over the grass, flower beds, paths. The quince had lost their fuzz and were shiny, all the other trees were bare, and my old garden shoes were still standing side by side in their niche under the porch roof . . ."

Evelyn pushed reassembled photos and photo scraps onto a piece of cardboard and cleared a place for it at the foot of the bed. She had heard Adam's story only once before, but as he retold it now it was as familiar as if she had been there herself. She could see all the things she hadn't thought about till now, because she wouldn't be seeing them ever again: the gate, the garden, the house, the three steps up to the door. She heard the adhesive seal being ripped open and felt the chill pouring out at Adam. The chill surprised her too. The washing machine in the guest bathroom was missing. The pane in the door to the hallway was cracked. How dark it suddenly was as he closed the front door behind him. The fridge and the stove had been hauled away, the kitchen tiles were covered with broken dishes like from a *polterabend* the night before a wedding—she had to stop at the kitchen door and stare at it. And the mixer tap was missing from the sink.

Evelyn made sandwiches. The butter was soft. She had to put her shoulder to the living-room door. Something heavy scraped across the floorboards. As she worked her way through the crack, she could see what she already knew. Nothing was left untouched. Hoping to open the door wider, she first tried shoving the bookcase that held their records to one side, but it was wedged against the upended and plundered writing desk. Shredded photographs or crumpled letters and bills everywhere. She immediately began to gather things up. She picked up pieces of records only if there was something she could read.

It wasn't until she had worked her way across the room to close the window that she noticed its crossbar was broken and sagging. It took her hours to collect the photos, or what was left of them. She even managed to get the desk back on its feet and shove it to the wall.

Now she poured the hot water over teabags in a glass teapot. Back in the hallway she opened the door to the cellar, reached into the corner behind it, found the flashlight, moved slowly down the stairs, and shined the light into the darkroom. It was empty. In the midst of all this devastation, this emptiness comforted her too. All that was left of the jars of preserves in the entryway were circles in the dust on the shelves.

Adam laughed. Katja said something. Evelyn had finished the open-face sandwiches, and now cut them into quarters, garnishing them with chives, horseradish, and mustard, and between each an alternating pattern of cornichons and mustard pickles. Arranging them carefully, she took her time, as if Adam's story would last only as long as she kept busy.

She just glanced into the bath and other rooms. It was the same everywhere. She was afraid of going upstairs to the studio.

Evelyn handed the platter to Katja and Adam.

Through the open door she could see the smaller of the tailor's dummies hanging on the hook that held the Christmas star. The larger one lay slashed open on the floor. Something stinky had been poured over the rolls of fabric. As she turned around to descend the stairs, she couldn't help noticing the large snow-white bra draped on the door handle. She had picked it up herself that day. She had been certain that it would in fact be there glistening white amid the wreckage, as shiny as the quince in the garden. She took it with her.

But did she really still not know what to do with it? She held a lighter under it and once it caught fire, hurled it like a torch into the living room.

Adam laughed again. No, it wasn't laughter, but "laughter" was the only word Evelyn had for it.

Adam tossed the butt of his cigarillo into the yard and closed the window. Evelyn wanted to hear more, she was also prepared to make more sandwiches, to wash and dry dishes. What mattered was that he went on speaking. And it was only now Evelyn realized that she could believe Adam again.

54

LAST THINGS

STEPPING FROM the subway car, Evelyn let the others overtake her. For a moment she stood there alone on the platform. It belonged to her now, to her route back from the university. It was still unspoiled by worries, untouched by bad memories. And she herself was not the person she knew, but the someone she had always pictured when she thought of the future.

Startled by Adam at the top of the subway stairs, she stopped for a moment. Although she was happy to see him waiting for her.

"Where have you been?" he cried once only a few steps separated them. He looked at his watch and waved Katja and Marek over.

"Am I too late?"

"Actually we were on our way to a pastry shop, so we wouldn't arrive empty handed."

"I thought Gabriela and Michaela were going to bake something for us?"

"Who?"

"Our new apartment mates."

"For the pupil's first day of school—well, belatedly," Marek said and handed her a small traditional cardboard cone full of goodies.

"Congratulations," Katja said and gave her a hug.

"Thanks," Evelyn said. "But all I have for you is this." She extracted the half-full mustard jar from her pocket.

"That's hardly all," Katja said, holding up her hand with its ruby red ring. "Besides, there's only one of these!" She snapped the glass with her finger, eliciting a bright, echoless tone.

Evelyn hooked her arm under Adam's. They crossed the street and walked along beneath the chestnut trees.

"Michaela and Gabriela," Adam said.

"Nice monikers," Marek said.

"And from excellent family," Katja said.

"What do you mean, 'from excellent family'? What are you talking about?" Adam said.

"But it's true, you're now members of a very upscale shared-apartment community. Also known as a SAC."

"We used to call them a kommunalka."

"Right!" Marek exclaimed. "The old kommunalka."

"I'd rather have something of our own, doesn't have to be so special, but with our own bathroom and toilet, if only because of the baby."

"In this neighborhood you won't find anything like that."

"Or a cellar," Marek said. "I once lived in a cellar apartment."

"Would be my choice."

"But not with a pregnant wife, Adam. You can ask them both to be godparents."

"And there really is a garden?"

"You look out onto a garden, but it's only for the people on the ground floor, who also own the place. They'll definitely have no problem if you want to set the buggy out on the lawn, or let Elfi scramble around a bit."

"And the security deposit? Can you cover it?" Adam asked. "We'll spoon-feed you that as quickly as we can—"

"Spoon-feed?" Marek asked and smiled.

"Pay me back bit by bit, in installments. No problem, really it isn't," Katja said and thrust her arm under Evelyn's, so that the four of them now took up the width of the sidewalk.

Evelyn was moving as if in a dream. She heard the voices of the others, but wasn't about to let anything disrupt this new life of hers. With each step that brought her closer to her own room with its hardwood floors and a ceiling of fine plasterwork and that huge kitchen, the more certain of herself she felt.

"And why is this palace so cheap?" Adam asked.

"Actually not that cheap. We have their parents to thank. They want reliable people living with their daughters," Katja said.

"And we're reliable people?"

"Why sure, no drugs, no counterculture, refugees from Communism, studying to better yourselves, hard workers, and good looking to boot—those are the folks that need to be helped. Besides, Evi will be teaching them Russian."

"You?" Adam stopped in his tracks.

Evelyn shrugged and pulled him along.

"You're lucky," Marek said. "You've all had great luck, nothing but a clear road ahead."

"How old are they?"

"Around twenty-two, twenty-three, but still studying. Michaela knows a lot about music and Gabriela all there is to know about politics. Two brains. Gabriela's already working on her dissertation, something to do with the Near East. She wants to become an ambassador, and I'll bet anything she makes it. I won my first bet with you, too." She leaned forward to cast Adam a glance.

"Can you study politics?" Adam asked.

"Sure, you can study anything here," Marek said. "But they look like they're barely out of high school. But then I never can tell a woman's age here."

They stopped at the pastry shop. The line was out the door.

"You can get your rolls here every morning, or apple strudel with vanilla sauce," Katja said.

"Fresh manna daily," Adam said.

"They promised they would bake something," Evelyn said. She didn't want to wait in line. She felt sure of herself only when they were walking.

"I haven't even told you that Frau Angyal called," Katja said.

"Frau Angyal?" Adam exclaimed. "Where did she get your number?"

"Probably from Michael."

"Isn't that grand! Hasn't he paid his bill yet?"

"She just wanted to know how we are all doing."

"And what did she have to say?"

"Nothing much—other than that you should get in touch sometime."

Adam had to make way for two women exiting and carrying a large package of pastries.

"Let's go, this is going to take forever," Evelyn said.

"But then we won't have anything to bring," Katja said.

"So what? We'll be punctual at least." Evelyn tugged Adam on ahead. The other two followed.

"And what if all of a sudden you decide to come back to your villa?" Adam asked and waited until Katja had linked arms with Evelyn again.

"But I won't want to," she said and gave Marek a kiss.

"Well then, come on everybody," Evelyn said.

"Once Adam has really made a start of things," Katja said, "and once you make a start of things too, you'll be able to live anywhere, or almost anywhere."

"What are you talking about? How am I supposed to make a start of things? It works differently here, very differently. Until a few days ago I still thought we had the choice—but that's over. Don't you understand?"

"No, why's that?" Katja asked.

"Adam's caught on," Marek said. "He knows it's all going to be 'the same old same old' everywhere—that's the phrase, isn't it?"

"Yep, 'the same old same old,' " Adam said.

"It wouldn't help Adam if he took off to Poland now," Marek said. "But a bowl of the same old still tastes better here."

"That's if there's something in the bowl," Adam said.

"Now that's enough," Katja said. "Sounds like somebody's funeral. Do you guys believe in any of it?"

"You mean, does the number thirteen bother us, our new address?" Adam asked.

"No, I mean whether you believe—in God or whatever?"

"Where did that come from?"

"I'm just asking."

"What about you?"

Katja shook her head. "I've been asked a couple of times here if I'm Catholic or Protestant. At least I've got me a Catholic now."

"Oh no, no, I'm not one anymore, please, no way," Marek said and raised his free arm as if in self-defense.

"Hopefully my Persian won't ask me," Adam said.

"Oh, no problem."

"Evi was baptized, to make her elegant grandma happy. Right?"

"Yes," Evelyn said, "but that was the end of that."

"Looks like I need to play catch-up—anyway, they're gonna hold a mass baptism here shortly," Adam said.

"Oh, I should never have brought it up."

"Look at the mess they've made for the last two thousand years. And then they get upset over our lunkheads because they believe the means of production should no longer be in private hands—"

"Please don't," Katja suddenly said in full earnest. "If there's something I never want to hear again, then it's that."

"But that's not my point—I can still follow that argument somehow. But I just don't get this other stuff, how a grown adult can actually believe in eternity, sin, hell, and the whole whoop-de-do."

"If they drum it into you from early on, you end up believing it."

"But that's no excuse," Marek said.

"Listen to the man. My uncle, my mother's brother, was in the

Party too and believed it all. But after sixty-eight he had had it—aft
Dubček that was it, for good and all," Adam said.

Evelyn could see the house by now. There was light in most of th
windows, it looked downright festive.

"That's no comparison," Katja said. "There's something religiou
stuck inside every human being, you can't make any headway again
that."

"Is what I'm saying wrong? Tell me, is it wrong?"

"Dammit, Adam, don't get so upset," Katja said. "What people her
believe shouldn't matter to you. It's all baloney."

"Baloney," Marek repeated. "Baloney!"

"Those two windows on the second floor, those are yours."

"Are those Christmas decorations?" Adam asked.

"Next week is the first Sunday in Advent. You'll be having a birth
day here soon, are there to be some invitations?"

"If our two angels haven't tossed me out by then . . . or if Evi hasn't."

"And then we'll dine on baloney," Marek said.

"You do it," Katja said, handing her bundle of keys to Evelyn. "Th
big jaggedy one."

What were words, any words, compared with this key? Evely
thought.

The gate opened with a soft click.

55

FIRE

"THEY'RE REALLY VERY NICE—nice, and sharp as tacks too," Evelyn said as she entered the room, waving a Polaroid picture. "And we have the small toilet practically to ourselves." She walked over to Adam, who with one hand on the window handle was pressing his forehead to the pane. Next to him was the magic cube, each of its sides all one color.

"What were you doing?"

"We were setting up quarters for Elfriede in the vegetable bin, works perfectly, exactly six degrees Celsius."

"Are you sure she isn't dead?"

"Gabriela pricked her leg with a toothpick, she responded but didn't wake up. No need to worry. Besides—if she was dead she would have dried out and feel a lot lighter."

"But it won't be quiet enough for her in the vegetable bin."

"Why's that? In March or April we'll take her out again. Have you seen the CD collection? Michaela is writing a paper on Haydn's *Creation*."

"I know it—quite well in fact."

"Do we have it?"

"We had it, with Peter Schreier and Theo Adam."

"About this time day after tomorrow," Evelyn said, putting her arm around Adam's shoulder, "you'll have your first working day under your belt."

"At the patch-and-cobble shop."

"I've heard you say that alterations are the hardest thing to do." She removed her arm from his shoulder. "Katja wants you to sew something for her, and Michaela is already thinking it over . . ."

The wind yanked at the last chestnut leaves. Piles of raked leaves were being strewn across the lawn, to be caught again in the rose bushes and hedge.

"What a spectacular view, and come spring—"

"Where'd you get that sweater?"

"It's practically new."

"Must have been knitted for somebody on a mountain rescue team."

"Orange looks good on me. See, here I am." Evelyn showed him the Polaroid. "You have a pretty wife, don't you think? So far no one's noticed a thing." She passed her hand across her belly.

"It's a little early, I'd say."

"All the same, from the face or just general look, with some women you can tell right off. This is a present for you."

"Thanks," Adam said as he took the photo.

A magpie landed on a branch just outside the window.

"Don't you like it here?"

"Depends on what you mean by 'like.' "

"What time is it?"

"Three after four."

"Should I make some tea? Or coffee? When we have a little money I'll buy us a real tea service, maybe something Chinese, like the one Marek gave Katja." Evelyn gave Adam's cheek a peck and sat down at the table. "I'm going to buy another couple of albums."

"What for?"

"Who knows how long they'll be such a bargain. Gabriela would lend us her camera. Sharp down to the last detail. And when our snookums comes—"

"Please don't say 'snookums,' 'snookums' is ghastly."

"When our baby comes I'll start an album, one for each year."

"Plenty of time for that. You need to worry more about school. Don't you ever have any homework?"

"I work at the library." Evelyn paged through the album with Adam's models. "It was a really great idea to gather up all these photographs. I don't know if I could have done it. I might have just run away. Why they went to the trouble of tearing them up—think of the effort it took. Flogging would be too good for the bastards! Makes my head swim just thinking about it. But you know, if they do actually manage to pull it off over there, we might consider, in a couple of years maybe, whether—"

"Go back? To the neighbors who stole my bike, robbed us of everything that they didn't smash to smithereens."

"Neighbors? Why the neighbors?"

"I saw it at the Kaufmanns', leaning against the wall. It was my bike."

"You mean they tore up the pictures? I don't believe it."

"Or watched and did nothing."

"What about selling it?"

"The house? What am I going to get for it? The whole shebang isn't worth anything. You've been watching too—one West to ten East, in two weeks it'll be fifteen, and it'll just keep going like that. If I hadn't exchanged my money it'd soon be worth nothing."

"You need to buy up stuff there and sell it again here. Jewelry and china, old coins and chests, anything antique."

"Especially jewelry—my best wishes, but for that you're going to have to look for another man."

"It wouldn't take all that much effort."

"I'll be putting in my time at the patch-and-cobble shop."

Adam stared out at the garden. Evelyn looked through the photos.

"You could make one outfit after the other and I'd wear them. I'd be your model. That'd work, once people get a look at it."

"It's a matter of body type, the walk, the figure—"

"Wouldn't matter, once you present it and if I come along. Or you can create a whole new collection just for me, for me with my big belly. You've never done something like that, have you?"

"Oh Evi, what's all this?"

"Just picture it, early June, sunshine, blue sky, everything green, the mountains—our baby will be coming into the most beautiful world there ever was."

"You think so?"

"Well, then tell me one that's ever been better. Is there a time you'd want to go back to?"

"And Michael will help us make it to two hundred, and after that we can become immortal."

"Not a bad idea. And nobody needs to be scared of war anymore. They can put all that money to a sensible use, not just here but around the world. Pretty soon there'll be a thirty-hour workweek, and instead of a year and a half in the army, it'll be a year of everybody doing something useful."

"And the lion shall lie down with the lamb."

"Why do you have to say that?" She tried to catch his reflection in the window, but he was standing too close. "Do you really believe it will all just go on like before? That would be absurd."

Adam shrugged. The Polaroid shot had slid off the windowsill and now lay backside up in front of the radiator. Evelyn tore off a piece of cellophane tape and taped her picture to the window.

"So that you'll look at me again once in a while. Do you want tea or coffee?"

"Doesn't matter."

"Tea or coffee?"

"Whatever you want."

"Okay, tea," Evelyn said.

Gabriela was in the kitchen peeling apples, dough still clinging to her fingernails. "For tomorrow," she said, "Sunday breakfast."

"Can I lick the bowl?" Evelyn asked. "I haven't done that for ages."

Gabriela shoved the blue plastic bowl across the table, reached to pull the utensil drawer open with her pinkie, and handed her a teaspoon.

"Thanks." Evelyn started scraping the bottom of the bowl. Gabriela spread slices of apple across dough rolled out on a cookie sheet.

"Want some?" she asked, pushing a strand of hair from her forehead with the back of her hand and offering Evelyn two leftover slices of apple. "Would you like to help me peel?"

"There's more?"

"Those go in the oven after the strudel."

"Baked apples?"

"More like a casserole, with cinnamon and topped with vanilla sauce."

"Aha," Evelyn said. She set the well-scraped bowl in the sink and held the kettle under the tap.

When she had finished with the apples and the teapot, and glass cups stood ready on the tray, Gabriela took off her apron and offered Evelyn a cigarette. They sat at the table and smoked.

"You can't imagine how much I'm enjoying all this," said Evelyn. "As if I had never lived anywhere else."

But after only a few puffs she stubbed her cigarette out again.

Adam wasn't in the room. Evelyn set the table, with the sugar bowl and a saucer of apple slices in the middle, and poured the tea. It wasn't until she heard Adam's voice and laughter coming from the garden that she noticed one of the windows had been tipped open. There was a smell of fire.

The first thing she saw was her straw hat on his head. Adam was holding the opened album in front of him like a musical score. He pulled one of the large reassembled photographs of his women out and dropped it into the flames. He did this without haste. He turned the page, pulled the next one out, tossed it on the fire. One page fluttered up again, only half burned, curled up, and perished in the heat.

What frightened Evelyn the most was the symmetry and calmness of his movements.

Two women were standing at the fence and gesturing in Adam's direction. The man from next door was trying to climb over the hedge. He was holding a spade above his head like a rifle and shouting something. A male voice could be heard from the ground floor, then a window slammed shut.

Adam went on paging, pulling out photos, tossing them on the fire, and laughing. The bottle beside Adam's feet was stoppered with a blue-checked rag.

From one moment to the next the fire collapsed. The flames crouched low to the earth. Adam clapped the book shut.

The man with the spade grabbed the bottle and took it somewhere out of her line of sight. He quickly returned and started beating the fire with his spade. Sparks scattered. Adam stepped back to make room for a second man. Both men were yelling as they raked wet leaves over the embers and stomped out the last few flames.

All at once Adam looked up at her over his shoulder, as if he had known she had been standing there all along. He doffed his hat, smiled, nodded to her, and set it back on his head. Evelyn felt a chill run up her back.

She closed the window and retreated into the room, until all she could see were the two women at the fence, and then not even them. She bumped against the table and just stood there. The magpie hopped along across the bare boughs and branches of the chestnut tree, all the while rocking back and forth as if at any moment it might lose its balance. In the windowpane was a reflection of the ceiling lamp. Beneath it Evelyn saw herself and the whole room around her, looking much larger than in reality, almost huge, and right in the middle she saw, small but in bright colors, her own image.

ACKNOWLEDGMENTS

I have Péter Bacsó to thank for the idea of sending a tailor and his wife from the East German provinces to Lake Balaton in August 1989.

The following films and books, among others, spurred my imagination: *Kein Abschied—nur fort,* a film by Joachim Tschirner and Lew Hohmann, 1991; *Und nächstes Jahr am Balaton,* directed by Herrmann Zschoche, 1979/1980; *The Swimmer,* by Zsuzsa Bánk, translated by Margot Bettauer Dembo (New York, 2005); *Heimspiel,* by Ines Geipel (Berlin, 2005); and *Balaton-Brigade,* by György Dalos (Berlin, 2006).

A large portion of this book was written in 2007 at the German Academy Rome Villa Massimo, a paradise of a place. The role of patron was played by the Federal Republic of Germany, those of angels/cherubim by the staff of the villa. The other stipendiary fellows became my fellow exiles.

My warmest thanks to them all, and especially to my family.

CHRONOLOGY

MAY 7   Local elections in the GDR. For the first time in the republic's history, individual citizens (from oppositional groups) participate in the count and claim massive ballot fraud.

MAY 20   Gorbachev in West Berlin, viewing the wall: "Nothing is eternal."

JUNE 16   Imre Nagy, premier during the 1956 Hungarian resistance to the Soviet Union, is buried with full honors after a ceremony on Heroes' Square.

AUGUST 8   Arrival of 170 in West Germany aboard a special train from Vienna after crossing illegally from Hungary.

AUGUST 19   Mass flight of GDR citizens during a pan-European picnic on the Hungarian border with Austria. Approximately six hundred storm a normally locked border gate that was to be symbolically opened during the picnic.

AUGUST 24   Hungary tolerates the crossing of the Austrian border by GDR citizens. Those in the West German Embassy in Budapest are allowed to leave the country.

SEPTEMBER 4   After prayers for peace in Leipzig, many demonstrate for freedom to travel. This is in fact the first of the Monday demonstrations.

SEPTEMBER 7   One hundred GDR citizens cross from Hungary to Austria.

SEPTEMBER 10   Hungary "temporarily suspends" the twenty-year-old agreement with the GDR on repatriation of refugees. Gyula Horn announces that the estimated sixty thousand GDR tourists vacationing in Hungary will be allowed to travel to the West from midnight and will not be required to show an exit visa.

SEPTEMBER 11   Neues Forum, the first attempt at organized political opposition in the GDR, constitutes itself. Hungary opens its border with Austria. Thousands surge across.

SEPTEMBER 13   More than fifteen thousand GDR citizens have crossed to Austria from Hungary since the eleventh.

SEPTEMBER 25   Eight thousand demonstrate in Leipzig for freedom of expression, the right to hold meetings, and the authorization of the Neues Forum.

OCTOBER 2   Monday protesters in Leipzig number twenty thousand. Police break them up violently.

OCTOBER 7   The official fortieth anniversary of the GDR. Honecker meets with Gorbachev.

OCTOBER 9   The GDR experiences its largest demonstration since June 17, 1953, with seventy thousand gathering in Leipzig's Karl-Marx Square.

OCTOBER 16   More than one hundred and twenty thousand parade through Leipzig.

OCTOBER 18   Erich Honecker resigns from all offices. He is replaced by Egon Krenz.

OCTOBER 23   Three hundred thousand demonstrate in Leipzig. There are large demonstrations in four other cities.

NOVEMBER 4   Approximately one million demonstrate in East Berlin.

NOVEMBER 6   Five hundred thousand attend the Leipzig demonstration.

NOVEMBER 9   The collapse of the wall. The Council of Ministers decides to open the GDR's borders to the West and with the Allied sector of Berlin. Masses surge forward to the crossing points in the wall (9:00 p.m. Central European Time).

Between August 13, 1961, and November 11, 1989, 188 people died in their attempts to cross the border between the Germanies and Berlins, the last dying on February 6, 1989.

NOVEMBER 10   Berliners gather on top of the Berlin Wall at the Brandenburg Gate. East German border guards start to demolish the wall.

NOVEMBER 11   Seven hundred thousand GDR citizens visit the Federal Republic of Germany.

DECEMBER 2   Krenz, the entire Politburo, and Central Committee of the SED resign.

A NOTE ON THE TYPE

This book was set in Janson, a typeface long thought to have been made by the Dutchman Anton Janson, who was a practicing typefounder in Leipzig during the years 1668–1687. However, it has been conclusively demonstrated that these types are actually the work of Nicholas Kis (1650–1702), a Hungarian, who most probably learned his trade from the master Dutch typefounder Dirk Voskens. The type is an excellent example of the influential and sturdy Dutch types that prevailed in England up to the time William Caslon (1692–1766) developed his own incomparable designs from them.

Composed by North Market Street Graphics,
Lancaster, Pennsylvania

Printed and bound by RR Donnelley,
Harrisonburg, Virginia

Designed by Maggie Hinders